A
Measure
of
Undoing

a novel

David Kos

This book is a work of fiction. Any resemblance to actual people and places is coincidental, with the exception of the patients at Can Tho Children's Hospital. Many of these children were real victims of the United States Government's use of the chemical weapon "Agent Orange" during the war in Vietnam.

Printed in Victoria, Canada

NATIONAL LIBRARY OF CANADA CATALOGUING IN PUBLICATION DATA

Kos, David, 1944-
A measure of undoing / David Kos.
ISBN 1-4120-0573-6
1. Vietnam--History--20th century--Fiction.   I. Title.
PS8571.O789M42 2003   C813'.6   C2003-903456-9

Published by Maipenrai Press
131 Webster Drive
Salt Spring Island, B.C.
Canada V8K 1Y4

in cooperation with

TRAFFORD *on-demand publishing service*

Suite 6E, 2333 Government St., Victoria, B.C. V8T 4P4, CANADA
Phone	*250-383-6864*	*Toll-free*	*1-888-232-4444 (Canada & US)*
Fax	*250-383-6804*	*E-mail*	*sales@trafford.com*
Web site	*www.trafford.com*	TRAFFORD PUBLISHING IS A DIVISION OF TRAFFORD HOLDINGS LTD.	
Trafford Catalogue #03-0942		*www.trafford.com/robots/03-0942.html*	

10   9   8   7   6   5   4   3   2

For my children: Kristen, Gretchen and Dylan

Acknowledgements

My thanks to Kay Kos for her constant encouragement, support and assistance throughout this writing effort.

Thanks to Kristen Sanderson for her research assistance.

Deep appreciation to the people of Vietnam, especially friends and colleagues at Can Tho University.

"What difference does it make to the dead, the orphans and the homeless, whether the mad destruction [of war] is wrought under the name of totalitarianism or the holy name of liberty or democracy?"

Mahatma Gandhi (1942)

Nearing midnight. The passionate tempo increased in the rice paddies on the country side of the canal. Bull frogs, desperate to replay the pleasure, croaked their pleas to an indifferent gender. Victims hoping for victory.

Seb Kloster felt an indifference as well, but his was a more kindly one. He had just finished his fourth pipe and, rolling onto his side with knees bent towards sleep, he felt the gentle victory of disregard. He was at peace with himself.

Peace had never come easy for Seb, but over the years Ky - Madame Ky - more than any other woman - had given him a calming pleasure. Long before him, she had pleasured men. First, at fourteen, she had sold herself from homelessness and hunger to Madame Guc. On a train of houseboats listing in one of the Mekong's many canals which carved into Can Tho City, virgin Ky became General D's girl. Madame Guc's eight boats served the special needs of the South Vietnamese officers. Then, American military advisors, invited as guests of the Vietnamese officers, found Madame Guc's "Venice." High ranking officers only, and virgin Ky only for General D. For three years, until General D's car was ambushed by Viet Minh insurgents, Ky was his. She thought herself fortunate. A boat of her own with oiled teak floors, silk curtains and windows screened from the insects of the night. Catered meals. Long lazy hours of reading, of learning English. Then, without warning - at any hour - General D.

After the ambush she became just another one of Madame Guc's girls, serving the needs of the South Vietnamese officers and their special guests, the Americans. No longer virgin, no longer special, she lost the privileges of General D's power. Between visits she cooked her own meals, washed her own clothes and had few lazy hours for reading and study. During the visits she recast herself from domestic to coquette to courtesan - shy, sexual and, if required, sadistic. She no longer had her own grand boat, but - with the others - would wait out the hours in Madame Guc's lounge - the first boat - until this Vietnamese general or that American colonel would choose her. For three teenage years she was General D's choice, then for ten more she was chosen by other men.

In the spring of '75 the Americans left. One year later Seb Kloster arrived, and within the month he had his first visit to "Venice." Madame Guc had retired with her wartime savings to a handsome house once occupied by French then American generals, several of whom had been her most faithful patrons. She had arranged for herself a proper pension: ten percent of the brothel's income from opium and auxiliary services to be paid once a year during Tet, the Vietnamese New Year. For her life-long cut she had sold the "Venice" enterprise to Ky - now Madame Ky.

Once in position, Ky - only twenty-eight - proved herself a shrewd businesswoman and a caring madam to her "sisters," as she called them. For Seb, she proved to be both Kama and Cassandra.

Now, after over two decades of living alone, Ky's "Venice" became home to Seb. He continued to rent a flat near Can Tho Children's Hospital, but rarely did he spend time there, especially at night. Ky, less in superstition than in memory of the Chinese mother she had lost to malaria, renovated and moved onto Boat #8, Seb's lucky home-away-from-home.

"Chien Bot," Ky whispered to her sleeping lover, "The frogs are sleeping; you must get up." It was almost a daily ritual now, this tender wake-up call. It had begun as a tease of Seb's obsession with *ech chien bot* - fried frog legs.

"You have to meet the new doctor at eight . . . at the hospital."

Seb growled gently, "What's the time?"

"Just six, but you must walk off last night."

Last night still lived within Seb, and he liked the mellow morning it promised. A walk would not only ruin the mellow, it would invite the melancholy he feared.

2

"No guarantee he'll be there," Seb said, "and no guarantee I'll like him once he gets there."

"No, Chien Bot, no guarantees. Here's some coffee, but you'll have to get out of bed if you want your all-American breakfast."

Those had been Seb's words, originally, years ago. He had come to relish Vietnamese food - except for breakfast. The traditional morning dish, *pho*, proved delicious at what he considered the proper time - lunch - but rice noodles shingled with no-name meatballs and slivers of liver were not an appetizing beginning to the day.

So he indulged in his all-American breakfast of two eggs, a local ham-of-sorts, baguettes - a leftover of France's one century rule - in lieu of toast, and a second cup of exquisite Dalat coffee. As he ate, he watched the coffee drip slowly through the aluminum filter balanced atop the glass. It was his daily reminder of all that was most beautiful here: that slow, fluid tempo of a passing day, the warm nuances of human contact and the cream-brown color of Ky.

After a silent breakfast, Seb moved behind Ky and, pressing himself against her, he combed her smooth black hair with his fingers. He whispered "Jasmine," her nickname, into her ear. Without further words, he left Ky's house of good fortune and walked reluctantly alongside the slow canal for two hundred metres until he reached Nguyen Trai Street, hectic with hawkers, school children and *cyclo* drivers.

He scanned the maze of machines and men, searching for Hao. The other drivers knew Seb's choice was Hao, and, without resentment, shouted Hao's name over the cacophony of bleating horns, hawkers' squalls, children's whoops and the very harshness of the language itself.

Hao and Seb went back twenty years; the friendship had been set in motion by the explosion of a dormant landmine strategically placed under a bamboo grove trail by long-gone American soldiers. Hao was carried into the Children's Hospital. The father bowed slightly, silently, and with outstretched arms presented his son to the American doctor. The boy, no more than ten, lay semi-conscious on top of the reception counter.

3

Blood trickled through the home-made tourniquet of rags which somehow held thigh to shattered knee and calf. The toes, the foot, the ankle gone. Dr. Seb - as he was called by patients, nurses and other doctors - lifted the boy into his arms and, bowing slightly and silently to the father, carried Hao to the emergency room. After removing the soaked rag, he poured a dilution of hydrogen peroxide and water into the open wound and wiped away the blood - wet and dry. The boy cried out once. Then, without anaesethetic, Seb knifed and sawed through the leg, above the knee. The boy cried out - once more - and fell unconscious. Seb overlapped the skin below the thigh muscle and stitched the amputation with sutures made from the tendons of rats' tails. Three days and nights of fitful sleep followed, broken by howls of pain and frequent whimpers of fear. On the fourth day Hao was released, and returned on the back of his father's bicycle to his anxious mother and three older sisters. He would never till his father's fields.

Seb's saving Hao had come three months into his two year stint as a volunteer doctor at the hospital. By then, he knew that a boy in Hao's condition would be a liability to the family's survival on the farm. He made Hao's father a deal. The boy could have free board and room at the hospital - he would sleep underneath the reception counter, the same counter he had been laid upon after the explosion. In exchange, Hao would guard the bicycles of the doctors and nurses.

Five years later Seb made Hao a deal without the father. He would buy Hao a used *cyclo* - a motorized trishaw- to taxi staff and patients to and from the hospital. In return, Seb would get free rides as long as the cyclo lasted. Now, twenty years into their friendship and fifteen into the taxi business, Hao backfired his cyclo towards an already sweating Seb.

"Good morning Dr. Seb. You work early this today."

"I hope not," Seb shouted over the morning din. "I want to go and come back within the hour. Today is Sunday, Hao. Good Christians rest on Sunday, you know."

"I know you no Christian Dr. Seb. And I know every day you want Sunday since you with Ky."

Seb feigned shock. "I'm not with Ky, Hao. I was just visiting . . ."

Hao laughed in friendly conspiracy. "Long visit Dr. Seb. In old time, I take you from you house to hospital to you house to Ky to you house - every day. Now I take you from Ky to hospital to Ky. No need go you house. Save gas. Thank you, Dr. Seb."

Hao cocked his right wrist upward, giving the throttle full flow. Seb stepped up and into the double seat behind Hao, careful not to cut skin or clothes on the sharp shards of metal making up the scarred body of Hao's immortal machine. The patched canvas canopy, hinged to both sides of the cyclo by crane-legged metal struts, sheltered Seb from the growing sun. When he had first found southeast Asia, like so many white foreigners, he had a craving for the sun's heat. Now he found it unforgiving, even vindictive. He remembered the cool comfort of Ky's boat and promised himself one hour at the hospital - max.

Hao killed the engine one block from the hospital, letting the cyclo coast down the street and through the open iron gates. He stopped in front of the large double doors and looked through the barred windows to the reception counter he had called home until he and Seb became partners in the taxi trade.

Seb jumped cautiously out of the back seat, slapped Hao's hand with imaginary money and, backing towards the front door, teased, "Thanks partner. Another day, another *dong*. Can you come back in an hour . . . sober?"

Hao smiled as Seb turned to face the hospital and the queue, at least forty strong, of sick and injured children awaiting admittance. Anxious parents, mostly mothers, stared vacantly at the foreign doctor. Seb acknowledged their presence while avoiding eye contact. Even after twenty years - long and weary years after his initial volunteer stint had finished - he could not face the reality of statistics; many of these children would not see next week. And he knew, but could not convince these stoic parents, that their children could as easily be saved - if at all possible - by his Vietnamese colleagues. He further knew that his own professional interest and energy had been compromised

5

by that fatigue brought on by the failure - he felt his failure - to make but a moment's difference in a millennium of suffering. And this knowledge, his daily epiphany, made going to work more difficult, leaving easier, and living with Ky and his pipe all the more addictive.

He shuffled sideways - a hermit crab in a sea of suffering - through the double doors.

Dr. Trang Anh Nguyen, a teenage twenty-eight, a pediatrician and an instinctive optimist, approached Seb as he was wiping the morning's sweat from under his chin.

"Good morning Dr. Seb. Thanks for coming in on a Sunday. I know it's your holiday, but we thought it would be good for you to welcome the new doctor since he's an American."

"Morning Professor Trang." The "professor" was both a truth and a friendly tease, and the first name "Trang" showed a friendship beyond titles. She had recently been appointed to the medical faculty of Can Tho University as an assistant professor. Throughout most of traditional Asia, teachers, especially professors, are given a higher degree of respect than other professionals, including doctors since doctors were once their professors' students. Seb respected both this ancient Confucian concept and Trang.

"What's this morning's lecture, Professor? The symptoms? The diagnosis? The medical miracle for today's disease?"

Trang warmed to Seb immediately. She savoured the teasing irony of his daily greeting. He had been her mentor during her internship at the hospital.

"No lecture today, Dr. Seb. But there is a delay, and I'm sorry I couldn't find you. Linh went to your flat at seven this morning but there was no answer. You're a deep sleeper."

Seb, showing an unusual flash of embarrassment, countered, "Yes, the ageing process, I guess. What's the delay?"

"I'm not sure why, but the new doctor has been detained in Saigon. The Immigration Office insists that a hospital representative come immediately."

"Oh, Professor, why must these foreigners disturb my peace? Why have you put up with the likes of us - French, Chinese, Americans, Russians - over the centuries? We're more trouble than we're worth."

"Not you, Dr. Seb. We think you're worth - how do you say - your pounds in gold."

"Weight in gold," Seb corrected, "Weight in gold. Aah . . .okay. . . I'll go. When Hao comes by in an hour, tell him I've gone to the big city. Can you give me a quick - but safe - ride home so I can grab a change of clothes, my razor, a good book ?"

The ride on Trang's scooter - five minutes to his flat and another ten to the Ministry office - equalled fifteen minutes of nostalgic pleasure for Seb. He loved women, especially Asian women, and most especially Vietnamese women in *ao dais*. Seb could not remember Trang in anything but an *ao dai,* that sensual combination of loosely fitting silk pants covered by a form-fitting silk dress, slit high on both sides. He thought of the *ao dai* as the *yin-yang* of fashion - the male and female in harmony, especially when in motion. Trang - dressed in an *ao dai* of white trousers and a blue tunic, driving her motor scooter and walking into his flat and into the Ministry office - was the pleasure of memories in motion: of the women he had known and of the woman he had come to love - Ky. Not simply sexual, not only sensual, Seb was experiencing the pure pleasure of remembering why he couldn't imagine living anywhere else.

2

The five hour trip from Can Tho to Ho Chi Minh City became for Seb a chance to replay his twenty years in post-war Vietnam. Middle-aged angst invited him to reflection.

Then the city had been called Saigon. There had been few cars, hundreds of motorbikes and thousands of bicycles and hand-pulled carts. The smooth ebb and flow of traffic had mirrored the rhythm of Asia's war-worn Paris. Now, with thousands of cars, and motorbikes and bicycles in the millions, the tides of traffic flooded the streets with noise and smoke. Still, the rhythm andante of the people prevailed. Seb admired this loyalty to ancient movement. It encouraged him to moderate his own life's rhythms.

Then, as a newcomer to country and culture, Seb had always found a hotel room in the former European centre of Saigon, near the colonial Continental Hotel, the old Opera House and the embassy avenues. Then, he had felt a need for foreign company. Now, he shied away, preferring his Vietnamese contacts in Cholon, the Chinese quarter. In Cholon, the past of Vietnam was present, and, knowing the language, Seb felt a sense of cautious belonging.

He asked the Ministry's driver to stop the car at Phung Hung Street, the southern gateway to Cholon. Like a sweet-toothed kid, he felt his belly rumble in anticipation of his walk through the market. He barely touched pavement when a man of his own middle age, lying belly-down on a mechanic's trolley, placed both arms - amputated to the elbows - on the ground to position himself between Seb and the first market stall. Seb pulled a 2,000 *dong* note from the money roll in his pocket and carefully slipped it into the prone beggar's tin cup, which was nailed to the right front corner of the trolley. Without a word the man rolled on and Seb walked towards the line of cloth and canvas umbrellas.

First, the fruit vendors, females from ten to an ancient fifty, in peasant pajamas. The older women, squatted on their haunches, still as stones. The younger ones, caged into work by their squatting elders, gave listless effort to the chores of cleaning and stacking the fruit. They were specialists, selling only mangoes or only papayas or only melons. Seb never sensed any outward show of competition, but he knew the day's take could be the difference between rice or rice with vegetables or rice with meat and vegetables. He stopped to buy a single coconut from a startled teenage girl in black pajamas and wearing the conical hat common in the countryside. With quick, deft machete strokes she carved a diamond-hole in the top and shyly offered the coconut, a straw in the hole, to the foreigner. Seb's *"Cam ong"* - thank you - brought a nervous smile followed by an immediate look away.

He browsed slowly through the vegetables while drawing up the milky juice. Finished, he lay the coconut on the ground, and before he straightened, a boy-waif began whittling away at the nutritious meat.

Bowls without end of noodles: thin - yellow, white and clear; thick - yellow, white and clear. And, as if central to the market's theme, hills of rice separated the fruits, vegetables and noodles from the fish and meat.

On the make-shift tables, small fish swimming in plastic bags of water, and underneath larger fish, drowning in air while flip-flopping on plastic mats. Crabs, prawns and shrimps, all to be sold rather than eaten.

Seb was far from being a vegetarian, but other than his craving for fried frog legs and a distinct liking for fish, he seldom ate meat. Perhaps it was the association he made. Because meat was expensive, it usually was consumed in quantity only on special occasions: most weddings, some funerals, and at Tet. And, with the meat and other dishes came too much potent liquor. Too often meat meant too much alcohol, too little sleep and too heavy a hangover. Midday sun-baked banquets only worsened his condition.

On the left, a dozen young pythons writhing over each other in a chicken-wire cage. A felt-yellow duckling waddled anxiously on the snake's spines, searching for escape. On Seb's right a pig, cut up into pieces and placed on a table as if it were a correctly positioned jigsaw puzzle: at the top, severed ears above the decapitated head; the stomach and entrails dead centre; the hocks at the bottom above the hooves. Flies scratched at the dried blood between the pieces.

Buckets full of frogs.

From the food market one could continue straight ahead into household goods, plastic and fabrics. Seb chose a left turn, into a narrow alleyway. Here, shaded by high, white-washed walls only eight feet apart, women without men were everywhere, catering to that vanity of gender which had always intrigued, Seb. He was taken by the universal truth he had witnessed in his travels throughout exotic Asia, primeval Africa, sophisticated Europe and fashionable America: women, regardless of age, love to preen, to make common beauty unique. But he had misunderstood their intent. He had always thought that women, whether in downtown New York or up-country Sweden, preened for the sole purpose of attracting men in competition with other women. About ten years ago, Ky, walking this same alley with Seb, had made myth of Seb's truth. Yes, women competed with each other, but not for men; rather, for recognition of their own beauty by other women. Even now, Seb instinctively rebelled from Ky's truth.

A woman, aged beyond her forty years, slouched in a bamboo chair, relaxing into a pedicure. Seb saw that her toenails had been filed to sharp points, much like fingernails, before being polished a crimson red. For whom? Her husband who slept by day and gambled through the night? Her market mates, who themselves were slouching in pedicure posture? Seb counted eight such cosmetic stations, every two fronting a beauty salon specializing in shampoos, cuts, perms and facials. His thoughts bounced south to Ky, Kama-Ky. Every day, with rare exception, she treated herself to a mid-morning shampoo, every week to a manicure and pedicure, and every month to a cut and style. For whom? Seb? Her brothel mates? Other women? Seb never tired of his misunderstanding for, regardless of intent, women's vanity fed his own.

At the end of the alley Seb faced a single wooden door, the entry to Ky's Saigon home, her reward for lonely years of long nights with men without love. To the left and right were four more doors, each an entry to the courtyard of an extended family. Ky's family included Seb and her sisters of Venice, and her Saigon home served as a retreat from the working world of Can Tho. The middle of three rooms was reserved for Seb and Ky, but tonight he would sleep alone.

It was evening, too late to contact the immigration authorities, but early enough to catch a nap, have a bath and a couple of beers. He was in no rush to meet his American guest. He wanted to eat alone, to enjoy what he called his umbilical urge - a cheeseburger with the works, french fries and beer - at Queen Kangaroo, an Australian pub specializing in American dishes. This ritual was a rare acknowledgement by Seb of his American self. Cheeseburgers and french fries were in his blood. He could remember challenging his two brothers and sister to "eat-the-most-contests" on Saturday hamburger nights. They lost. But he didn't like American beer, watery and without body. Vietnam's BGI, another remnant of French rule, was half the price of a Bud and European good. Besides, it was a political decision for Seb. He was convinced that American beers and their man-in-the-saddle sales pitches - much like the Marlboro ads - caused red necks and hard hearts.

Whenever he went to Queen Kangaroo he experienced a twofold pleasure: the warm welcome by Queenie, the Vietnamese wife of the Australian owner - now dead, and the anonymity of being a nobody to the Western journalists, bureaucrats and business types exchanging their expertise over nightly drinks.

It was past eight when Seb swallowed the last of his beer. He knew his time alone was nearly over. The young doctor would be confused and anxious, not knowing what might happen to him in this strange, foreign culture.

To save time, Seb took a car taxi to the Tan Son Nhat Hotel on Saigon's northern outskirts, near the airport. He asked the reception clerk, a young man in a wrinkled white shirt too long in the sleeve, for the room number of Mark Gullens, Dr.

11

Gullens. The clerk's tie was 1950's narrow, his black hair plastered down.

"Oh, Mr. Mark, he not in room now. He there," pointing as he spoke to a circle of couches separating the main lobby from the hotel restaurant. "He laughs too much."

Seb turned around to see an overgrown cherub of about thirty years, holding court with three delicate ladies-in-waiting. He approached the four, bowed gently to the three women who sat opposite the man, and with a telltale wink said, "Sorry for the interruption Dr. Gullens. My name's Seb Kloster - from Can Tho Children's Hospital."

Gullens was startled more by the wink than the words. He rose excitedly to his feet and thrust forward his right hand as he spoke, too quickly, "No problem Mr. . .uh . . Klausner . . Glad to meet you. I just knew someone would rescue me." He paused a fast second or two. "I'd like you to meet . . .gee . . I've forgotten . . "

Gullens nervously asked each her name and repeated it - incorrectly to Seb. They remained seated, bowed their heads slightly and smiled forgivingly as Gullens introduced Lan as Lamb, Mai as May and Sao as Sew.

"Nice to meet you. Thank you for giving Dr. Gullens such a warm welcome. I'm sure he appreciates your kindness," Seb responded in Vietnamese. They were awed by this foreigner's near-fluency in their language.

He turned to face Gullens, "I understand you've had some trouble. I'd like to help if I can. Let's go to the lounge for a drink."

Gullens was floundering. In a foreign country, in the company of three beautiful women, and under the counsel of a total stranger . . . he tapped his right foot nervously on the tiles, trying to regain his balance. He spoke again, staccato, "Well, maybe Lamb, May and Sew can join us." Two second's silence. "What do you think?" Another second. "Are you staying here? Which room?" A split second. "Where's the lounge? I'm hungry. Can I . . ?"

"Let's go to the restaurant then," Seb interrupted, "You can eat, I'll drink. But it's best we go alone . . for now. They will understand." And, before Gullens could answer, Seb continued, only in Vietnamese, looking at Lan, Mai and Sao, "Thank you again for your kindness. Perhaps we will see you later."

As the two men were leaving the lobby, Seb thought just how eternal waiting was in Vietnam: waiting to get on a ferry, to sell today's produce, to gain admittance to a hospital, to sell oneself to a stranger. They - the traveller, the vendor, the sick, the lady-in-waiting - possessed a patience Western minds could neither understand nor appreciate. They had the unique capacity to remain static in a hyper-changing world. These three women, at one time too young and soon-to- be too old to wait in hotel lobbies, have waited for centuries. They have waited through the Chinese, the French and the Americans. They were all, in their own time, ladies-in-waiting.

Seb followed Gullens into the restaurant, and for the first time took measure of his burden. Gullens looked athletic, but a plumpness softened his body, even his face. By American standards he was of average height, but this plumpness made him look larger than he was. To the Vietnamese this symbolized strength and prosperity. Once seated, Seb measured Gullens' face: small ears, small bright eyes, smallish nose and mouth, small teeth. Something was missing. It wasn't a matter of proportion, but a lack of completeness. Gullens looked in-waiting, a bit like bread dough before kneading. Unrealized potential. Even his beard, darker than his light brown hair, was hit and miss, like prairie grass.

Gullens wanted an American dinner. "I was warned by my uncle, a Vietnam vet, to take it easy with foreign food until my insides get used to the different spices and all."

Seb smiled, remembering his own early days in Asia. "Actually American food is foreign here, and they have their own way of cooking foreign American food. Chances are you'll be disappointed." He waited briefly, then continued, "You're better off to . . .you know . . .when in Rome . . Just stick to the cooked dishes, avoid raw vegetables and drink beer, not water. You'll be okay."

"I'm game. What do you recommend?"

"First time, just try some fried spring rolls or ginger chicken on rice."

Gullens ordered and devoured both with a gusto Seb hadn't experienced in himself in years. He laughed, "Well, here comes another American invasion." He took a liking to Gullens' innocent enthusiasm. He wondered if it would last.

"So, Dr. Gullens . . "

"Call me Mark, okay?"

"Okay Mark, what happened when you arrived?"

"I don't understand the fuss. Customs said my visa's not valid."

"Why?"

"Cuz on the form, where it said purpose of visit, I checked 'Other' and wrote 'medical work'."

"Do you have a work visa?"

"I don't know. What's the difference?"

"Let me see your passport," Seb said with a studied patience.

"Don't have it. Some ass in uniform said they would keep it until all my papers are okay."

Seb sensed in the raised voice a ready disposition towards confrontation. Youthfulness, he thought.

"Okay. Not to worry. Tomorrow I'll check with Customs."

Gullens moved in. "Yeh, I'll go with you. They can't just . . ."

"Yes they can Mark. And, you can't go to Customs. Without a passport you are, so-to-speak, under house arrest."

"House arrest! That's bullshit!"

"No bullshit," Seb cautioned. "This can get serious if you don't keep cool." He paused. "Let me look into it tomorrow morning. You relax and enjoy your jet-lag. Just don't try to leave the hotel or - guaranteed - you'll be leaving the country without seeing Saigon, Can Tho or the hospital."

Gullens looked down at the empty plates in front of him. A long awkward silence. Then, he bounced back and with spontaneous enthusiasm he almost shouted out, "No problem . . .Jesus, I forgot your name . . "

14

"Seb."

"No problem, Seb. I'll just have another chat with those gorgeous ladies in the lobby. They sure are friendly."

"Enjoy yourself. Remember though, it'll cost you. They've got to make a living too."

"You mean . . ."

"Yeh, they're working girls. It wouldn't be fair to take their time unless you plan to do something."

A sheepish silence. "Well I . . . "

Seb took this moment to shake hands and, with a closing wink, wished Gullens a good night.

In the morning, after his all-American breakfast in the rooftop restaurant of the Rex Hotel, Seb walked the short distance to Customs and Immigration. He knew Vuong Quoc Phai, the Assistant Director, who ten years ago had been the chief customs official in Can Tho. *Duong day* - connections - are a traditional part of Vietnamese life, and Seb believed in the divine efficacy of certain time-honoured customs. Casual conversation about mutual acquaintances and the obligatory tea set the stage for the formal discussion to follow.

Mr. Vuong approved of Gullens' stay in Vietnam with two caveats: one, Gullens must leave the country after three months and apply for a proper work visa before reentry, and two, Seb would be responsible for Gullens during his three month stay. Seb knew better than to argue either point, even though he felt unduly burdened by the latter. Why, he thought, should he be held responsible for a total stranger? Mr. Vuong's observation that they are both Americans and both doctors wasn't a compelling reason to draft him into parental service. Nevertheless, Mr. Vuong's very position compelled.

With the necessary documents and Gullens' passport in hand, Seb returned to the Tan Son Nhat Hotel just in time to witness Gullens in the thick of a luncheon orgy.

"Hi ya Seb! Pull up a chair. Here's a feast fit for . . ."

"About a dozen jocks in training," Seb interrupted as he sat down, rocked his chair on its hind legs and slowly absorbed the scene: six dishes - all main courses - an Australian white wine and cans of beer in a bucket of ice.

"Jesus Mark, you can't possibly begin to eat all of this."

"Truth is . . ." Gullens mumbled, his mouth midstream between consumption and conversation, "I probably could. However this is for all of us, including you."

"Us?"

"Yeh, there's an American businessman and his wife staying at the hotel. He's picking up the tab, so enjoy."

"Where are they?"

"In their room, I guess. He invited me to join him for lunch, but he left as soon as he ordered. A phone call to Texas I think. Anyway, it's here, so dig in!"

"Yeh, I'll need a shovel, for sure." Seb paused to take a second measure of his burden - the round, ruddy face with its small features, the nervous energy, the innocent enthusiasm.

"Mark, before I eat and the others return, let me tell you what's happened."

"Shoot."

"Everything's okay - sort of." Seb consciously became more serious. "First of all, you screwed up by coming to Vietnam on a tourist visa rather than a work visa. Secondly, you screwed up by hassling the customs officer and by threatening to contact the American Embassy."

"Shit Seb, I didn't hassle anyone. I only wanted to get going, and I thought the embassy part would set them straight."

"Set them straight?" Seb's voice gnarled. "This is Vietnam. They won the war, and it really pisses them off every time some American forgets his history lesson."

"Hell, I was only . . ."

Seb refused to listen. "Think about it Mark. A Vietnamese visits the U.S. Arrives at San Fran airport. He's questioned, then detained by U.S. Customs. He threatens to contact his embassy - Vietnamese - wherever it is. . . What the hell do you think U.S. customs would do to the poor bastard?"

"Yeh, but . . ."

"No buts, Mark. Just listen. Customs has given you permission to stay here for three months on your tourist visa on the condition that during that time you are my responsibility. Now, there's no way I want to play father-figure at my age but, god dammit, if you want to stay, we have no choice - neither of us. So think about it, because three months with me as your Papa could prove fatal to both of us."

"Sorry, Seb, I really am. I didn't mean to cause trouble."

17

A smile showed through Seb's seriousness. "I'm sure you didn't, so let's drop it and start from here . . . Eat everything on your plate son - or no dessert."

They both laughed in harmony.

They had just finished when they saw a man followed by a woman approaching the table. "This is the fella I mentioned," Gullens whispered, "The one who's buying lunch."

Gullens rose first and Seb followed. The man was massive - well over six feet - fat, and he carried his body stiffly, like a patient recently removed from a body cast. The woman was beautiful. Better than the girl next door. Blond, pixie-cut hair, green eyes, a swimming suit figure and full lips framing a TV smile. He was in his late forties, she about twenty-five.

The huge man took control immediately.

" Name's Dick Samuelson," he announced, and presented his business card to Seb.

Richard J. Samuelson, III
President and Chief Executive Officer
SAMUSAN SHOES, INC
Liberty, California. U.S.A 96369

Seb quickly passed over the phone and fax numbers and the e-mail cipher. "I'm Seb . . . Seb Kloster, and I'm afraid I'm cardless." He smiled slowly.

"Well, in these parts a business card's the key to opening doors, markets and banks. Understand?"

"Yeh," Seb replied, "I understand."

"Enjoy the lunch? On the house . . . of Samusan Incorporated." He sighed his benevolence. "My apologies. I was phoning my eldest son, Ronald. Texas plant not proceeding on schedule. But, we'll correct that, pronto."

Gullens wanted recognition. "Here you are, Mr. Samusan . . .there's plenty of food left."

The woman interrupted, smiling. "I'm sorry Mr. Gullens, but . . . . "

"Please, just call me Mark."

18

"But Mr. Samuelson already ate in his room. A special diet. And it's Mr. Sam-uel-son. Sam-u-san, that's the company."

" Yeh . . . U.S.A. in it, you know. And this is Mrs. Sarah Samuelson, my new bride."

Sarah offered her hand to Seb. Ivory piano fingers. "Pleased to meet you Mr. Kloster."

The conversation stood still, so Seb retreated slightly. "Glad to meet you." Then he turned towards Gullens. "Mark, I'm going out front to check if our driver's arrived. You better get ready to go. Nothing urgent, but the road to Can Tho . . . ."

"Can Tho . . .well, what a coincidence," boomed Samuelson, "This trip is a combination of business and pleasure. I should have said pleasure, then business. We honeymooned in Hawaii, Tokyo, Bali and Singapore. Vietnam is business. And, Can Tho's my target. That's where we're headed as soon as I arrange transportation."

Seb repeated, "The road to Can Tho is a bit risky, especially at night. We should leave soon."

"You mean dangerous?. . . Bandits?. . .Guerillas?" Samuelson asked.

"No, not at all. The war's over, you know. It's just that there's too much going on: bicycles, motorcycles, buses and trucks . . .sometimes no headlights. Farmers drying rice on the road and pulling or pushing carts, old women walking, kids playing, the odd drunk. If it moves, it's on the main road - only one. We don't want to hit or be hit."

"Give me ten minutes, Seb, and I'll be ready to roll. Maybe Mr. Samuelson . .uh . Dick. . you can catch a ride with us."

Sarah smiled again. "That's very kind, Mark. But Mr. Samuelson will need three cars. I mean one car and two vans - personal belongings and business materials."

And Seb added, "Our car is booked - fully. Anyway, it's a Ministry car so we can't just..."

Samuelson broke in, "You mean a government car?" His voice tensed. "You work for the Communists, Mr. Kloster?"

19

"Not really. I'm a doctor. I work with sick folk - some communists, some not. Mainly with kids." He looked to Gullens. "Hurry Mark, your ten minutes are almost up."

"I'm outta here. Nice to meet you Dick .... Sarah ..."

"Mr. Samuelson," she corrected, smiling.

Gullens was unperturbed: "Thanks for the lunch. Hope to see you soon - in Can Tho."

Gullens left, and Seb, after small conversation about California wines and the recent world series, excused himself. He left the restaurant, crossed the hotel lobby, opened the front door before the doorman noticed him, and signalled the Ministry driver forward for pick up.

Gullens came out of the elevator into the lobby, disguised as an American: His short-cropped hair covered by a San Francisco Forty-Niner cap, mirrored dark glasses, black long-sleeved shirt, black denim pants, black Nike running shoes. And he brought America with him: a mega-backpack, a zoom camera around his neck and a Samsonite in each hand.

Seb saw him struggling across the lobby. He re-entered the hotel, and, taking the two suitcases, said," Come on, my son. Time to go home."

Again, they laughed, together.

Between the hotel and the car, thirty metres, Gullens felt his chest cave in and his throat tighten and close. The sun had peaked above, greeting him with the static-hot welcome of Vietnam's humid dry season. Seb saw the sweat spill instantly down Gullens' forehead and under his jowls. His black shirt darkened with blotches of wetness.

Seb sensed Gullens' discomfort. "You'll get used to it .... the sweating. You'll sweat - guaranteed. But it will cool you down - guaranteed. A couple of months of beer will thin your blood and you'll sweat less - guaranteed." He laughed gently, alone.

Everything Seb had described about the road from Saigon to Can Tho was true - plus some - in Gullens' eyes.

Leaving the city, even in midday, was a bumper-car course of metal on wheels, a great challenge with a definite sense of purpose but with little direction.

The suburbs showed the recent changes. Concrete houses where rice paddies once were. A Catholic church. A Buddhist temple. A Cao Dai Cathedral, its enormous eye of God looking out from above the front doors. The odd roadside market, a miniature of its city cousin.

Then came the countryside, more rice paddies than houses, and for every house an ancestral grave on a high mound, safe from monsoon floods. Raised, foot-worn dirt paths between paddies - avenues of gossip. Pajama'd women, steeped knee-deep in paddy water, tending green shoots of rice. From above, their cone-shaped hats looked like so many tiny thatched roofs. Outhouses on stilts in the deep middle of shallow ponds, with wobbly wooden planks linking toilets to land.

The ferry at My Tho crossed the mother river, the Mekong River. Young women selling fruit, boys hawking watches and cigarette lighters dangling from large cardboards, tiny girls selling chiclets and doublemint gum - their dirty hands motioning to their hungry mouths. Men, forty to eighty - most in one piece, some in parts - begging. Young, healthy men in their teens and twenties, staring with quiet curiosity.

The driver showed his Ministry card, then drove to the head of the line. Once the inbound cars and foot passengers had disembarked, a ferry worker coaxed the vehicles onto the open deck. The Ministry car had a front row, ring-side seat. To the right of the ferry, five near-naked boys jumped helter-skelter in and out of the muddy river. Beyond the boys, clothed mothers and daughters washed clothes and themselves. Between the two, a lone water buffalo, chained to a stake, wallowed in the cooling pleasure of water and reeds. In front, *thuyen cheo*- river boats. Pajama'd women in conical hats Xed their arms and pushed forward on the long oars, moving the boats briskly with or so very slowly against the heavy current. Family houseboats. Craft and produce boats. Water taxis.

The ferry first coughed then churned its way from the dock. At once, the young women, the cardboard boys, the tiny gum girls with dirty hands, and the men - whole or in part - queued up to stare into car windows, hoping for money earned or begged. Seb said nothing. He pushed open the car door and slid

21

gracefully through the surrounding crowd to the front of the ferry. Gullens baulked. The press of noses on glass, the staring eyes and open mouths paralyzed him. Five minutes into the crossing, just past mid-river, he steeled himself and opened the car door. The faces retreated, honourably, and Gullens sidled cautiously to Seb's side. They studied each other, silently.

Silence was essential. For Seb, a recharge of energy and purpose. For Gullens, a new understanding of his confusion.

Another two hours by car and another ferry across the Mekong. The press of faces seemed remarkably similar. During the second crossing Gullens chose to stay in the car, his small eyes staring blankly at a travel book, *Vietnam: The Land and the People*. The others' eyes pierced the windows and stained the pages of the book. He closed his eyes.

Dr. Trang had arranged accommodation for Gullens at Can Tho University guesthouse. Two ash grey concrete blocks, separated by a driveway, had been built in sullen Soviet style by the Americans during their war in Vietnam. The six bedrooms, shared bathrooms and communal dining room had been home to a parade of experts - political, economic, military, academic, even religious - from the United States. After the Americans, there followed Soviets of the same ilk - minus the missionaries. Then came specialists from other nations, less chauvinistic than their American and Soviet predecessors.

The trip had taken longer than planned. By the time they arrived at the guesthouse, the foreign guests had retired and the staff had left. The gates were locked. The driver, tired, hungry and tense, bounced his hand against the horn five or six times. Hung, the old watchman, was already on his way to whiskey-sleep, and his slow totter towards the gates caused the driver to hit the horn again. Hung looked at the car then down to his chain of many keys. After slow study, he chose the key to the double gates.

"Well, here's your home-away-from-home," Seb welcomed Mark. " This is where I stayed when I first came to Can Tho twenty years ago. What was good enough for the old man should be good enough for the kid." A weary laugh.

Gullens said nothing, not because of what he saw - his new home - but because of the exhaustion of culture. Too much in too short a time. Centuries crammed into hours.

"I've got to be going. Hung will show you to your room. If you're hungry, fifty metres up or down the road you'll find food."

"Thanks Seb, I'll be fine. Just a little out of it, I guess."

"Well, a good sleep and you'll bounce back. Breakfast's at seven in the dining room - that building." Seb pointed to the left block, "I'll be by before noon - okay?"

"Okay. And thanks again."

Seb watched Gullens follow Hung to the building on the right. The young doctor carried his two suitcases while the old man shouldered the pack. The door opened and shut, and they disappeared into the interior darkness.

The driver offered Seb a ride home but he declined, wished the driver a good night's rest and hailed a passing cyclo. He was only minutes away from Ky's.

She was lying on her right side, her arms hugging the pillow under her head. Seb slipped soundlessly out of his clothes and into bed, beside her.

His nakedness touched hers. His face near her raven hair, his chest against her upper back, his knees crooked behind hers. He listened to the quiet, easy breathing of his lover and felt the serenity of her sleep.

Intimate nightness . . . inviting sleep.

Then his maleness awoke, and a growing stiffness searched for her. His left arm reached around her waist, his hand cupping the soft fullness of her right breast; he cradled it to the other, his thumb lightly touching her left nipple to hardness.

Her breath quickened and she rolled half onto her back, lifting her knee towards heaven. His hand wandered down, from breast to belly to warm and welcome dampness. His fingers tipped her own hardness until she opened to his. He entered slowly, fully, and held his stay, returning his hand to the hollow between her breasts, cupping one then the other upward. He lay still, swelled within her.

23

Slowly she rocked her back against him, then away - slowly, then back and away, back and away . . . . He stopped her rocking and began himself, sliding slow strokes deep within her . . . then out, teasing her tender edge. She moaned, and he slipped deep into her again, held, then slowly almost out again . . once more . . . once more again . . again . . each stroke slow . . until she pulled him deeply into her and rocked back and away in rhythm with him.

She squeezed his swell, held tightly, moaning. His breathing quit as he flooded into her. She trembled, then trembled again, then his seized breath sighed release.

They lay still, still together, and they slept deeply through the darkness.

4

Long before daybreak. Seb was lying on his left side and Ky was curled behind him, her left hand lost in his hair, her right arm around his chest - the hand capturing the heart. He could feel the warmth of her slow breathing on his shoulders. Again, he stirred and grew.

"Oh my Chien Bot," Ky murmured. "You are always ready to play". Her right hand left his heart and roamed through his belly hair to grip him. "I must hold you down."

Seb groaned in the pure delight of the moment, in the "*joie de vivre*" she gave his mornings. "Let me go! I must get up," he teased, as his hand held on to her hand which held him hard.

And in the softness of morning memories, they dozed off, leaning against each other.

"Dr. Seb! Dr. Seb! Are you there?" A long polite pause. "Dr. Seb, I know you no home. Dr. Trang sent me you home. You no answer so I come here" A longer pause. "Dr. Seb! Dr. Seb!"

"Morning Hao. Just a minute, I'll be right out." Seb could tell by the sun's piercing angle that it was after 10 o' clock, but he couldn't understand the commotion. He rolled over, straddling Ky without touching her, his legs and arms outside hers. His lips brushed below first one then the other ear, "I love you Jasmine - absolutely."

Seb knew he had to move quickly, before Kama took control again. He got up and went to the toilet. Then he splashed his face and sponge-soaped and rinsed off the night. The cool waterfall from the hinged urn above cleansed his body and readied him for the reality of his day.

As he dressed, his eyes scanned his sleeping lover and his mind mused on her mastery of the moment. Ky, Seb thought, never seems weighed down by her past - hunger and

25

homelessness - or frets about her future. She seems to be in a constant present, and this knack to be in the now negates yesterday's ghosts and tomorrow's devils. He envied Ky's easy indifference to her own fate, and he wished he could be less conscious of self, of purpose, of results, of meaning. He wanted simply to be - just like Ky.

Hao was leaning against his cyclo, his stump-of-a-leg pointing at Seb in mock accusation. "You sleepy man, Dr. Seb. You feel O.K.?"

Seb looked the accused for a moment, then recovered. "I'm just fine partner. What's up? What does Trang want?"

"She worry about new doctor. She worry he have big trouble in Saigon." Hao sucked in the smoke from a cigarette.

"Doctor's fine. We'll go by the hospital to tell Dr. Trang, then we'll pick him up; he's at the University Guesthouse." Seb scowled at Hao who was caught in a coughing fit. "Dammit Hao, you're going to die before seeing forty if you keep sucking on those cigarettes."

Hao knew the lecture. "I know Dr. Seb. But I die, I come back again . . have two good legs next time. Be handsome, rich man."

"Quit the bullshit Hao." Irritation reddened his neck. "Hao, you've had TB . . . still do. That and smoking's going to kill you - just watch."

"No problem Dr. Seb. You watch me in new life. I no smoke . . . I no drink . . . I have pretty lady like you . . . .I . . . "

"You win, partner . . . let's go."

The cyclo weaved through the traffic. Hao preferred a quick squirm around a car, truck, bus or cart to using the brakes, and he had little patience for pedestrians. Seb could only sit back and let Hao perform. He had convinced Hao, after a head-on collision with another cyclo, that the habit of driving on the wrong side of the road - a short-cut to save gas - could prove not only dangerous but expensive.

After calming down Trang at the hospital, Seb and Hao motored on to the guesthouse. Gullens, in what seemed his primary position, was seated at the first of the three tables in the dining room. He had missed breakfast and was early for lunch; consequently, he was eating alone.

Marie saw Seb enter and dashed towards him. She grabbed his arm with both hands, shaking it like an antique pump handle.

"Dr. Seb, you no look good. You skinny. You need a wife to feed you."

With his free arm Seb hugged her, pulling her against him.

"Ah, how's my beautiful Marie? And how's baby Thao?"

" Thao fat - look good, but you skinny. You eat now."

"Yes Marie," and he sang as best he could, "so warm and tender, .. Marie..."

She was the first person Seb had met when he first arrived - so long ago - at the guest house. Then, she was a pre-teen orphan living in a French nunnery behind Can Tho's only Catholic Church. By day she - along with other children whose Catholic families had fled the north four decades ago after the Vietminh victory over the French - was schooled by the nuns. In the evening she, along with seven other orphans, worked to pay for board, room and tuition by doing menial chores: washing dishes and clothes and cleaning guestrooms.

Seb had gently teased the child that when she reached the age of twenty, he would marry her if she wished. During his one year stay at the guest house his proposal, "Sweet Marie, will you marry me?" and her sincere reply, "Oh yes, Dr. Seb, I will," had nurtured a fast friendship. By the age of twenty, Marie knew better. By twenty-two she married, and at twenty-five she gave birth to baby Thao with assistance from a midwife and Dr. Seb, now Uncle Seb.

"Marie, I've found a husband-to-be for beautiful Thao. Of course, he seems a bit old for her now, but when Thao turns twenty, Doctor Mark here will only be in his mid-forties - at the height of his career."

"You promise me long time ago, Dr. Seb. But you no marry me. Now you promise man to my daughter. I no believe you. You hurt my heart. Now you hurt Thao heart too." She stared at him sternly, in mock anger, then laughed full-out. Her cheeks and belly shimmied in rhythm to her sounds.

Marie, even as an orphan child, had leaned towards plumpness and now, as manager of the guesthouse, she could eat without end. Stout, more than mere fat, she was an imposing presence, unlike the sylphlike fragility seen in most Asian women. That stoutness combined with a cherubic face and a rollicking nature provided the guesthouse residents the comic relief required to see their daily glass of life half-full.

"Here you *pho*, Dr. Seb. Breakfast for lunch."

"Thanks Marie. Dr. Mark will be staying here for three months, at least. Please feed him well, so I can work him hard."

Marie chuckled. "Dr. Mark work hard at lunch. He have good appetite, not like you Dr. Seb. You skinny."

Gullens was finishing a second go of soup, stir-fried greens, shredded meat and rice just as Seb was beginning his *pho* - rice noodle soup with slices of beef, tendons and meatballs. Seb looked at the empty serving bowls usually prepared for two.

"Well Mark, it looks like you've made yourself right at home."

"Yeh, this is damn good food. Don't know exactly what I'm eating, but it's damn good."

Seb sprinkled lime, mint leaves, bean sprouts, chili and fish sauce into his bowl of *pho* and picked up the *dua* - chopsticks.

Gullens watched. "I was gonna try some of the sauces, but my stomach's sometimes queasy so I didn't want to chance it so soon."

Seb spoke between inhales of noodles. "Seems to me your stomach's doing fine. This fish sauce is to the Vietnamese as soy sauce is to the Chinese. It's addictive. Makes you want to drink lots of fluids, which is good for the body in this climate. The red sauce is made from chilies . . . spicy hot, but once you get used to it, it's good for you too."

Gullens doubted Seb's wisdom. "I don't know. Bad for the bowels - no?"

"No, not once your guts adjust. The cuisine in most tropical countries is flavoured with spicy sauces. Good for the heart too - a stimulant. And it will help you get used to the real heat - outside."

Gullens looked through the open window and felt the hot, earthy wafts of humid air spinning off the ceiling fan. "Well, my guess is the sun's going to take more getting used to than the chili sauce. I'm thinking heatstroke and I'm not even outside yet!"

Seb smiled in sympathy. "It'll get hotter by the week until the monsoons come in June. By the way, you're scheduled to meet Dr. Trang at the hospital, so I'll finish and we'll be off."

"OK Seb." Gullens eyes wandered the dining room, a stark and ghostly room, especially when not filled with guests. He noticed three rectangular light areas, each about eighteen by thirty inches, on the back wall. "I wonder what was up there?" pointing to the wall. "Looks like pictures of some sort."

"Yep, Marx, Lenin and Ho Chi Minh. Ho was in the middle. They watched me eat every day for a year, twenty years ago. Only recently taken down . . . . I think in connection with the lifting of the American embargo. Since then, the government has been trying to make foreigners - especially capitalist foreigners with money to invest - feel welcome. So those pictures had to go."

Gullens' small eyes narrowed. "Wow! From Karl Marx to Macdonalds, almost overnight. That's progress."

"Don't be so sure. They suffered the American embargo for nineteen years . . .still, they survived. However, I'm not sure they can survive an invasion of junk food, junk music, junk movies . . .you understand? American junk values."

"Why junk?" asked Mark, as he nervously played pencil with one chopstick on the stained tablecloth. "That's free enterprise . . it guarantees . . "

"Nothing," interrupted Seb with an unusual loudness. Then in a quiet, careful voice, "Not now Mark, we've got to go. Later, if the mood suits - although I seldom feel the mood anymore - we can talk up a political storm. Just a word of caution. It's best not to delve too deeply . . .to ask - uh - political questions. They have answers, but they're different, depending on whether their family fought for Ho or for the USA . . . or - like many in the Mekong Delta - got caught between the two."

Seb paused and followed Gullens' silence with his eyes. He continued, "Politics in America equals taxes, unemployment and interest rates. Here, it was about life and death . . . for entire families . . .even villages. The war was in their backyard. In the States, it was on TV."

Seb lifted the bowl to his lips, drinking up the pho broth. Gullens watched him, without speaking.

"Since the war they have worked together . . had to . . enemies now colleagues. It hasn't been easy, but they've done it. To me, that's amazing. Hell, in the States they still fly the confederate flag in the South . . . hundred and thirty years after the Civil War." Seb stopped abruptly, pushed his bowl to the centre of the table and stood up, looking over Gullens towards the front doors. "Anyway, enough for now . . .let's go."

Seb and Gullens approached Hao who was bent over the handle bars of his cyclo, coughing violently and spewing phlegm onto the dry, thirsty asphalt.

"Hao, I'd like you to meet Dr. Mark. Mark this is Hao, my very good friend, my trusty business partner . . . and your first patient in Can Tho."

"My first patient?" Gullens questioned, reaching for Hao's hand in greeting.

"Yes, you can see Hao has TB, and yet he smokes every waking minute. His chances of seeing forty are nearly nil. But he needs a second opinion - yours. Good luck Dr. Mark, this patient takes patience!"

Hao's limp hand folded within Gullens' firm handshake. He was exhausted from his coughing fit. His eyes were reddened and teared and sweat beaded on his forehead. He grinned, mischief showing behind the tears. "Welcome Dr. Mark. You no worry. I be okay. Dr. Seb just angry me because he sleep and I wake him. He feel better soon. Me too."

5

To any passerby, Can Tho Children's Hospital, by Vietnamese standards, was a monument to modernism. The off-white concrete structure, occupying an eighth of a city block, gave the impression of economy, efficiency and quality. And, the makeshift kiosks and vendor carts bordering the hospital's high metal fence gave promise of hope, good health, even happiness. Cheap children's toys, soaps, lotions and basic medicines - mostly local - were there for anxious parents to purchase. The balloon man was there too, blowing up, twisting and pinching balloons into fantastic shapes.

Within told otherwise.

Dr. Trang, lovely in a bright yellow *ao dai*, was waiting to welcome the new doctor. Seb knew she had been ready since he left her, over two hours ago. As he made the introductions, he noticed for the first time an engaging shyness in Gullens. The young man was almost formal in greeting Trang, and he even seemed to bow a bit as he spoke. "I'm really looking forward to working with you and your colleagues. I hope I can be of help."

Trang responded in kind. "We have been waiting for you. I am sure you will be very helpful. Thank you . . . I only hope you don't become too tired from the work. It's very difficult, as Dr. Seb has told you."

"Actually, I've told him next to nothing. Didn't want to scare him away before he even arrived." He turned to Gullens. " By the way, we go by first names here, so from now on you're Dr. Mark."

Trang smiled at them both, discerning the contrast between experience and innocence, wisdom and wonderment. "Dr. Mark, let's have a cup of tea and I will tell you about our work. Then, you can visit the wards."

With Trang in front, they went into a small reception room adjoining the lobby. Two couches, covered with shiny red naughahyde, and a long, sort-of-coffee table were the only pieces of furniture. A naked bulb, unlit, hung loosely from the high ceiling. There was no fan. A Chinese thermos and a Vietnamese tea set were strategically placed on the table: the thermos, the teapot and a single cup on one side, two cups opposite.

Trang poured the boiling water from the thermos into the teapot, leaving the tea to steep as she spoke. "This is the only hospital for children south of Saigon. Over three million children in the region. But we only have one hundred and eighty beds, so we're always full."

"Flooded would be a better word," suggested Seb. " There are often two, sometimes three to a bed in the wards."

Gullens was nonplussed. "But that's impossible!

Trang stared at the teapot, absorbing the painted images of sampans below, limestone mountains and seagulls above. She had never visited beautiful Halong Bay in the north. Her mind tried to wander there, to her father's family.

"With so many children, how do you decide whom to treat, to admit to hospital?"

Without leaving Halong Bay, she said, "We . . . I mean the Director and the doctors must decide. If a child will live without our help, we don't treat him. If a child will die, even if we try to save him, we send him away. If we're not sure whether a child will live or die, we take him. We do our best for him." Trang's face dropped, her eyes leaving Halong Bay, staring at the floor. Her long, silken hair slipped over the front of her stooped shoulders.

"So, our overall success rate isn't very good," added Seb. "Even when we take them in, we don't have the equipment, the supplies, even the medicine . . . We don't . . . ." His voice trailed off .

Trang returned to the conversation, her head raised, her voice energetic. "But we have a wonderful staff . . . very dedicated . . . doctors, nurses, even two pharmacists."

"But no godamn medicine," Seb said with restrained emotion.

Trang countered, "We do have herbal medicines, but not antibiotics . . .usually. . . sometimes, we do."

"Why not?" asked Gullens.

"Ask the American president, the U.S. congress," snapped Seb. "Ask them about their embargo against Vietnam, including an embargo on medicine. Ask them." Seb stood up, glanced at Trang apologetically. "I'm going to make my rounds, excuse me." He left the room without looking at Gullens.

"I'm sorry, Dr. Mark . . .Dr. Seb is very tired."

"But I thought the embargo was lifted?"

"It was. So we can get medicine now if we have money, but we have very little money. Let me show you around. Then, you will understand."

Trang led Gullens to the laboratory. There was one long counter covered with chipped green and white tiles. On the counter, in the very centre, was an antiquated centrifuge, used for blood samples. There were empty test tube racks on either side and an old Russian microscope nearby. Nothing else. Two wooden stools served as furniture. No one was working there. "We couldn't keep our two lab technicians. We had a national budget cut two years ago . . we couldn't pay them. The doctors try to use the equipment themselves."

Gullens surveyed the meagreness. His eyes moved from the centrifuge, following the electric cord to the power outlet. He saw a hole in the wall with wires snaking out everywhere, leading nowhere. The cord from the centrifuge was connected to the lone outlet, lost in the maze of wires.

Next Trang showed Gullens the single operating room, down the corridor from the lab. He could hear pride in Trang's voice. "We just received the new surgical lamp," pointing to a tall white stand to the right of the operating table. "From the U.N. . . . World Health Organization."

Gullens nodded as he scanned the room. A dark green tile floor, white tile walls, blinking florescent lights. Hygienic to the naked eye. He opened the doors of the surgical cabinet: scalpels, forceps, tweezers and what looked like instruments for tonsillectomy. They were bulky, too heavy, unlike those in American hospitals. Trang said, " Our surgical instruments are from Russia. Some are American. When the U.S. army left, we took them . . .a long time ago . . I was only a little girl then."

"What kind of surgery is done here?"

"Well, we can do all the basic operations - tonsillectomy, appendectomy. Three of our doctors are general surgeons, so they do the difficult procedures."

"If the hospital is full, why isn't the operating room being used . . . now, for instance, in the middle of the day?"

Trang retreated towards the door. "I think we need anaesthetics . . .the next shipment is coming soon . . . Please follow me now . . to see the children."

The intensive care unit was at the end of the corridor, a twenty-bed room. All the beds were occupied, not only by a child but also by the mother. Gullens learned that eighty percent of the children were from the countryside, some as far away as two hundred miles. Fathers remained at home, working in the fields. Mothers and children travelled by public bus. Some children died before reaching the hospital, some were admitted, others not. The mothers had no money for lodging, so they slept with their children, either in the bed or on a straw mat on the cement floor. The hospital had no money to feed the patients. The mothers bought cooked foods - noodles, rice, vegetables- from the vendors outside the hospital gates. The hospital provided a single grey sheet - bleach was beyond the budget - and a worn blanket.

Gullens stepped slowly beside Trang, his hands in his trouser pockets. His shirt was sweat-wet from the heavy, humid air. The hair just above his ears was damp, and a darker shade than ususal. "What major illnesses do the children have?"

"At least half suffer from severe malnutrition - very, very weak. Also, acute dysentery from polluted water."

"Don't they sterilize their drinking water?"

"Most don't. Kerosene is expensive. Wood is hard to find. They don't know they should. Their parents didn't."

Gullens moved to argue the point, but Seb's earlier words of caution reined in his voice. Trang continued, "polio, malaria and dengue fever and bilharzia. Accidents too . . . many, many accidents . . fire . . bus . . and birth deformities . . from the war . . " Trang's final few words were whispered, then she stopped altogether. She stood still, inviting Gullens - by hand gesture - to make his first rounds in intensive care.

The two nurses on duty watched as Gullens went from bed to bed. Other staff, curious about the young American doctor, stood outside, looking through open, wooden-shuttered windows. The mothers didn't move, but most smiled shyly, sadness in their eyes.

A young boy semi-conscious, his arms and legs outstretched. Dengue fever. His mother, in flowered pajamas, on the bed beside him. One hand gently touching his forehead, the other tightly gripping his bony wrist. On his blanket, below pink flowers and shoots of green grass, the word "Lucky" sewn in capital letters. An International Red Cross donation.

A baby, perhaps three months, in a blue nightshirt. Orange gloves, too large, covering tiny hands. His face a cold blue. A portable electric heater on the sill near his bed. This time a father, his sun-browned hand curving carefully over his son's little chest. His face showing the sorrow of coming loss.

A strong looking boy, sitting upright in the middle of the bed, his back to Gullens. Third degree burns from a kerosene lamp fire. The tinderbox thatched hut devoured in flames. The boy's dead skin sooty, the new skin a painful pink. Too painful to lie down. No bottle on the iv stand; only a baseball cap and a conical straw hat. Waiting alone.

A very young girl, under four years, naked on her back, her reedy legs open. No blanket. Second degree burns on her belly and chest. Her face, free of burns, pinched in silent pain. A mother's boiling pot of rice. The mother, in striped pajamas, stooped in desperate guilt.

A baby girl, only weeks old, under a green blanket. Gullens lifted the blanket. A surgically constructed anus where her navel once was. Dioxin. Agent Orange. Twenty years after the war. Silence. No chance.

Another baby girl, this one in a faded blue dress, screaming in agony. Her right forearm and hand ballooned to a grotesque popeye form, ready to burst. Amputation tomorrow, if anaesthetic available. Dioxin. Agent Orange.

35

6

That afternoon at the hospital had totalled Gullens - an emotional wreck. And, he had yet to put in a single day's work. A frigging first visit, that's all it was. He didn't even finish Trang's tour. He knew - and she had sensed - that intensive care had been too much too soon. She had reacted graciously, suggesting that a visit to the wards should be delayed until his body could adjust, could build up some immunity - a matter of contagious diseases. He agreed. A doctor, yet he agreed. He left the hospital without seeing Seb again, without wanting to see him. He flagged down a cyclo-taxi and showed the driver the address. Marie had written it down, guessing that Gullens - like most foreigners - would be unable to pronounce the words so as to be understood. Our alphabet, their language. Even so, the cyclo driver sped past the guesthouse, and stopped only after Gullens yelled out some strange foreign sounds. "Stop! Stop here! Please stop!" He paid the driver too much. Marie had warned him to bargain before, not after. He had forgotten. He didn't care. He opened the gate and shuffled quickly across the driveway, an interloper in his own home. He did not want to be seen, to make polite conversation. The interior stairwell was stuffy hot, hotter with each rising step. The second floor hallway held steamy, heavy air, immovable. He couldn't breath, and he was drenched in sweat. Finally, his own room. Alone. He turned on the ceiling fan, and the heavy air moved sluggishly around the room, warm not hot. He took off his clothes - everything - and fell naked onto the bed. The fan squeaked as the blades turned. He stared up, and the constant squeak of the whirling blades calmed him, hypnotized him. He blocked out the day, the people, the country. He fell asleep. When he awoke two hours later, he felt disoriented. Where? Why? What next? He needed more time. He showered off the sleep and sweat and put on a change of clothes. Then he left the guesthouse, avoiding contact with anyone, and walked the two blocks to the river.

The Can Tho River flowed leisurely, forming the city's western boundary. The setting sun gave the water an amber glow, the steady ripples shining in the fading light. Boats lined the shore. On deck, the making of dinner. Babies cried softly in homemade cradles or sisters' arms. Young girls bounced about - half in play, half encumbered by mothers' demands. On shore, young boys ran higgledy-piggledy after a balloon ball, kicking it about without goals. Circles of men squatted on their haunches, their loud banter and raucous laughter puncturing the evening air. The smell of whiskey.

Gullens wanted to be alone, away from human sights and sounds. But here, people were everywhere, like thistle back home. He felt the distance - his own - between himself and them. He wanted it that way. He didn't know why. He even chastised himself for thinking so. But it was what he wanted, what - he whispered to himself - he needed right now.

As he walked past the boats he could smell the women's cooking and the men's smoking and the whiskey. He wasn't hungry in the least and he never had smoked; didn't like it. He entered a light industrial area just as night came and, sensing the immediate darkness, he turned his eyes towards the river. It was gone, lost - save for the shiny ripples - in blackness. He stopped and peered back, searching for the families and their boats; he saw nothing, only night. He was lost, and his stomach knotted in ache for the familiar. Yet, he didn't want to return to the guesthouse, not now; perhaps never. He sat down on the ground, facing the lost river, lost in thought.

In the States, when he had first seen the notice on the interns' bulletin board asking for a volunteer to work in Vietnam, he became impulsively intrigued. He wanted to do good. Sure, it sounded schmaltzy, but he really did want to help, to make a difference. He planned it out. A year in Vietnam. Back to the States. Join a clinic. Establish his practice. Marriage, but no rush. Children, maybe . . later. Now, facing the lost river and himself, nothing made sense. Not the U.S. Not Vietnam.

Alone. America too far. Vietnam too near. "What next?" he wondered. In the blackness of the night, the steady flow of the lost river was his only reference point. He stood up and, more in confusion than in purpose, he proceeded forward into the industrial core. He shuffled slowly, feeling the uneven road with its many dry potholes beneath his feet. He heard occasional voices, but saw no one. He saw movement - a stray dog, a cat - he couldn't be certain. Far ahead, it seemed like miles, lights and the faint hum of motors.

He continued in slow shuffle for an hour long ten minutes, until the road opened onto a long wide area filled with makeshift tables and covered by rows of thatched roofs. The length and breadth allowed some vision. He was certain the scurry was of rats, rummaging through the rotting fruits and vegetables. Sporadic diving caught his eye, then disappeared into the night. He guessed bats.

He recalled a weekend camping trip with his father and his best friend, Luke. The two buddies had shared a tent across the smouldering fire from his dad's. They were explorers. They jabbered well into the night, spooking each other with tales of horror. Then, when they finally tried to sleep, their silence invited a scurry over here and a dive up there, "Look! Shit! What's that?" "Beats me! Holy Mole! Are you scared?" Their answers were a halting breathing, a sleepless night and good morning bravado over a campfire breakfast with his father.

His mind returned to the deserted market, and he realized that his past experience had lent perspective to the present. He inhaled deeply, joshing to himself about his state of confidence, then and now. Had nothing changed?

The dim lights of Hai Ba Trung Street greeted Gullens as he left the empty market. Along the east side was restaurant row - small cafes, Vietnamese and Chinese. Tipsy tables and rickety chairs crowded the sidewalk fronting the cafes. Gullens sat down in the first chair in front of the first restaurant, the Bong Mai. A young girl, her hair in a page boy cut, offered him a menu. He smiled at her vaguely and asked, in words and hand signals, for a beer. He studied the menu, hoping the exercise would bring him back to reality. The list of dishes - in

Vietnamese with a local version of English opposite - included snake, frog and turtle. He wasn't hungry. When the girl returned with a beer, he guzzled half instantly and then finished in three thirsty gulps. "Another Ba-Ba-Ba please," he said to the girl, pretty in her white pajamas and pink plastic sandals. Before she brought the second beer, the empty can was gone, swiped by a shirtless, barefoot streetboy. He skipped away, glancing back with a conspiratorial grin, then crossed the street - zig-zagging through the traffic - and sat down between two girls, both younger than his own seven or eight years.

Gullens connected. His last day in the States, his older brother's home. A nephew, Tommy, and a niece, Rebecca, six and four. Crayons and two coloring books on a beige carpet. He looked directly at the three street urchins, huddled together as if strategically planning a second foray. They were seated on the base of a huge statue, which he recognized, even in profile, to be the figure of Ho Chi Minh, called *Bac* (Uncle) Ho by children. The silver statue faced north, allowing Bac Ho to oversee his sovereign nation, from the Mekong Delta to the northern Red River Delta, nearly one thousand miles away.

Again, too much too soon, and Gullens found himself reeling. War movies, recently read history books, even childhood TV images of aerial bombings and body counts and street protests filled his mind, knocking him down, into himself. He laid two ten thousand *dong* notes on the table and walked away, aimlessly. He passed by other cafes, mostly empty. Too early in the evening, he thought. A group of tourists - a bus load full - had taken over the street, forcing bicycles and cyclos to the sides. He heard German and French, and perhaps Dutch, and certainly English - British and American. He hesitated, only long enough to hear words he recognized, and then hurried by, his eyes averted, searching for escape. The Quoc Te Hotel on the corner. He entered and slumped furtively into an ersatz leather armchair. He closed his eyes and tried to shut his ears to the noises outside. He slouched there a good while, like the reclusive resident bachelor of an Irish boarding house. His very posture, fetal and defensive, preempted any social interaction. He was left alone.

39

7

"Chien Bot, how is the young doctor? Is he happy here?" Ky asked. She was sitting on the edge of the bed, brushing her long hair which touched the small of her back.

Strange, mused Seb as he watched Ky, on western women he preferred short-cropped hair that just grazed the nape of the neck. Long, luxuriant hair better suited Asian women. "I'm sorry, Jasmine, what did you say?"

"How is the young doctor? Is he okay?" repeated Ky. Only one pipe and he had freed himself from the other world. "Oh, Mark Gullens. Seems to be doing better now, working hard. But his first week was tough. I thought he wouldn't stay."

Seb inhaled a second pipe of opium. The pungent scent wafted over the room. Ky rarely smoked, but she enjoyed the scent and delighted in Seb's company when he was under its spell. It always calmed him, sometimes soothing him into a deep and peaceful sleep and, on other occasions, seducing him to her. She knew better than to continue with her questions about the other world. She waited for him. A third pipe meant sleep.

He placed the long bamboo pipe carefully on the rattan bedside table and lay down on his back. He combed his fingers through the length of her hair. She turned towards him, glowing, "I'm very happy now, Chien Bot." Then she slipped on top and straddled his waist, and, leaning forward, she took her brush to his brown, grey-singed hair. Her breasts showed full under her sheer, silk tunic.

"Me too," he whispered back, and he shut his eyes to enjoy her.

In the morning they slept in, undisturbed by the activity along the canal. Seb and Gullens had arranged workshifts to suit their respective natures. Gullens was a morning person, full of early energy, while for Seb mornings meant a slow and leisurely prelude to hectic afternoons and evenings at the hospital.

Breakfast offered Ky a second chance at conversation. "The young doctor, Dr. Mark, is he okay?"

"Well, I think so," Seb answered, still reluctant to return to the workaday world. "He seems very quiet though. When I met him in Saigon, he was really in motion - in high gear - talking non-stop. Now he's rather quiet."

"Maybe he's sad. Maybe homesick. Does he have anyone?"

"In the U.S., it's possible. But here, no. Anyway, he's working long hours. Too long for his own good. But he's done well. He's a skilled surgeon . . . his techniques are state-of-the-art. He's been a big help to the other doctors. They like him."

Ky circled back to Gullens' mood. "It's good Dr. Mark helps others, but who helps him? He needs someone . . ."

"Jasmine, please don't play matchmaker. He's been here less than a month. I'm sure he can take care of himself." The coffee had finished dripping into the glass. Seb removed the filter and poured thick, sweet cream into the coffee.

"You need more cream, Chien Bot. You are not very sweet this morning . . . . . . sweetheart." Ky giggled, remembering the 'sweetheart' that Seb had taught her long ago. She sipped her own coffee, the colour of her almond eyes. "Madame Guc is having a party for my girls, to celebrate Tet before everyone goes away. Please invite Dr. Mark - for Saturday night."

"Dr. Mark's not ready for your girls, Ky. It would be awkward for him."

"Awkward? What's awk-ward mean?"

"I mean uncomfortable. He's not used to .. "

"Girls? Oh, not true, not true Seb. Do you remember when we met? You were awk . . . uh . . . .not comfortable that evening. But, by midnight you were very comfortable, sleeping with me."

"Yes, but . . . okay, you win . . again. I'll tell him today. But he might not come. He's been keeping to himself lately."

"You tell him. Let him choose . . . Papa." She giggled again, a gentle reminder to her lover that life is to be lived, not worried.

In the afternoon Seb met Gullens at the hospital. The young doctor had just finished his surgical duties and, to Seb's eye, looked more tired and tight than ever before.

"Good day, Dr. Spock," Seb said, as cheerful a greeting as he could muster sensing Gullens' condition. "How goes the battle?"

Gullens' small eyes were but slits, hardly open as he spoke. "What a day! You know the anaesethetic that came a couple of weeks ago? Gone! Totally gone! We need more now, right now. Not tomorrow. Now!"

Seb was non-plussed, startled by Gullens' aggression and by his own recognition of his younger self. "Of course Mark, you're right. We need more anaesethetic, but . . ."

"But? Bullshit Seb! No fucking buts . . . There's over a dozen emergency ops - three urgent staffs - ready to go. We need the gas now - not tomorrow."

"I know . . .I know . . .sorry Mark." He had nothing else to say, to offer Gullens. He remembered well the long waits for anaesethetic or antibiotics. "How about a late lunch or an early dinner . . on me? Half an hour . . meet you in reception. Yes?"

Gullens nodded. He peered directly into Seb's eyes in an angry, almost accusatory way. Seb smiled sadly and pivoted, walking away from his mirror image.

Gullens was waiting in the reception room, his body lying the length of the red naughahyde couch on which he had sat so stiffly upright when he had first visited the hospital less than one long month ago. His eyes were closed, but the twitching of his crossed feet hanging over the arm of the couch told Seb that he was awake.

"Mark, a change of plans. No more operations for a few days . . ."

"Few weeks . . . few months," Gullens intervened weakly.

"So, we both have some free time. The director has arranged a car for us, for the rest of the day. It's about time you had a break and saw a bit of the delta."

Gullens acquiesced, a matter of no options and no energy. They walked out of the hospital and into the sun, its fierce glare blurring colours and forms.

"By the way," Seb squinted as he spoke, "you've been invited to a party . . . Saturday night. Ky wants to meet you. A lot of good food, music, some pretty girls . ."

"I don't know. I'm not sure what I'll be doing," Gullens mumbled.

"You'll be going to a party - guaranteed."

A car pulled up and stopped, blocking the entry to the driveway. "Oh, I forgot to tell you. We have a proper guide for today's tour . . .young, bright and beautiful."

Trang waved from the front passenger seat, beckoning the two men to hurry. "Hello Dr. Mark. Dr. Seb asked me to be your guide today. Do you agree?"

Seb joked, "I'm his boss, so he has no choice," as they seated themselves in the back. "Where are we off to, Ms. Tourist Guide?"

"We are going to Soc Trang to visit the famous Temple of the Bats."

"Excellent choice. Let's show our American tourist the Soc Trang market, famous for *ruou ran* - snake whiskey."

Gullens made an effort to react in kind to Trang's goodwill and Seb's stabs at humour. And, as the car left Can Tho behind, heading south, he felt the city and the hospital take leave of his shoulders. He sat forward, lighter now, and followed the passing landscape with his work-weary eyes. Rice fields bordered the straight, rough road. People were there - peasants bending over tender shoots of rice and children walking the side of the road - but they weren't everywhere as in the city. He rolled down the car window and breathed in the humid country air.

The drive, only forty miles, took two hours. Old women walking, men on bicycles, boys on water buffaloes, hand-pulled carts, cyclos, the odd old bus and truck, and rice drying on both sides of the sun-baked road made progress pleasantly slow.

Trang and the driver exchanged pieces of their lives - family, work, even a bit of politics. The subject was broached

43

only after the driver had mentioned his father's death by American napalm. He had been scorched alive, his flesh melting into the metal of his bicycle.

Seb remained quiet, pretending sleep. His mind flashed back to his green youth, to his uncle's ranch and to the long, lazy summer days of fishing and the cool, cricket nights of sleeping in his bunkbed. "If I ever return to the States," he murmured within himself, "I'm going to be a country doctor, hobby farm n' all."

Soc Trang broke the spell of conversation, reverie and sleep. The road became congested, and all progress stopped abruptly on the bridge, just before the market.

"Let's visit the market and have something to eat," Trang suggested.

"Good idea, - otherwise it's barbecued bats with the monks at the temple." Seb looked to Gullens for laughter, but none came.

Gullens choked out, "Not really, Seb. First snake whiskey and now barbecued bats. You've got to be bullshitting."

"What do you mean, bull-shit-ting, Dr. Mark?"

"Nothing, Trang," interrupted Seb. "It's an American way of joking, that's all."

"You bull-shit-ting with me, Dr. Seb," Trang said, and both men laughed the pleasure of her innocence.

They left the car on the bridge, to the driver's concern, and approached the market- Trang between the two. It was Gullens' first experience with the hustle-bustle of market ways: the clamour and jostle, the sweet and savoury smells, the scenes of barter and haggle, and the sizzle of stir-fry. Gullens recalled his nocturnal shuffle through Can Tho's deserted market. The difference, he ribbed himself privately, was night and day.

He was recharged. The boisterous banter between sellers and shoppers, the bawdy chuckles of the drinking men, the hide-and-seek of children - it was all contagious, and Gullens pleasured in the market's infectious magic. The strangeness of sights and sounds was lessening and, although he still felt an outsider, he was no longer lost. Yet, some market customs puzzled, even repulsed him: live ducklings fed to caged pythons, dead cobras - snake whiskey Seb called it - coiled up and staring out from inside huge glass jars, live frogs layered a foot deep in plastic buckets, fish flopping on the ground - drowning in air, dead animal parts baking in the midday heat.

Gullens looked at Seb, and Seb waited for the question, "Why don't they just kill the poor buggers - the baby ducks, you know . . . the fish . . why let them suffer?"

Seb had felt the same, for a long time. "The western mind would think that life is cheap here . . .that they're insensitive, even cruel."

"Well?" challenged Gullens.

"Well, the truth is elsewhere. We cage our chickens in batteries - the poor cluckers never see the light of day. We kill young calves for veal and keep pigs in concrete pens. We even shoot up cows to give more milk and we dye meat red so it looks tasty, all packaged up in styrofoam and cellophane wrap."

"I agree," Gullens said, "but . . ."

"We're just more efficient than they are. Technology of the marketplace, I guess. And what's the result? The highest meat consumption in the world along with the highest rate of heart attacks. The waste of resources and the destruction of the environment. And the silly fact that kids don't know milk comes from a cow's udder, not from a milk carton in their local spic n' span supermarket."

"Yeh, yeh, Seb. For sure we've screwed things up." Gullens seemed on the defensive.

"And here they do what they've done for hundreds of years, probably what our own ancestors did not so long ago - before tractors and conveyor belts and pesticides. Here, they're real folks struggling to survive, that's all."

"That's all, I agree," entered Trang into the discussion. "While you were talking about food, I ordered some. Follow me," and she pointed to a row of low wooden tables and wooden stools - more suitable for children than adults - in front of ten or twelve homemade food trolleys.

"Fast food at its best," Seb said. They sat down to a lunch of deep fried spring rolls and steamed rice pancakes -

rolled up and stuffed with mushrooms and meat, and beer for the men and tea for Trang.

Seb knew Trang had already paid for the lunch. "Dammit Trang. This outing was my idea. Now you've gone and spent a week's salary on food for the fat foreigners."

On the stunted stools Seb and Gullens looked like giants, and Trang could not resist, "I think both of you should talk more and eat less, then we little people can eat more and catch up with you." She grinned as she deftly dipped a spring roll into a spicy, sweet sauce.

Gullens was having difficulty pinching the tiny rolls with his chopsticks. Seb teased him, "Use your fingers, my friend, or else I will eat your share before you do."

"No way! When in Rome . . .you know . . ." retorted Gullens, and with the skill of a drunken surgeon he squeezed the stuffing out of a pancake roll, leaving minced meat and mushrooms on the table and the pancake hanging limply from his mouth.

"You use your fingers, it's okay Dr. Mark, I'm not bullshitting with you," joked Trang, and they all, even Trang, belly laughed - they at her skillful use of language, she at her own sense of humour.

The bat temple was located a few miles beyond Soc Trang. A narrow road, shaded by tall palms, led to the temple gate. The Soc Trang area had a large population of Khmers, descendants from the era - prior to the Eighteenth Century - when the Mekong Delta was a part of the kingdom of Cambodia. Most of the monks were of Khmer or mixed ancestry. Within, the grounds were surfaced with golden grains of rice drying in the sun. Two men, holding long rakes with teeth on both edges, were shifting the rice into parallel rows, like waves of sand after the sea's retreat. A temple, exquisite in its simplicity, stood alone, its several spires curved in prayer towards heaven. The gilded tiles reflected the sun's brilliance, producing a hazy halo above the roof. Above the entrance were painted ten figures, signifying the stages of life: from birth and infancy through childhood and adolescence to adulthood, old age and death. The first and final images were of a globe - a coming from and returning to universal wholeness.

Trang climbed the short flight of stairs and entered the temple, careful to step over the sacred threshold. She chose three joss sticks and set them smoking in a decorative urn, situated immediately in front of a sitting Buddha. Kneeling down, she bowed her head to touch her prayered hands in worship.

Seb and Gullens stood in silence at the threshhold. A monk approached them from behind and in Vietnamese said, "Welcome to our temple, please enter."

Seb gestured Gullens inside. Trang rose from her prayer and introduced herself and the two Americans to the monk. He was well over six feet, half a head taller than Seb. His lanky frame carried a strong, sinewy body, unbefitting a monk's image. Even his robe, a long saffron skirt and a deep red cloth hanging toga-style over his chest - his right shoulder naked - seemed ill-matched, inappropriate to ascetic life. He smiled easily, his wide grin ready for laughter. He told Trang, who translated for Gullens, the history of the temple from historic times - when Cambodia ruled - to the present.

The monk then led them behind the temple to a grove of trees, the sacred refuge for thousands of fruit bats. They hung upside down from the branches, like so many black socks drying on a clothesline. They slept motionless during the day. Then, in the stealth of darkness they flew away to raid the fruit trees of neighbouring farms, quick to return to their sacred refuge before sunrise. Gorged by their marauding nights, they settled in the trees within the temple grounds, safe from a farmer's wrath.

He introduced Heo, the holy pig, as if it were a member monk. Born with extra hooves on its hind legs, it was considered a curse by a local farmer and donated to the monks. Strict vegetarians, they nurtured it to a slothful and contented four hundred pounds.

And, with a great grin and equal pride he showed off a dugout canoe, at least forty feet in length. Races were held throughout the delta, and the monks, eighteen strong, routinely paddled to victory, their logo - a flying bat on the prow - first to cross the finish line.

Gullens, in the short span of an afternoon, had forgotten time and found release from the tensions of his own world. This other world, where bats honoured their hosts and cursed pigs found sanctuary, had enthralled and entranced him. On the return he fell into a dream-like doze, he a saffron-robed monk paddling to victory in a dugout canoe.

8

Seb returned to the hospital the following day to find the original Gullens - hyperactive, talkative and positive, his glass half full.

"*Chao ba. Chi co khoe khong?*" Gullens greeted Seb in Vietnamese.

"*Toi van khoe, cam on anh,*" replied Seb with a chortle. "I'm fine, thank you. But why do you want to know about my health, Doctor? Anyway, a thorough examination will prove me male, not female, as you addressed me."

"My God," exclaimed Gullens, "How could I make so many mistakes in so short a sentence?"

"Not to worry. You will be admired for your effort even while being laughed at . . and you'll be corrected . . repeatedly."

"Yeah, I know. Trang made me repeat every word - too many times - until I got it right."

"Even then," cautioned Seb, "she probably wasn't completely satisfied. But she'll be a good teacher, not so strict as some old, bona-fide language prof. Ky taught me over the years, but I still screw up, she says."

"Well, we made a deal." Gullens was excited. "She will teach me Vietnamese and I will help her with cool words. Her English is excellent, but she wants to learn American slang, like bullshit." He smiled broadly, his narrow eyes bright, as he relived yesterday's excursion. "By the way Seb, do you have a minute? I . . .well, I just want to bounce something off you . . ."

"Of course, as long as it's not in Vietnamese." Seb grinned, hiding his recognition of Gullens' worried tone. "Let's go across the street for a coffee."

They crossed Tran Hung Dao Street, one of the city's major avenues, in jittery starts and stops, hoping to avoid collision with the chaos in motion. Once on the other side Seb

49

caught Gullens' shoulder and turned him back towards the street. "Look at them Mark . . over there . . those two women crossing. They weave through this crazy traffic without worry. Why? How can they do that?"

"Why?" Mark repeated. "I don't know. Why?"

"And why do we shit our pants when we cross?"

"Well, we're doctors. We know . . ."

"I don't think so. I've seen many foreigners play dodge ball in the traffic and I've never really seen a calm face. Why?"

"You've got me, Seb. I really don't know."

"It's just something that's had me thinking time and again. Very interesting . . Let's have that coffee. My treat . . I'm your elder, and in Asia you must obey your elders' every word, even if it's bullshit." Both men laughed aloud, in mutual appreciation of yesterday.

Coffeehouses, ubiquitous in urban Vietnam, had once been the social venue for French youth. Their fathers were busying themselves in civil service or business enterprise - along with occasional liaisons, while their mothers were serving tennis balls or sharing gossip over coffee and croissants, giving the lost generation the opportunity to commiserate for hours, over cafe au lait, their common plight - the decline of French colonialism and its many comforts.

Then, with the coming of the Americans, the wealthy Vietnamese, sycophants of the French colonialists, took to the coffee houses to bemoan, over *ca phe sua* - white coffee, their common fear: Ho Chi Minh and the communist hordes from the north.

When the Americans left, along with thousands of Vietnamese collaborators and profiteers, the coffee houses became the social in-spot for local professors, university students, small-time entrepreneurs and the masses of unemployed.

Seb and Gullens found a table on the patio, shaded by a palm-thatched awning. Seb glanced at the television set above the coffee bar inside. "They used to play taped music, starting at six in the morning. It was too loud, but at least it was music. . . . Vietnamese songs. Now they show videos, usually Kung-Fu

50

crap from Hong Kong. These poor guys," pointing to a group of young men sitting as close to the TV as possible, " fill their empty days staring at the glitz and glamour of life elsewhere."

"That's a recipe for frustration," Gullens remarked.

"And social unrest and then what?" asked Seb, rhetorically. "But let's get back to the life and times of young Mark Gullens . . . You wanted to talk?"

"Yeah, if you don't mind Seb. I just want your . . . well, you've been here a long time. You know these people . . and you and Trang are close friends."

"Oh, it's about Trang, is it? I should have guessed."

"It's nothing, really. I'd just like to see her . . you know . . .socially . . nothing serious . . just for company . . a movie maybe."

"Well, I can understand why. She's beautiful, of course. She's bright . . .has a great sense of humour. Most of all she's got spirit - a joy for life and a deep caring for others."

"So, you think it's possible?" Gullens hurried his next question. "Is there a proper approach . . you know . . culturally speaking?"

"Anything's possible Mark. Probable? I honestly don't know.""

You mean there's a problem? Does she have . . .uh . . .is she seeing someone?"

"I don't know. I don't think so. But that might be the least of your problems."

"Why Seb? What are you getting at?"

"Trang's family fought with Ho . . .against the Americans. She was young when her brother died, tortured by the South Vietnamese soldiers under U.S. military control. But the family remembers."

"That was over twenty-five years . . a quarter century ago . . That's past history now."

"For you, yes. Even for Trang, perhaps. I've always been boggled by the willingness of most Vietnamese to forgive, and the younger generation . . .maybe because they didn't suffer directly . . .are actually eager to know foreigners, especially Americans."

51

"So . . .problem's solved. Trang's young and I'm American. A match made in . . uh . .Can Tho." He laughed lightly, sensing a chance.

"It's not that easy Mark. Her family . . .they're very important to her. Her father's a leading communist official in the Mekong. I've met him several times . . .with Trang . . they're very close . . she's his youngest. He's always been polite, but distant . . and I don't think that distance is easily . . uh . . bridged. He saw too much during the war . . on both sides. . .Trang's told me a little . . And Trang's mother, she's still in mourning for her son, her only son."

"Jesus Seb, I understand . . their loss n'all. But it doesn't seem fair . . after all these years . . that Trang is caught up in all of this."

"She's not just caught up, Mark. She cares. Her family comes first. In Vietnam, you marry a family, not just a woman . . .Trang would never go against her family's wish, even their unspoken wish."

"Which is?" Gullens asked, tensely.

"I really don't know. I'm just telling you the situation as I see it. I could be wrong."

Gullens' eyes narrowed, focussing on the drops of filtered coffee slowly filling his glass. Impatient, he lifted the tin filter from the glass and set it aside. "Why can't people just live and let live? Why all the baggage? The war's over, goddammit!" He poured the thick condensed cream into his glass. "All I want to do is take her to a goddamm movie. I'm not talking marriage."

"Mark, listen." Seb looked kindly at Gullens, almost fatherly. "I understand where you're coming from. Me too, the U.S.A. But things are different here . . . Cultures are different. . not better or worse. . .just different."

"For Christ's sake Seb, what's that got to do with Trang and me?"

"Everything. Do you think you're culture-proof? Well, you're not. Whatever values you have, they were determined by your culture - parents, school, church." Seb paused. "Even if you've rejected . . let's say church values . . you still relate to them . . only, in a negative way."

"I don't understand. What's your point?" Gullens finished his coffee just as Seb was taking his first sip.

Seb continued. "This. Even if there weren't the war and the politics to deal with, there's still the culture."

"So?"

"So you must . . you said so yourself just yesterday . . when in Rome do as the Romans do."

"And what's that supposed to mean?" Sarcasm slipped into Gullens' question.

"Well, it means that you must relate to Trang in a Vietnamese way. It means a movie is too big a move, so-to-speak. Coffee, yes . . but don't invite just Trang . . . it could embarrass her."

"Embarrass her? A cup of coffee? Come on Seb."

"Yes. If she's seen with you . . alone . . even over an innocent cup of coffee . . it could . . culturally speaking . . mean the beginning of a serious relationship. A movie . . just the two of you . . could mean the possibility of marriage."

Gullens bounced his empty glass hard against the table top. "I don't believe it! I just can't believe a frigging cup of coffee equals marriage!"

"It might not Mark." Seb continued in a soft voice. "But for Trang, in the eyes of others . . especially her family. . ."

"There's the family again. Where's Trang's individual rights? Her freedom to choose?"

"That's the cultural part, Mark. . .that's the problem. In America we were taught . . conditioned I think . . to believe in individual rights." Seb hesitated, then proceeded. "I'm not so sure . .with the right to bear arms . . that bullshit . . that individual rights are the best way to go . . that's another issue though."

"Oh? I see. In communist Vietnam . . no rights . . no freedom to choose. . . not even your date . . " Gullens had the glass by both hands - in a choke hold..

"Has nothing to do with communism. It's culture, Mark, not politics. You have individual rights back home . . .date whomever you want. That's good. They have collective responsibility, especially to family. That's good, I think. Two goods . . in conflict."

"Seb, are you trying to tell me it's a no-go?"

"No, not exactly. I'm just suggesting you go slow. . . and realize there's no guarantees."

"I'm not expecting a guarantee."

"Good. Then, invite her and a few of her friends for coffee. Next, a day's outing . . a picnic sort of thing . . with Trang and others. Then, maybe a movie or a concert. . ."

"With others." Gullens completed the sentence. "My god Seb, now you want me to be a recreational director for Trang and her friends. Ridiculous!"

"Slow down Mark. You're going too fast."

"Too fast?" exclaimed Gullens incredulously. "I'm still at home plate. I'll never even reach first base."

"You might, but you'll have to walk, not run," Seb liked the word play. It eased the moment, sharing a common ground. "Just never try to steal . . "

"Out at third," Gullens barked, enjoying the pun as well. "Game's over."

"Maybe. . . maybe not . . With time, you will sense Trang's feelings. As long as she's enthusiastic about going here and there with you, it means you're still in the ballgame. Eventually . . it will be a while . . you could suggest a lunchtime rendezvous . . .an opportunity for just the two of you."

"Wow! What's that mean? A home run? Marriage?"

"Possibly. Certainly, it means she really cares for you."

"And then . . next?"

"By then, you'll know what to do, I'm sure."

Gullens sat back and sighed deeply, exhaling the exhaustion of his emotions. "Seb, I can't believe that our cups of coffee together could travel so far."

"Sorry, if I went on too much. Just remember, my son," Seb smiled fondly at Gullens, "when in Rome . . ."

"Right now, I wish I were in Rome. Beautiful Italian girls, who smile when you whistle. Romantic nights without mosquitoes, red wine instead of snake whiskey . . ."

Seb stood up to leave, laughing as he did. "Ciao, Romeo, Ciao."

Gullens watched Seb cross the street, struggling through the maze of traffic, a frightened foreigner, even after all these years.

9

It was the last Thursday of the month. Poker night with Hank at the Rainbow Cafe. Just the two of them, for the last ten years, playing cards to the tunes of country- western music. Hank was his nickname, after cowboy crooner Hank Williams. Han Shu Li was his real name, a descendant of a Chinese family that settled in Vietnam at the turn of the century. Restaurateurs.

When the U.S. military set up base near Can Tho, Hank was twenty-five, the number one chef in his father's restaurant. Within a month of the Americans' arrival fighting broke out, and the restaurant, Can Tho's largest, was razed by a cluster of hand grenades. By whose hands, they didn't know. They had been careful not to take sides. For one week the family hid in an underground shelter, beneath the gutted kitchen. Hank's father, too old to start over, retired to play mahjong in China alley, a back street near the open market. Here, in street-level shops smelling of mustiness and camphor, were herbs, potions, medicines, electrical gadgets, plastic and metal kitchenware and a miscellany of new and used items. The clicks of abacus beads counting. In the back rooms were black market treasures smuggled in from Hong Kong - western liquor, perfumes and medicines. In the alley behind the back rooms were old men sitting on stools playing mahjong. The clicks of ivory tiles colliding. Upstairs, above the shops, families lived - grandparents, parents, children, spinster aunts. The constant rise and fall of Cantonese conversation.

Hank had grown up upstairs, above his father's restaurant, and the only work he had ever known - since the age of twelve - was down below, in the kitchen. Without a kitchen he was nothing. So, after the restaurant's demise, he jumped on his bicycle and rode to the U.S. military base on the outskirts of Can Tho. He became the number one chef in the officers' mess. Every night after dinner he scrubbed down the kitchen while the officers drank rum and coke and played poker long into the night. Hank Williams and Patsy Cline sang of lost loves and cheating hearts. Billy Joe Stillwater, a Cherokee from Oklahoma, took a liking to the quiet chef. He nicknamed him Hank and, in a crude and convoluted sort of way, he taught him the ABC's using hand-scribblings of country-western songs as textbooks. Hank not only learned to speak English, even though he was too shy to speak out in a group, he learned how to croon the greatest hits coming out of Nashville during the war years. He sang loudly to the Vietnamese kitchen staff, but fell silent as soon as the officers entered the mess. Then, it ended. Billy Joe and a couple of the other officers gave him their cassette tapes before the evacuation. But there was no one to share them with until Seb stepped into the Rainbow Cafe one night for dinner.

In the early years following the war's end, few foreigners came to Vietnam and fewer still strayed into the Mekong Delta. So, when Hank first met Seb he wanted to revive the camaraderie he had witnessed in the officers' mess. He had not been included, but he remembered the vicarious pleasure of witnessing the fringe benefits of war - drinking and gambling to Nashville rhythms. In Seb he saw a chance to relive the past.

Seb knew the game of poker well; he had poker-faced his way through many all-night sessions in his college days, before medical studies took away his leisure life. And, although rarely a heavy drinker of hard liquor, he had enjoyed his university nights out with the guys.

Now, the guys numbered only two; nonetheless, it served their respective needs. For Hank, an occasion to replay bygone times; for Seb, an escape from the suffering reality of dying children.

The last Thursday of the month had been a ritual for more than a decade. Seb would show up shortly after nine, when most of the evening's diners had left - replete with gourmet cooking and country songs. Hank would greet him at the door and lead him to his favourite table, shaded by a fig tree growing just inside the entrance. Seb, without exception, would order two salad rolls and a plate of *ech chien bot* - fried frog legs - and a large bottle of BGI beer. Hank, his own best chef, would cook up the frog legs while singing "Jambalaya" and Linda, his daughter - the poised and pretty maitre-d' - would serve a platterful to Seb. Then Hank would sit down at the table and, while Seb indulged in his addiction, Hank would reminisce about the officers' mess, the drinking and gambling and his friend, Billy Joe Stillwater. They would never talk about the war itself, but Seb knew that Hank had sided with the U.S. once he had taken on the chef"s chores. Hank knew that Seb's favourite songs from that era had been different because Seb, when they began this Thursday night ritual, had given Hank tapes of Bob Dylan and Credence Clearwater Revival. Hank had listened to and had come to like CCR, but Seb never heard him play the Dylan tapes. Once Hank had said that Dylan sounded like a sick frog, too sick for eating. Seb figured there were other reasons, but he never asked.

Tonight was no different, except for the scene at the back. Four foreigners and two Vietnamese were seated at two tables pushed together. One foreign face was picture-perfect, and Seb instantly recognized the young wife of the tall American businessman he had met in Saigon at the time of Gullens' arrival in Vietnam. She was even more attractive than he had remembered. It must be the short pixie hair he thought, musing briefly on his hypothesis regarding western women. Seb's eyes moved to her left, to her husband. Even from this distance he showed a singular stiffness in his shoulders, and he sat straight back, looking like an oversized mannequin on display in a department store window.

Seb sidled towards his table, hiding behind Hank and the fig tree. He was hoping to go unnoticed. But, just as he was sitting down, he heard a blustery voice call across the room.

"Doctor, over here. You must join us." The stiff man stood up and in long, ungainly strides crossed the room and stopped, looming large in front of Seb's table. Conversation ceased, as all eyes followed the wooden figure. "Evening Doc. Can't remember your name, but a familiar face is a blessed sight. I've felt like ol' General Custer here in the Mekong. No white faces around." Sweat stuck to his neck, above his rigid collar.

Seb stood up slowly, and hesitantly shook the outstretched hand. He couldn't believe the squeeze, the intensity of the handshake. "Kloster, Seb Kloster. And I've forgotten your name as well," he lied.

"Dick Samuelson from Liberty, California, just south of San Diego. In the shoe business, remember?" Before Seb could answer he felt Samuelson's hand fixed firmly on his arm. He pulled back, " Yeah, I remember now, in Saigon . . . at the Tan Son Nhat Hotel."

Samuelson was oblivious to Seb's reluctance. "That's right. You and that young doctor. What's his name?"

"Mark Gullens"

"Gullens, huh? How's he doin'? Must be tough for him, being alone with all these foreigners around."

Seb's face flushed, and he felt sweat beading at his temples. "We're the foreigners here . . .and Mark seems to be doing quite well. He has been warmly received by the hospital staff."

"Well, anyway," and again Samuelson's hand reached rigidly for Seb, this time catching his shoulder, "it's good to see a white face. American to boot. Come on over. Meet the gang."

Seb started to balk, but noticing that everyone, diners and staff alike, were frozen in anticipation, he moved forward.

"This is my friend Dr. Kloster," he said boastfully. "You know my wife, of course." Just as Seb was nodding his head in recognition, she rose slightly from her seat, leaned gracefully over the table and extended her hand, her slender fingers held out seductively. "So nice to see you again, Dr. Kloster. Dick was hoping to find his American friends down here." She was wearing a silk *ao dai*, her svelte figure touching tightly against the blue tunic.

"Nice to see you again as well," Seb said, softened by the hand he held. Her emerald eyes captured his, and he felt uneasy, not in full control.

"And this is my crew. John Murphy from our Dallas plant and Wayne Reynolds, our marketing manager from Miami. Here, sit yourself down," and in one rigid, rapid motion he grabbed a chair and set it opposite his own and next to the two Vietnamese men.

Seb looked at them and, before being seated, he introduced himself in Vietnamese. Mr. Bui and Mr. Luu took out their wallets and produced their business cards, one side in Vietnamese, the other in English: Red Dragon Development, Inc. and Victory Exports, Inc., respectively.

"Sorry," recalling his introduction to Samuelson in Saigon, "I don't have a card. Maybe next time." Seb grinned, knowing he never would.

Samuelson took over. "Didn't know you could speak their lingo, Doc. Must've taken some time."

"I've had twenty-plus years to practice, but I still make mistakes" replied Seb.

"I'm betting on this place not to make mistakes. Haven't been able to get a decent meal since Saigon. Nothing but foreign food. Mr. Bui here recommended the Rainbow Cafe. Said it specialized in American food."

Seb tensed up. "Yes, Hank serves excellent foreign . . .I mean American cuisine. The hamburgers are especially tasty." He could hear the sarcasm in his own voice.

"Hamburgers are for barbecues on the deck. Tonight it's steaks...rare...all around. Mr. Bui and Mr. Luu have never eaten steak. Well, they're going to tonight." Samuelson dabbed the trickles of sweat from his neck with his napkin. "They'll never want to go back to rice and noodles."

"Rare?" questioned Seb.

"Yep, rare . . .the only way to cook a steak. Anything more, you end up eating a shoe. And I should know . . being in the shoe business." He laughed loudly, proud of his sense of humour.

Seb looked knowingly at the two Vietnamese, and then straight at Samuelson. "They've never had rare meat. Guaranteed, they won't like it. Why not well done . . . for them?"

"Not tonight, my friend. I've been eating their food for a full month now. Tonight they're eating my food, my way - rare."

He circled his eyes around the table, looking not for agreement, but acquiescence. "And what will you have . . a hamburger?"

"*Ech chien bot.* Fried frog legs," responded Seb, hiding his irritation.

"Frog legs!" Samuelson shouted out. "Not frog legs!"

"Yes, frog legs . . delicious . . they taste like chicken that's gone to heaven."

"Hell, eating frog legs. You're going to end up croaking all night and full of warts."

"No more than you'll be mooing and giving milk." Seb retorted caustically.

Samuelson's wife let out a spontaneous snicker. "Imagine that . . two grown men . . one croaking like a frog and the other mooing like a cow . . The perfect farm . . milk too . . . delicious!" Her green eyes glistened and her full lips opened to release a giddy laughter. John Murphy and Wayne Reynolds joined in. Mr. Bui and Mr. Luu looked at each other, not certain what they should do. Seb took it all in, poker-faced.

"That's enough, Sarah," Samuelson scowled. "It's not all that funny."

Seb intervened to ease the tension. "Sarah? Oh yes. A beautiful name. Reminds me of a southern belle."

"Well, she is from Texas . . . same town I came from."

"And the same town I hope never to see again," she countered.

"Enough Sarah. I said enough. You've had too much booze . . Don't know what you're talking about." Samuelson's sweating increased, his shirt half- moon wet under his arms.

"I'm talking about me . . . . about what I want."

"Goddammit girl, not here!" His face knotted as he snarled, and his stiff shoulders lurched forward - his right hand held high and rigid.

"Look! Here come our steaks," John Murphy said. He was an enormous figure, but his voice came out in a timid squeak, like a boy frightened by an angry father at the supper table.

Hank helped his daughter Linda serve the dinner, a steak with baked potato and greens on each plate. Seb met Linda's eyes and smiled reassuringly. He then turned his eyes towards Sarah, hoping to do the same.

Sarah's head was bent low, her half-closed eyes looking vacantly at the plate before her. She seemed to sense Seb's concern and raised her eyes to him - now wet - and smiled furtively, then bowed her head again.

Seb tried to lose himself in salad rolls and frog legs, but the terse exchange between Samuelson and his wife left him without appetite. He glanced sideways, to inspect the steaks given to Mr. Bui and Mr. Luu. Hank had broiled the steaks to a medium brown and had sliced slits halfway through the meat to ease the cutting for the two men. Even so, they awkwardly speared with their knives and forks, the steaks skidding into the greens. Mr. Bui's potato fell off the plate, onto the flowered tablecloth.

Samuelson peered over. He had rolled up his shirt-sleeves and was clutching a knife in one hand, a fork in the other. "What happened here?" pointing to their plates with his knife. "Your steak's not rare Mr. Bui . . yours neither Mr. Luu. What the hell's going on ?"

"No worry, Mr. Sam-u-son," Mr. Luu stammered, just as Mr. Bui was stabbing at his wayward potato. "It tastes too good . . just like you tell."

Hank overheard. "Sorry sir, it's my fault. Too many steaks to cook. I forgot."

Seb spoke up, before Samuelson could have his way. "Worked out just right Hank. They like their steaks, just as you cooked them. No apology necessary." He paused. "So, how about some good ol' country-western music to go along with this cowboy feast?"

Hank put a tape in the cassette player - Johnny Cash's Greatest Hits - and the odd collection of diners settled into dinner and cautious conversation. Only Sarah remained quiet, picking sparingly at the potato and greens. She did not touch the steak.

10

Seb left the Rainbow Cafe early that Thursday, forfeiting the pleasure of a poker night with Hank. His mind whirled around the evening's drama and its protagonist, Richard Samuelson. Why the stiffness in his body? Why the social bravado? Why the flare-up with his wife? And Sarah. Why such beauty living with such beastliness? Why the ingenue? Why the silence? Her poise seemed a veneer, vulnerable to her husband's moods.

Eleven o'clock. He walked the other way back to Ky's boat, along the Can Tho River and past the long-distance bus station. There, he saw the nightscape that was Vietnam. The dirt-poor peasants waiting without expectation for a ticket to better times, the war-torn half bodies begging to see tomorrow, and the unemployed youth - moving to Saigon in search of anything other than the now, their possessions in a cardboard box. The buses ran unscheduled, departing when full, never before. They were leftover military buses - made in the U.S.A.- held together with ingenuity and wire.

Seb's stomach ached, not from food but fatigue. He was tired of their poverty and their disease and the desperation of their daily lives. And, he was nauseated by the bloated lives of the Samuelsons and their ilk: sybarites without eyes, without ears, without an inkling of the damage they do. Most of all, however, he was suffering from himself.

He turned his back to the people and, wending his way through rows of bicycles and cyclos and past all-night kiosks, he entered a dark, narrow alleyway, adjacent to the sailors' quarters and a shortcut to the canal and Ky's boat. He wanted to forget others and forgive himself. He wanted his pipe. He could smell the rot-gut rice whiskey and hear the bawdy laughter, but he saw no one - until he neared the end of the alley. In the blackness, he made out a lone figure leaning against the corner building, a dingy hotel with short-time rooms. When the figure straightened and moved towards him, Seb's eyes caught the glimmer of two shiny movements at his chest's height. He knew. They were earrings.

Darkness still separated them. She stopped, and in a gleeful tone she whispered loudly in Vietnamese, "You come with me. I make you happy tonight."

Seb slowed his pace, but didn't lose a step. "No thank you. Not tonight."

"Bac Seb! Oh! Bac Seb! . . . I no know you in the dark," she squealed, switching to English. "But I know your voice fast. Oh, I happy to see you again. Long time I no see you Bac Seb."

"Kim!" He knew her voice too, her English voice. "Kim . . what are you doing here?"

"I make money Bac Seb."

"Money? Kim, what are you doing? Where are your coconuts?"

"Sau and Tin sell coconuts. They bigger now. I too big. I sell me. Good deal, I think."

"Kim, you're only twelve."

"Thirteen, very fast Bac Seb."

"Too young Kim . . too young . . and too dangerous . . here. . .on the street."

" I be okay. I live on street all my life. I smart . . I make too much money for me and Sau and Tin."

Seb lost the words he wanted to say, but he felt he must do something. "Kim, you come with me, just for tonight."

"How much you pay ?"

"Nothing Kim . . I don't mean that. Just come stay at my place tonight."

"No thank you. I busy work." Kim's tone became at once distant and boastful.

Seb quickly weighed the options, knowing there were few. He thought frantically, afraid for Kim. "Okay Kim, not tonight. But on Saturday night . . this Saturday . . I'll meet you right here, about seven . . okay?"

"Why?"

"There's a party. I'll take you with me. You can meet some nice people."

"Nice? Good for business?"

"For business . . yes . . good for business."

"Okay. You got deal. Saturday night."

"G'night Kim. Please be careful."

"I too big now. You no worry. Goodnight Bac Seb."

Seb walked away, stunned. He thought aloud, "Is this real? Kim? . . a hooker?" Then he fell silent, listening to the war within his stomach. His pace quickened, and, as he passed by the boats bobbing gently in the canal, his memory wandered back to Kim.

She was eight then, about four years back. He had been enjoying a beer on a bench in the strip of park near the statue of Ho Chi Minh. Watching the boats laden with produce ply the river was a fascinating and freeing pastime for Seb. For Kim, it was a streetkid's chance to sell a coconut to a foreigner for a good profit. She knew from past experience that foreigners were easy prey to her ready smile. She smiled at Seb, proffering a coconut for the price of three thousand dong, about thirty cents. Seb knew better, but accepted. Her English was near nil, except for numbers, but she wanted to learn more. So she practiced that day with Seb.

"How are you?"

"What is your name?"

"Where are you from?"

"Are you married? Do you have children?"

"Do you like Vietnam?"

And Seb, drinking his mismatch of coconut milk and beer, began teaching her the basics as afternoon wore on into evening.. But for Kim, that was not enough. So they met in the park for an hour of English two or three times a week. And Seb bought a coconut or two each time for fifteen hundred dong, the local price. Her English grew with her, and by the age of twelve she knew street slang to go along with her smile. He called her "Kim the Coconut Queen."

Seb's wandering memory had taken over, and not until he found himself on busy Nguyen Trai Street did he return to the present and retrace his steps to Ky's boat. A soft peach glow shone through the bamboo curtains of the Venice boats, except the first - the lounge boat - which was floating in darkness. It was closed for the night, leaving Ky's girls and their men to their own pleasures. The guests at Venice stayed well into the night, not just the short hour allotted in the cut-rate hotels. On every bedroom boat were a mini-bar and paraphernalia for smoking and other sensual escapades. And there was music, not the noise screeching from taverns and all-night coffee houses, but music for the senses and the soul - sultry, dark voices backed by the plaintive strains of sax and trumpet.

Seb felt at home here, the merging of two worlds an ocean apart into a relationship founded on the mutual urgency to rub out past wounds and numb present fears. He was grateful to Ky for such sensual, soulful eloquence.

As madam, Ky managed the evening affairs, but once assignations were arranged and bedroom boats reserved, she was free to return home to number eight, the boat of good fortune. Usually, except for poker nights, it was Seb waiting for her. Tonight she waited for him.

All was quiet within. Seb removed his sandals and set about preparing a bath. He felt a need to wash away the night. He heated two large pots of water on the kerosene stove . To Seb, on par with an American breakfast was a hot soak, European style. Some years ago, when the renowned Hotel Continental in Saigon was undergoing renovations, Seb came into possession of two antique French tubs, one for his apartment and one for Ky's boudoir. The apartment had been plumbed, but the boat's system was primitive - a hose through the wall connected to a common pipe which ran the length of the moorage. The very act of preparing a bath was an unwinding experience. Seb undressed, fetched a bottle of beer from the ice box and settled into the steamy water. The outside air, hot and muggy, even at night, felt cool in contrast to the burning bath water. He slouched low in the tub, only his face and kneecaps showing above the surface.

"Me too," whispered the naked Ky, her hair in a topknot. She stepped over the tub's edge and into the water, forcing Seb to sit upright. She knelt down facing forward with her back to him..

66

"Welcome Jasmine. I was sure you were asleep, and I didn't want to wake you."

"Boiling water is not quiet Chien Bot. But I don't mind; I wasn't asleep. It was busy tonight and we had to ask one guest to leave . . he was very drunk." In Ky's brothel world there was a code of conduct. Non-compliance meant expulsion - only for the night of infraction. Refusal to leave meant permanent exclusion. Guests' conduct was monitored by Madame Ky herself, but she took advantage of police services when required. A succession of Can Tho's police elite - from the French era through the American period and into communist rule - were patrons of Venice.

"Who was the bad guy?" Seb asked, curious since such trouble rarely occurred.

"A colonel . . can't remember his name . . but I won't forget his face . . next time. He just came from Hanoi, so he thinks he's . . what do you say . . ? . a big frog in a small paddy."

"Pond, Jasmine, pond!" Seb chuckled, in love with her every word.

"But we didn't need the police. The girls refused to sit with him and General Trien . . his boss . . told him to leave."

Seb was impressed. "I think you, along with your girls, should run this country. With your connections you could reach the top."

"No connections, Chien Bot . . only a pretty face. Now my face grows old and no one wants me . . on top or bottom." Ky giggled coquettishly, knowing her teasing worked wonders for Seb.

"Don't worry my Ky, I will always want you . . any way I can."

"Thank you, my Seb. Next, you will want to marry me - okay?"

"Marriage? . . .Ah . . you don't really want to get married, do you? After all these good years?"

"Don't worry . . .we won't get married. But be careful what you say . . You said you will always want me . . and you know always lasts forever."

"Right again, my wise one." Seb rubbed the bar of soap between his palms and lathered Ky, from her hairline to the dimple at the base of her spine. With a sea sponge he scrubbed her tawny skin to a rosy hue, then rinsed her with an urn of cool water. He sudsed the soap again and, circling his arms under hers, he gently massaged first her breasts and then the hollows of her underarms, pulling at the velvety fringe of hair. Again, holding an urn, he let the water flow freely down over her shoulders, breasts and belly.

"*Cam ong*, darling . . That was wonderful. Now it's your turn."

"Okay Ky, but no hanky-panky . . understand?"

"No hanky . . just panky," Ky replied mischievously as she stood up in the tub to dry off.

Seb stretched out on the bed, lying flat on his stomach - his arms and legs angled outwards. Ky knelt on the bed beside him and rubbed coconut oil into her hands and onto his shoulders.

"Oh Seb . . your muskles are so tight. Are you angry?"

"Muscles . . mus - suls Ky, not mus - kuls," Seb murmured, his face half buried in a pillow.

"Mus - suls," Ky repeated, giving strong accent to each syllable. "But, are you okay?"She pressed her thumbs and fingers deep into his stiff shoulders, kneading the tension away.

"Oh, it was a wasted night. No poker with Hank. Some arrogant American made an ass of himself at the Rainbow, and I just wanted out . . that's all."

"Well, you're out now, so you can relax."

Seb felt a slight pinch of nerve as Ky put finger pressure to the back of his neck. "Ky, do you remember that young girl . . Kim . . the one selling coconuts in the park by the river?"

"Yes . . pretty girl . . she really likes you . . told me you will be her teacher for the rest of her life. Did you know that?"

"Yeh, she told me that every time we used to meet for English lessons. She said, 'if you teach me only one word, you are my teacher for life.' An old Vietnamese proverb, isn't it?"

"Proverb? What's proverb?"

"An old, famous thought."

"Yes, of course . . but it doesn't mean you must teach her for the rest of her life. It means she will always remember you and thank you."

"Well, I saw her tonight . . . near the sailors' bars."

"She won't sell many coconuts there . . not at night," observed Ky.

"She isn't . . " he arched his back and turned his head to face Ky. "She's selling herself . . on the streets . . She's only twelve, Ky."

"Very young . . younger than I was when I went to Madame Guc."

"I have to help her but I don't know how."

"How can you help her Seb? She's a street girl. She's lived on the streets most of her life. How can you help her now?"

"I don't know." he paused. "Get her into a training course . . for a trade, you know . . like sewing . . . or something."

"Seb, she won't do that. I know. When I was young, I was hungry . . almost all the time. I did anything . . even stealing . . just to eat. When I was older . . fourteen . . I found out that I would never be hungry again . . if I sold myself. I saw the beautiful women in pretty dresses . . they looked happy to me. They had money and somewhere to live." Ky stopped massaging Seb. "I wanted somewhere to live, so I went to Madame Guc."

Ky stood up on the bed and stepped softly onto Seb's back, balancing on one side of his spine, her painted toes pointing outwards. In slow, tiny steps she walked sideways up and down his back . . several times . . digging her heels into the muscles bordering his spine. Then, she turned opposite and walked the other side, cracking the tension underfoot. Seb's chest caved in against the mattress and he exhaled in short, muffled moans. He couldn't utter a word. Ky chose not to.

Then she knelt again, positioning herself between his outstretched legs. She dribbled coconut oil on his skin and kneaded - with more intensity than Seb could remember - his muscles, from his buttocks to his calves, first one leg then the other.

"Ky, what can I do for Kim? I feel responsible."

"For Kim? What about the thousands of other kids . . .in Saigon . . Hanoi . . Danang? . . . Will you help them too?"

"Come on Ky . . that's not fair. I know Kim . . She calls me Uncle."

Ky went quiet, but she quickened her rhythm as she rubbed deeply into Seb's thighs and calves, causing him to jerk in reflex when the pressure pained the muscle.

After massaging the soles of his feet and giving a tug to each toe, Ky covered Seb with a thin cotton sheet. She moved from the bed to the dressing table and sat there, scrutinizing her face in the mirror, as if she were counting life lines like so many passing years. She loosened her topknot and her raven hair fell down the length of her back. She began brushing in full, graceful strokes, her eyes peering sharply at those in the mirror.

"I'll take her Seb . . but not as one of my girls."

"I don't understand? What do you mean?" Seb turned over and sat up halfway, braced by his elbows on the mattress.

"Well, business has been good . . I need help, and so do the girls."

"Doing what?"

"Shampoo girl . . to begin. The girls enjoy being looked after. Then, manicures and pedicures. Looking after the lounge."

"Do you think she'll do it?" Seb asked, knowing Ky knew Kim, the real Kim, better than he did.

"I don't know . . it's all I can do." She stopped speaking and for minute long moments she stared into the mirror, through herself. "I can't let her be one of the girls. She's too young. Maybe in the next few years she'll fall in love . . get married . . have children."

Ky put the brush down and lowered her head, hiding from the mirror. "If she doesn't find someone by eighteen, she can work like the other girls, if she still wants to."

11

Hao ran his engine full bore. He knew Seb detested the din of honking horns even more than the uproar of engines. Seb opened the green slat shutters of his second floor bedroom window. "I hear you Hao. Goddammit, kill the engine."

"Kill engine," Hao shouted over the noise, "and you kill my business . . kill my business and you kill me . . kill me and you kill you, Dr. Seb, because you be very sad when I kill . . you love me too much." He howled in the pleasure of his tease, almost drowning out the sputters and backfires of his cyclo. Then, he fell into a coughing fit, his arms draped over the handlebars like a drunk.

Seb came out and locked the front door, the only entrance to his two storey apartment. "I won't have to kill you Hao . . you're killing yourself. Let's go . . we're late . . first to Ky's, then to Guc's."

Hao lifted his head, his teary eyes looking for sympathy. Instead, he sensed a serious tone in Seb's words, without a hint of tease. "Okay partner. You boss."

Seb wasn't playing his role. He wasn't even paying attention. "Hao, on the way to Guc's, I want you to go by Sailors' Road . . you know where?"

"Of course, Dr. Seb. I live too close there. Too much noisy . . no sleep . . too much sick . . need doctor." Hao looked back at Seb as he turned the cyclo towards Venice, ten minutes away. But Seb did not react, not even smile. He sat in the back seat, his knees spread out, his arms folded.

Hao too said nothing more until they reached Venice and saw Ky waiting on the canal road outside her boat of good fortune. He whistled, just the way Seb had taught him years ago, a wolf whistle in praise of Ky. "Wow! You too beautiful tonight Ky," Hao shouted. "Maybe you my girl. Dr. Seb too much sad tonight. . . he no fun."

Ky was especially beautiful, ethereal she seemed to Seb as he stepped down to let her into the back seat. She was dressed in an *ao dai*, one Seb had never seen before - all white with an embroidered peacock, its beak kissing the high collar and its plumage feathering over her heart. The bright blues and greens of the peacock contrasted seductively with Ky's full, red lips and dark eyes.

"Well Hao, I'll give Dr. Seb one hour. If he isn't any fun, you've got a date." Ky continued the tease, but there was no bounce in her voice.

And, when Seb did not respond in kind, Hao knew it was best to be silent. Seb, almost always, was ready for a give and take. Not tonight. So, Hao drove slowly along the canal, slackened by the silence amongst friends. The cyclo passed by a row of dilapidated fishing boats, alive with mothers cooking, fathers watching and children waiting. The smell of burning charcoal choked out the sweetness of the evening air.

At the corner of the canal and Sailors' Road Hao stopped, waiting for directions from Seb. "Hao, keep going to the next corner . . to the alley behind the hotel . . "

"The Viet Ngu, I know Dr. Seb." Hao coaxed the cyclo towards the corner, across the street from the hotel.

"That's good Hao. Thanks. Wait here Ky . . I'll be right back." Seb jumped out of the cyclo and began crossing the street. He noticed two women standing at the entrance to the hotel, but in the dusky light he couldn't be certain if either one was Kim. Before he reached the curb, they were waiting for him, smiling at him, offering themselves to him in Vietnamese, "early night discount." Layers of make-up and the near darkness could not belie their worn-out years.

"I'm looking for a young girl . . Kim . . Have you seen her?"

They eyed each other before speaking, suspicious of Seb's fluency and his interest in Kim. "Last night she was here. Not tonight. We don't know."

"But she was going to meet me here," Seb said in exasperation. "Do you know where she lives?"

72

Neither answered, but the taller woman touched Seb's shirt, pulling at a button. Seb backed up. He knew nothing would come of this conversation, least of all Kim. He ran back to the cyclo, unusually oblivious to the traffic bearing down on him.

"Careful," Ky scolded Seb as he lifted himself into the back seat. "You will be killed . . too many crazy drivers."

Seb didn't respond to Ky, didn't even hear her. "Hao, take us to Guc's now. Then, pick up Dr. Mark at the guesthouse and bring him to Guc's."

"Yes, partner . . uh . . Dr. Seb." Hao censored himself.

"Then," Seb continued, "I want to buy your time tonight. Could you return to Sailors' Road and look for Kim? When you find her bring her to Guc's"

"You no worry, I find her."

"Do you know what she looks like?"

"Sure Dr. Seb. I see her too many times in park."

"Well, she looks different now . . like a woman . . you understand?"

"I find her Dr. Seb. But you no pay me . . you my partner."

"Thanks Hao. Then, pick us up at twelve."

Madame Guc's house on the outskirts of Can Tho was steeped in foreign intrigue. Built by the French in the 1920's, it had housed a succession of generals, French and American. The last French resident, a General Bouchard, had lived a double life there - the dry season with his wife, the wet months with his French mistress. According to rumour, Madame Bouchard not only tolerated but encouraged the liaison, thinking it would keep him out of brothels. She never knew of the General's attraction to a young *fille de joie*, Guc, who first took to the trade at fifteen. Twenty years later, the last American resident of the house had been a CIA operative acting in the official capacity of a military liaison officer. A bachelor and a puritan, he vowed to rid Can Tho of its brisk sex trade, which had swelled with the coming of thousands of American soldiers. He twice tried to close down Madame Guc's Venice, alienating in the process his fellow officers, South Vietnamese and Americans alike. Just hours

73

before the fall of Saigon he was found in his study, hanging from a rope. A letter on his desk, addressed to a Private John Prescott, spoke to the loneliness of unrequited love.

Guc's house had contained four bedrooms and two full bathrooms on the second floor. The sitting room, dining room, study, one bathroom and a chef's kitchen were located on the first floor. Madame Guc had the upstairs renovated, converting the four massive bedrooms into eight cozy suites, each having two single beds. They were reserved for Guc's colleagues - ageing prostitutes without savings or shelter or the security of a male benefactor. The former study served as Guc's bedroom, and the kitchen, dining and sitting rooms were shared in common. Guc's generosity was founded on the simple principle of her appreciation for the women's service to Venice during their younger years. They were family. The evening's celebration, one week in advance of Tet, was an annual ritual hosted by Guc and her retired sisters-in-residence. The guests always included the working girls of Venice - Ky's girls now - and an escort of their choice. Most of the girls, especially the younger ones, arrived without escort. Certainly, they had a long list of clients, but seldom a special lover. Such commercial monogamy came with time and experience and the wisdom to weed out the fly-by-night patrons.

The sitting and dining rooms were decorated with festive red banners and *bong mai* - yellow peach blossoms. In the sitting room stood a large altar of teak wood, installed after the departure of the foreigners. Here residents and guests placed small dishes of food and lit joss sticks in honour of their ancestors.

The early evening music was in keeping with tradition. From a made-in-Vietnam ghetto blaster situated opposite the ancestral altar came the haunting sounds of ancient instruments: moon lutes, monochords, zithers, two-stringed fiddles, bamboo flutes, a percussion set of mother and child drums, small and large gongs, a wood block, a cymbal and a bell. Entrancing themes of springtime, the full moon, a missing lover, village life and great harvests evoked nostalgic memories of childhood, family, work and love, and gave full circle to the seasons of life.

Much later in the evening, after ancestral worship and a slow banquet of food and drink, *tan co* - pop music - set the mood for singing and dancing.

The dinner itself was an elaborate affair, offered by Guc not only to favour her guests but also to appease the kitchen god whose influence on the fortunes of the coming year was supreme. Chicken curry with lemon grass and ginger, salad rolls of vermicelli and shrimp, grilled pork in caramel sauce, fried frog legs - in Seb's honour, dried fruit candies and steamed rice cakes - all prepared and served by Guc and her sisters. A toast of snake whiskey by the men launched the feast, and Guc's presentation to each guest of a red envelope containing not money but a famous proverb concluded the sitting.

Gullens was intoxicated by the experience. Exotic women in a rainbow of *ao dais* moved gracefully about, in quiet conversation with their peers or their elder sisters. Distinguished men, outnumbered three to one, talked of sports and business, and whispered notions of this or that woman's beauty and charm. Tradition - in the altar offerings and ancient music of the early evening - gave way without protest to the drinking and dancing of the late night. And the food, both savoury and sweet, opened for Gullens new realms of pleasure in smells and tastes.

And now, it was his turn to open the envelope addressed to him. He disguised his shyness in a burst of showmanship. "Ladies and Gentleman, I will now open this envelope." He paused for effect, then tripped and stumbled over the proverb in Vietnamese, mispronouncing in monotone each and every tonal word. Titters of laughter filled the room, not in ridicule but in welcome.

Ky, sitting between Gullens and Seb, repeated the proverb then translated for Gullens, "Go out one day and come back with a basket full of wisdom."

Gullens, with a spontaneous flair for the comic, exclaimed, " It will take many baskets, but I am a young man with many days ahead of me to live and learn." Ky's translation brought a tidal wave of laughter and applause. Gullens beamed in appreciation and turned towards Seb. "How about that Seb?

Better watch out . . . A basket a day and within a couple of years I will be the wiser one."

"You already are. My basket's half empty, even after all these years, " Seb replied in self-deprecation.

Throughout the evening Seb remained quiet and often alone, out of touch and without appetite. Kim and his sense of responsibility for her dulled the pleasure of the moment, even the pleasure of Ky's company. Once the drinking increased and the singing and dancing commenced, Seb felt a sharp strangeness within and a desperate need to do something . . anything. Yet, he suffered a paralysis, an inertia of purpose which pained him physically - squeezing his bowels. The flow of liquor, the lively music and the seductive movements of delicate bodies only intensified the strangeness and the pain.

Finally, nausea moved him - out of the house and onto the verandah. Over the side railing he retched, spitting up what little food and drink he had in him. His brow dripped sweat and his hands trembled, like an addict in the throes of withdrawal. But Seb knew it was not the liquor or the food or the music or the dancing *ao dais*. He knew it was Kim.

Without words to anyone he darted into the street and flagged down a passing cyclo. Within a block of Sailor's Road Seb could smell the rice whiskey and beer. He leaned over to dry heave, and the sweating and trembling returned. Before the cyclo came to a full stop, Seb handed the driver twice the fare and leapt out onto the broken pavement. Reeling, he fell to one knee. He stood up slowly, his entire body in a tremble, his face ashen, his hair soaked in sweat. He knew where he was, but he felt lost. The harsh, rough voices of drunken men frightened him, and the stench of sewer assaulted his senses.

He shuffled slowly, one foot then the other, towards the alley where he had last seen Kim. Nothing. No one, not even the ageing hookers of early evening. Everyone's doing business he thought . . Kim too. Who is she with? Will he be gentle with her? Will he pay her or just fuck and run? Kim's smart; she'll get her money first. But she's small, not strong; she could get hurt. He accused himself aloud, angrily, "Why didn't I take her home that night . . pay her what she wanted . . let her just talk -

practice her English - and then sleep? Why did I leave her to the streets . . .to strangers? Coward! A fucking coward!"

With a desperate sense of purpose but without direction Seb wandered the Sailors' quarters, his eyes cast down in self-disgust. This time, he said to himself, he would buy Kim for the night to offer her Ky's help . . .Venice . . steady work and a place to live. He entered shabby lobbies of cheap hotels. A few wallflower hookers waited without hope for men with money. They knew it was too late. The night's drinking had doused the men's desire, and their only urgency was to piss, then sleep.

Seb felt the want of sleep heavy upon him. He turned back in the direction of Guc's. He would get Ky and return with Hao to Sailors' Road. He saw a queue of cyclos, the drivers ready to gyp the one-hour johns and all night drinkers. As he passed the cyclos, he recognized Hao's: on the front fender a maple leaf decal - a souvenir from a Canadian tourist. Hao was not there, but drivers pointed Seb towards the tavern across the street - a rickety three-walled structure of rusty, corrugated metal and a thatched roof. Inside, the raucous music and bawdy talk had fallen to a whisper, and the few men left were face down on tilted tables or slouched in slumber against the dirty walls. One lay prone on the cracked cement floor, awash in his own urine. Seb stepped over the man and walked to the far corner of the room . . Hao was sitting alone, face down.

"Hao! . . . Hao!" Seb shook him gently at first, then with some force. "Hao! . . . Wake up! . .Hao!"

"Uh . . oh . . Dr. Seb." Hao raised his eyes upward without lifting his face off the table. "Dr. Seb, I drive you home . . . .no problem."

"Where's Kim, Hao? Did you find her? Hao! Hao!" Seb panicked.

Hao's eyes closed and his speech slurred, the words crawling along the tabletop. "No see Kim . . . no find . ."

Seb seized Hao by the shoulders and flung him back, half upright on the stool. Hao's arms spread out in balance, and a beer glass fell into sharp bits on the floor.

"Goddammit Hao! You're drunk! You promised me. "

"I do it Dr. Seb . . I look Kim . . too much time." Hao rocked his head slowly side to side, trying to shake out words he didn't know. He looked up at Seb, and his eyes tried to speak when the words wavered. "Kim no here . . Kim go way . . I no know where . . .Saigon . . Hanoi . . ." His voice trailed off.

"Why Hao? . . .Why would she go away? . . Can Tho is her home. She's never even been to Saigon . . . she's never left Can Tho . . " Full panic seized Seb's voice.

"They take her . . . big business Dr. Seb . . . sell new girl . . .no sick . . too much money . . Yankee dollar. . . "

"No, Hao, no!" Seb's stomach twisted in pangs of repulsion and regret. "Where . . in Saigon? Do you know?"

"I no know . . nobody no know." Hao sat fully upright and looked directly into Seb's eyes. "Too much new girls go way. Now, too much rich man in Saigon . . like new girl . . no like old girl. Bad man go to My Tho . . Can Tho . . Ca Mau . . take new girl to Saigon. Too much new girl for rich man . . Yankee man . . France man . . Japan man . . too much money for bad man."

Seb slipped backwards, defeated, against the wall.

"You no find Kim, Dr. Seb. Kim go way."

12

Seb had been scheduled to go with Trang on a medical mission up the Hau Giang River from Can Tho to Chau Doc, not far from the Cambodian border. It was a biannual effort to bring medical supplies and offer health workshops to the remote villages strung along the waterways of the Mekong Delta. Seb suggested it would be an eye-opener for Gullens to see the countryside - the hometowns of many of the children at the hospital - and the virtually non-existent health care offered outside the major cities.

Trang bubbled with excitement in anticipation of showing Gullens the real Vietnam - by riverboat. There was a typical early morning traffic jam on the river: boats laden with produce jostling for position to dock and distribute their goods, water taxis carrying legions of peasants - men, women and children - to the market to buy, sell and barter, and ragged waifs waiting on shore to beg or steal another day of life.

Trang and Gullens arrived in the hospital's only ambulance - a converted cargo van. They transferred the medical supplies to a waiting boat, a gigantic wide-bottom canoe with a square stern on which perched a belching, outboard motor with a spear length propeller shaft, designed to navigate the shallows of the river's tributaries. Within a quarter hour Trang, Gullens and Si, the helmsman, were heading upriver - against the slow, heavy brown current. Workshops had been scheduled for Long Xuyen and Chau Doc, the two major towns along the Hau Giang River.

Long Xuyen was a religious smorgasbord, serving up not only traditional Buddhism in Vietnamese temples and Chinese pagodas and Christianity in Catholic and Protestant churches, but also the Caodai and the Hoa Hao sects.

Caodaiism was based on the ideal principles of religious tolerance and inclusion, and, in an effort to encompass all, Ngo

Minh Chien, the mystic founder, had sainted in his divine pantheon Joan of Arc, William Shakespeare, Victor Hugo, Vladimir Lenin and the Chinese revolutionary Sun Yat Sen. Above the ornate portico of every temple a massive, omniscient eye looked out to greet both the devout believer and the curious tourist.

The Hoa Hao sect, founded in 1939 in the Mekong Delta, was as individualistic as Caodaiism was collective. Hoa Hao theology encouraged a direct contact between man and God rather than through institutionalized rituals. This denial of established authority had often put Hoa Hao believers in confrontation with the reigning government of the era, from the French in the forties to Catholic President Diem's South Vietnamese troops in the fifties.

Chau Doc continued the religious banquet. Cham Muslims and Chinese and Khmer Buddhists complemented the Vietnamese majority. Unique to Chau Doc was Sam Mountain and the Temple of Lady Chua Xu. Every other turn on the steep ascent led to a temple or pagoda, each distinctive in architecture and ornaments. Statues of elephants, lions and dragons guarded the temples' treasures and the resident monks. The most renowned temple, dedicated to Lady Chua Xu, was at the bottom of Sam Mountain. Legend told of Thai invaders who had attempted to steal the statue, perched atop the mountain. As they moved the statue downhill its weight increased twofold, and the Thais, sensing its supernatural power, retreated. Years later local virgins, aided by Lady Chua Xu's divine intervention, carried the statue to the bottom of Sam Mountain where a garish temple was built. For hundreds of years thousands of pilgrims - regardless of religious belief - from throughout Vietnam and neighbouring countries converged on Chau Doc to pay homage to and seek favour from this sacred lady of legend.

These cultural sights, punctuated with eating escapades featuring python and turtle, captivated Gullens - body and soul. He was humbled by the wealth of history of these peasant folk and honoured by the warm welcome offered him. And he was stunned by the poverty of the people and the virtual absence of medical care.

Community clinics were located in major centres, but they seemed a presence without purpose. The staff was underqualified and poorly paid - thirty dollars per month - less than a cyclo driver. Professional diagnosis was a mix of oriental folklore and occidental science, and the medicines were a miscellany of herbal concoctions and expired black-market western drugs. Preventative treatment was considered an unnecessary expense by the peasant patients and, consequently, women suffered the birth of unwanted, unaffordable babies, children were laid waste by cholera and polio, and old people died too young.

Trang and Gullens presented health workshops with an emphasis on preventative care, from the basics - potable water - to the sophisticated - vaccinations and birth control devices. They preached to the converted few. The others, in keeping with the stoic fatalism of their ancestors, honoured the old superstitions and shied away from modern miracles.

Gullens performed with missionary zeal, praising the powers of immunization, western medicines, even surgery. He shirt-soaked through the morning sessions, and, after heavy lunches and restless naps, he returned to his preaching. His afternoon shirt was sweat-wet within minutes. In his left hand he held a light, palm-leaf fan, awkwardly swatting away invading flies and cooling the burning air. In his right he gripped a stick of chalk to write strange words in a foreign language on a sun-cracked chalkboard. His damp fingers softened the chalk stick to a mushy white and words which came out clear in his speech became a muddy blur on the board.

A lone gecko timidly claimed his territory, the upper left corner of the chalkboard.

Trang translated the gospel according to Gullens to the passive, patient audience of forty, most of whom were medical staff from isolated village clinics. They had travelled up to six hours through the darkness in war-time, worn out busses, to hear the legends of western medicine and to renew friendships with their colleagues from far-flung villages. Two hour lunch feasts of food and drink required a long nap for recovery, especially for the men. The afternoon audience shrank to twenty - all women but two.

After two days in Long Xuyen and three in Chau Doc, both Gullens and Trang were empty of energy. The searing heat had sapped Gullens' body and the polite indifference of the listeners, his spirits. Trang's energy had been lost to Gullens. Every evening after a long day's workshop Gullens would sulk his way through dinner. Trang, anxious to buoy his spirits, would review the successes of the day. Gullens saw only failure. Each compliment offered by Trang was countered by criticism from Gullens.

"Jesus, Dr. Trang. They don't even care. They didn't learn a damn thing."

"That's not true Dr. Mark; they learned . . But they also knew . . ."

"Knew what?"

"That what you offered - as good as it might be - isn't for them . . not now . . not for a long time."

"Why not?" Gullens shot back defensively. "It's a helluva lot better than their snake oil and jungle juice."

Trang waited for his words to lose their sting; then, she continued. "Two reasons. First, they know that what you offer is impossible to get. Even now, after the end of the American embargo, vaccinations and antibiotics are too expensive for them . . for their clinics and their patients."

"And?"

"And even if they could afford to buy your medicine, they wouldn't, not for a long time . . . years."

"Why not, Trang? That's crazy."

"To you . . . but not to them. Tradition. Their grandparents and parents believed in the old medicines - Vietnamese medicines. Now, they believe in the same; even though they have listened to you, they will need time to change. Maybe, their children will learn to use your medicine - antibiotics . . "

"Not just antibiotics," interrupted Gullens, "inoculations to prevent disease, birth control to prevent pregnancy . . . preventative medicine. Don't you understand?"

82

"I understand, Dr. Mark."

"Well, then?"

"You must wait for them to understand . . and to accept. They know nothing about foreign medicine." A heavy pause. "But, they know about foreign bombs. The bombs killed their loved ones. How can they believe foreign medicine will save them?"

Gullens thought through Trang's comment. "Then, why do they bring their dying children to the hospital . . in Can Tho . . for western medicine . . even for surgery?"

"They have no choice . . . They know their medicine didn't work - this time . . They are desperate. They will do anything for their child."

"When it's too late?"

"Yes, often it's too late."

Gullens stopped, too tired to continue. Trang needed the last word, for Gullens' sake.

"Dr. Mark, when Dr. Seb first came, it was much worse. Now, in the cities, many people have been vaccinated . . .there is less disease. Still not good, but less than before. Drinking water . . the most important change. Parents in the city know the water must be clean for their children. So, they boil the water."

Trang watched Gullens as she spoke; he was listening - passively.

"Then," she continued, "the people in the city visit their relatives in the countryside. They tell them about clean water . . medicine . . vaccinations . . even birth control. The medicine and vaccinations are too expensive, but the water is free. They will learn to boil it. Then, many children . . coming to our hospital dying from dysentery - will stay at home . . . healthy."

Gullens smiled sadly. "It just takes time."

"Yes, Dr. Mark, it takes time."

The ride downriver was smooth, much faster than fighting the heavy current. Darkness closed in, about one hour upriver from Can Tho. The moon shone full in the sky, shedding its cool light on the hot evening, as the boat cut into the rolling water like a sharp knife slicing soft fruit. Sweetness in the air.

Si leaned back against the stern, his right hand held firmly to the rudder arm.

Gullens and Trang sat snuggled into the prow, both facing forward.

"Trang . . . should I say Dr. Trang?" he asked hesitantly. "Can you see the man in the moon?"

"Trang please," she answered with equal hesitation. "There is no man in the moon . . . only a rabbit."

"A rabbit? Unbelievable! Incredible! Impossible!" joked Mark with exaggeration, shouting to be heard over the engine noise and the lapping of the waves.

"Yes, Dr. Mark . . a rabbit."

"Trang, for sure, it's a man in the moon. Look! Can't you see the eyes, a bit of a nose and the mouth - the shady part at the bottom?"

"It's our moon, not yours Mark." She shouted her words, but fell to almost whispering his name. She sensed her own shyness, then repeated with conviction, "It's our moon, not yours . . . and it's a rabbit - sideways. See the ears, the curved back . . . the tail?"

"That's no rabbit," Gullens argued mischievously.

"It's our moon - in Vietnam - and it's a rabbit. That's the final diagnosis, doctor."

"Perhaps, doctor." Mark pretended agreement. "But, maybe a second opinion . . . a second diagnosis is necessary."

They laughed loudly over the thump-thump-thump of the boat bouncing on the water.

Gradually, Gullens felt the tension of the journey leave him, each laughing spell lightening his heart and recharging his spirits.

"And Trang . . or should I say Dr. Trang?" An elfish grin, his small eyes bright in the moon's glow. "I have one more case for you to diagnose . . . . are you ready?"

"Ready Mark. Or should I say Dr. Mark?" A girlish giggle and a casual flip of her long hair with her hand.

"Okay. Here goes. It's going to be fast, really fast, so listen carefully. . . Okay?"

"Okay."

Gullens began prestissimo: "When a doctor's doctoring a doctor, does the doctor doing the doctoring tell the doctor being doctored how to doctor . . or . . does the doctor being doctored tell the doctor doing the doctoring how to doctor?" He smiled, proud of his pace and enunciation.

"Yes! Yes! Yes! Do that again Mark," exclaimed Trang, in quick rhythm with his words. "Say it again . . please."

"No! No! No!" Gullens continued the beat. "It's not a yes or a no . . . you must decide which doctor . . ."

"What?"

"Okay. I'll do it again." Gullens repeated the tongue-twister, this time in moderate measure.

"No! No! No! " Trang sang out in laughter, more caught up in the cadence than the content. "Do it again, as fast as you can . . . please?"

Gullens showed a slow smile and, with mock seriousness, repeated the question in a sluggish pant, stretching out the last letter of every other word, "Whennnn a doctorrrr is doctoringggg . . ."

"Oh Mark! You are soooo funnyyyy." mimicked Trang, and their laughter drowned out the thumping of wood on water.

Trang looked forward, catching the first sight of Can Tho at night. "When I was a small child . . . during the war, Can Tho was dark at night. We were hiding from the bombs. Now look! Can Tho is full of bright lights. . . isn't it beautiful?"

"Yes, it is." Then, without consciously willing to, without even realizing what he was doing, Gullens put his hand on Trang's shoulder, pressing her soft, raven hair to her skin.

Without words, Trang looked to the side, away from Gullens and towards the far bank of the river and beyond - to a grove of dark palms in the distance. Her eyes squinted, as if she were trying to see past the grove, to the invisible horizon. She could only see the night-dark jungle.

Gullens felt the lead weight of his hand on her small shoulder, and he wanted to retreat. But his hand did not move. Inert. Heavy. Sweat on his palm, even in the evening cool of the moving boat, seemed to glue him to her.

Trang stayed her course, concentrating on the passing trees. She tried to choose a single tree, to study it. But she lost it to the jungle. She looked out, trying to see beyond. Then, she closed her eyes and stared blindly into the escape of the surrounding darkness.

Gullens begged his hand to obey, to lift off and away. He desperately wanted to start over, to take back the last few endless seconds, to say something funny. But suddenly it all felt so wrong.

Finally, he lurched backwards - his entire body, and with it came his arm and its heavy hand. He could feel the air cut the damp heat between his hand and her shoulder.

Trang slowly turned her head forward, again facing the city lights. In whispered words, inaudible to Gullens, she said, "There's the statue of Bac Ho. We're home now."

13

Seb rarely had felt at home in his own place. Ky's gentle company and the comforts of her boat of good fortune had made Venice his home away from home.

Now, however, almost a week since Kim's disappearance, Seb felt at home nowhere. When with Ky, he imagined innocent Kim, struggling for survival in a slave brothel in Saigon - a recycled virgin to satisfy the fetishes of foreign lust. When alone, he saw the cowardice within - the dedicated doctor who did good deeds in his surgical smock, but who cringed in fear of the darkness outside.

He started drinking - heavily. He had only once before drank so much for so long - during the mad-dog days and desperate nights when the American Congress, in patriotic reflex to President Reagan's fevered pitch about U.S. soldiers still missing-in-action, had tightened the embargo by threatening sanctions against third parties who had been cooperating with Vietnam. Then, even neutral, sovereign nations had felt the heat of American hate towards the Vietnamese.

Medical supplies dried up.

Gradually, the choke-hold eased and the flow of medicine resumed - to a black market trickle. Then, Seb dried out and returned to work. Now, his drinking was of his own doing, his lack of doing anything when it really mattered.

It was Thursday night, but not the last Thursday of the month - his poker night. Last Thursday the American - Samuelson - had stolen his poker night with Hank. Seb needed to escape the image of Kim - in Ky and, most of all, himself. Perhaps, he thought, he and Hank could make up for last Thursday's fiasco with a game of cards tonight. He wandered around the room, pocketing his wallet, a pair of reading glasses, a small accordion fan to chase away the heat and flies, and dozens of one-thousand dong notes to give to the many beggars between his place and the Rainbow Cafe.

Hank was standing outside, greeting passersby - potential customers - in his own friendly way.   He was comfortable with his life.   Two daughters.   Linda, the elder, would take over the restaurant business in a few years.   Meng Song - she only had a Chinese name - was studying to be a teacher.   His wife stayed comfortably at home - four blocks away - with her mother, an ancient woman of strong tradition and suspicious mind.   Hank and his mother-in-law had not exchanged words in years.   This arrangement left Hank some free time after an evening's work for country-western music, poker games and the odd dalliance.   That's why he drank ginseng root tea throughout the day.   He often told Seb - as if it were his own discovery, "Ginseng is good for everything, especially this thing," and he would point down, between his legs.   Then he would always laugh in self-conscious guffaws and add, "Is your thing up to anything these days?"

Seb enjoyed Hank's company, his bawdy humour, his poker strategy: a good hand shows a serious face, a bad hand tells a joke.   Seb knew Hank's ways and, bad luck aside, usually took the night's winnings.

Hank saw Seb approaching and, reading his mind, he did an about-face, sat down at their poker table - tipsy under the fig tree - and started shuffling the cards.

"Linda, play some country music," he shouted in Cantonese, "Doctor Seb is coming."

Seb entered, pretended to hang his cowboy hat and gun belt on the invisible elk horn rack, then sat down, facing Hank, the bar and beautiful Linda. "You all deal the cards, cowboy," Seb strained in Texas twang.

"You all cut first, cowboy," Hank said in reply, passing the deck across the glass table-top to Seb. "Seven card stud, joker's wild."

"Shoot, buddy."

Hank dealt the cards, five down with the last two facing up. "Linda, bring Seb a beer . . .B.G.I . . and I'll have gin-on-the-rocks," speaking English for Seb to hear.

"Me too Linda. Gin-on-the-rocks . . Thanks."

Hank paused, then said, "Seb, you never drink the hard stuff. Every time I want to give you gin . . . or bourbon . . or rum . . you take beer . . B.G.I."

"Tonight's different Hank. Tonight I'm drinking hard and playing hard . . So watch your money, partner."

Hank laughed in bits and pieces. He sensed Seb was acting different . . strange.

The night wore on, passing midnight, and Seb, even under liquor's sway, controlled the game and captured most of Hank's gambling money. But Hank was not a quitter, and he had just talked Seb into another game when out of the damp darkness staggered the tall, rigid figure of Samuelson, alone. He picked up a rattan chair from a nearby table, slammed it down between Hank and Seb and collapsed into it.

"Deal me in boys. I'm game to win a buck or two. You're dealing with a Texas Ranger now . . .so no tricks . . no dealing off the bottom . . no bullshit." Samuelson's eyes rolled as his slack mouth blurted out the words in a slurred drawl.

Seb tensed tightly, so tightly his forearm cramped against the table top. "Just finished Mr. Samuelson." he gritted out, "Sorry, you're too late." Seb could smell booze on Samuelson's breath. He also smelled the certain scent of brothel - a mix of rubbing oil and cheap perfume.

"What're you doing out this late . . . without your wife?" Seb needled. Then added, in soft-spoken sarcasm, " your lovely wife."

"She's asleep . . . I couldn't . . . This goddamn heat . . . never ends. So, I took a walk and, as luck would have it, I found myself a poker game."

Hank stood up and picked up the bottle of gin, the two empty glasses and the ashtray filled with butts. He always smoked more when he was losing. He walked away without a word.

Seb, however, was on a roll. "Not tonight. Another time. . . maybe . . when you're sober . . I don't take money from a drunk. . ."

"You sonna-va-bitch," Samuelson sprayed out the words, wet with spit. "I'll take the shirt off your back . . Hell, you'll lose your pants . . you sonna-va-bitch!"

"Sorry, not tonight. I'll take you back to your room . . . to your lovely wife. You can sleep it off . . to fight another day . . . another night."

"Okay goddammit . . you're the doctor . . " He paused, staring pie-eyed at Seb, "aren't you?"

"Yep . . . I'm the doctor . . . Let's go."

Linda brought an iced washcloth and Seb rubbed it over Samuelson's face. With Hank's help he got Samuelson standing up - stiffly sloshed. Seb grabbed him by the arm - instantly recalling Samuelson's fierce grip on his arm that Thursday night one week ago - and led him out of the Rainbow Cafe and up the street to the corner of Hoa Binh Boulevard. A cyclo was waiting, as if in anticipation.

Samuelson slumped into the cyclo, taking up the entire seat. Seb remembered that Samuelson and his wife had moved from the Quoc Te Hotel to a restored French villa, but he didn't know where and wasn't about to guess his way through the night.

He hailed a second cyclo, jumped in and motioned the first driver to follow. Within minutes he was in front of his house, half-drunk himself and burdened with an obnoxious, inebriated foreigner. He cursed his luck, cursed the sweltering night air and cursed the keys he struggled to find in his pockets.

"Dr. Seb? Is you? Dr. Seb? You fix me again? Please, Dr. Seb."

He knew it was Hao, but couldn't see him in the darkness.

"Drunk again, Hao," Seb admonished lightly. A boozy Hao was welcome comic relief to the pathetic Samuelson now leaning over the stair railing, retching out his night.

Seb saw Hao's silhouette against his front door. As he turned the key and opened the door, Hao fell backwards into the small foyer.

"Worse than usual, Hao? At least the booze quiets your coughing," Seb teased as he reached to turn on the light.

Hao lay flat on the floor, his lower back over the threshold, his one full leg dangling outside. Seb looked down, ready to pounce on Hao for his wayward habits. Instead, he reeled back, tripping over Hao's good leg.

Hao's forehead and face had been sliced up into rows of deep, razor thin slits. Dried blood stuck to his face. Had Seb not heard Hao's voice and seen his stump leg, he would not have recognized him. Tears welled in Seb's eyes and dryness choked his throat. He stared down at Hao and cried silent sobs of grief and anger.

"I try Dr. Seb . . . find Kim." Hao lifted his body halfway, bracing himself with the palms of his hands on the dark teak floor. "I try too much . . . They cut me too much . . . say Kim no here . . .You no look her . . They say tomorrow I look her . . . they kill me."

Seb understood. He knelt down beside him and rounded one arm under Hao's arms. He lifted him slowly on to his one good foot and - with Hao leaning on Seb - they entered the sitting room. Gently, Seb helped Hao lower himself on to the wicker day-bed, Seb's favourite reading spot. He pulled down the bamboo blinds and turned on the ceiling fan, letting the dark coolness soothe Hao's pain.

"I'm going to the hospital Hao. You lie still. Just rest. I'll be back soon, and we'll fix you up - good as new . . . okay?" Seb's voice cracked . . . words were lost in his effort not to weep.

"I know, Dr. Seb . . . you fix my face . . . then I have pretty lady like you . . .," he tried to tease. His words too were half lost, his to the pain of his wounds.

Seb left the room, only to find Samuelson lying where Hao had been, over the threshold of the front door - half in and half out. Seb cursed the sprawled Samuelson, "Get up, you bastard," he shouted, "Get up you son-of-a-bitch!"

He bent over and grabbed Samuelson by both wrists, and, using the door jamb to brace himself, he tugged and jerked. Samuelson, his stiff body gone limp, was dead-drunk and dead weight. Seb let him fall back with a thud, and then raced to the corner. There he saw Hao's cyclo - the tires slit, the engine hammered in, the entire frame twisted into a tangle of metal, the passenger seat ripped into so many shreds . . . a metre away, the canvas canopy charred black.

He ran the long block to the next corner and roused a sleeping driver and directed him to the hospital. There, he saw the huge grey building, brightened only by dim lights in the reception room and the half dozen ward stations. He gestured in recognition to the dozy guardsman, then entered. The squeaky creak of the door alerted the reception nurse.

Before she could question him or his presence, Seb blurted out in Vietnamese, "There's been an accident . . . near my house. I've come to get some things. I must hurry!"

She watched him running down the empty, deserted corridor until he vanished into the surgical area. He patted the wall with his hand until he found the light switch. A large bulb hanging from a frayed wire illuminated the room - its cracked ceiling, three resident geckos - frightened by the intrusion - an instrument cabinet and seven near-empty shelves of surgical supplies and medication.

Like a thief in the dead of night, Seb scoured the room, impulsively looting its treasures: scalpel, scissors, syringe and needles, sutures - real ones, not rat tail tendons - gauze, bandages, sponges, tape, even a tourniquet, and antiseptic and anesthetic solutions. He threw them into two small pillow slips which were shelved in a cupboard alongside surgical gowns, masks, sheets and towels.

He exited with a wave of his free hand to the startled nurse and sleepy guard. Again rousing the cyclo driver, he motioned him back to his house.

Samuelson was deeply asleep. Even then, even in these circumstances, Seb took the time to look at him, to stare him down. He was repulsed by what he saw: a rigid arrogance.

He jumped over Samuelson and rushed into the sitting room, to a semi-conscious Hao. Again, Seb's throat went dirt-dry and his eyes welled. He picked up a bamboo footstool and set it beside the day bed and turned on the lamp behind and above Hao's tortured face.

"This will hurt Hao," murmured Seb in warning.

He dabbed a square of gauze with antiseptic and gently patted the long slits etched across Hao's forehead and the smaller slits slicing horizontally down both sides of his face. Hao's head jerked slightly and his teeth snapped together and held, but he said nothing. Then, Seb rubbed between the slits - roughly - to wipe off the caked-on blood. He poured an anesthetic onto pieces of gauze and pressed them to the turned-out edges of each slit, softening the tissue and numbing the nerve ends in preparation for the sutures. From top to bottom of Hao's face - first the forehead slits, then those on each cheek - the open wounds were dabbed with anesthetic and stitched closed. Seb worked methodically, his hands steady, his mind focused. An hour later, he wiped the last of the blood away, blood which had trickled down from the slits to below Hao's chin and onto his neck and chest.

"That's it partner," Seb whispered into Hao's ear, "Operation Hao - over."

Hao moved slowly, just once, and fell into a semi-conscious sleep. Seb looked down at Hao and flashed back - over twenty years - to their introduction - an innocent boy maimed by the evil of war. He hunched over, took Hao's hand in both of his and wept silently.

The smash of a door slammed shut brought Seb back to the present and the presence of Samuelson in his house. He reacted instinctively, reaching the foyer in time to block the path of the stiffly standing figure of Samuelson.

"My head . . Oh God . . my head," Samuelson uttered in a near whimper.

"Wait a second," Seb ordered, and he slipped quickly into the kitchen and returned, carrying in one hand a glass of water, in the other double doses of aspirin and sleeping pills. "Here, take these . . I'll help you upstairs . . A couple of hours' sleep and you'll survive."

"You're the doctor, Doc." Samuelson slurred as he straight-armed towards Seb. He grabbed the glass, threw the four pills into his mouth and, in two loud, sucking gulps, swallowed the medicine. "Where's the bed Doc? . . Where am I, anyway? . . This ain't no hospital!"

"No. This is my place . . follow me." He led the rigid, wavering Samuelson up the stairs. Samuelson took ungainly steps, twice stopping to lean against the banister. When he reached the second floor landing, he lost his balance and fell against the wall, knocking down an oil painting given to Seb by a Mekong artist - a man Seb had treated for dengue fever. The woman standing steadily in her narrow boat in a Can Tho canal went hurtling down the steps to a crash landing below - the frame in splintered pieces but the painted canvas intact.

Seb watched as Samuelson fell forward and covered the entire bed with his body. He gave out several loud belches before starting to snore - the unrhythmic, irritating snore of a man out of sync with himself. Seb retraced his steps, picked up the pieces of the picture frame and the canvas, returned to the kitchen and sat down.

He wondered what to do next, and, as his mind raced in many directions and through all possible time zones - past, present, future - his heart began thumping . . louder . . faster. He checked his own pulse . . too loud . . too fast. He tried to free his mind and settle his heart, but time and circumstance took control. He felt he had no choice and, once acknowledged, he calmly - disregarding his racing heart - considered not the consequences, only his actions.

Seb looked in on Hao, saw him deep in sleep and closed the door to protect his peace. Then, furtively, like a thief in his own house, he opened the front door to a rising sun, leapt down the steps and into the street.

He returned within the hour, carrying a coil of rope around his right shoulder. His left arm stayed stiffly to his side, hiding a sheathed machete.

Again, he checked in on Hao, pressing his palm to Hao's forehead; no fever - no infection to poison his tortured body.

Upstairs, Samuelson lay motionless on his belly. Saliva had rolled off his lips, down his chin to further wet the sweat-soaked sheets.. Seb, to test the depth of Samuelson's boozy slumber, shoved him to the far side of the bed and, with a mighty pull, rolled him over on his back. Samuelson's only response was a choking cough followed by a slow release of sputum from his open mouth.

Seb moved rapidly, efficiently - as if he were performing emergency surgery. Holding the hilt of the machete tightly in his right hand, he rubbed the oiled rope over the upturned blade. With three swift slices he severed the rope into four five foot lengths.

He approached the bed - another purchase from the restoration sale at Saigon's Continental Hotel. First, he circled and doubled-knotted the rope around each of Samuelson's wrists. He pulled each piece taut around the sturdy bedposts and tied a triple knot. Then, he repeated the procedure to secure his legs; Samuelson was spread-eagled and tied down.

Sweat trickled lightly from Seb's temples and down his cheeks. He caught the fullness of the morning sun in his eyes as he brushed one cheek and then the other with the short sleeves of his shirt. Nine o' clock, he guessed. He hated wearing watches, rings - anything that reminded him of civilized man.

He looked down at his American Gulliver, pinned down by his arrogance and greed. He flashed back to Professor what's-his-name's course in English Lit. . . to Swift's Lilliputians, to his Houyhnhnms, to his disgusting Yahoos - modern man, then. Now, he gazed at the sleeping Samuelson. "Yahoo . . Yahoo . . Yahoo," repeated Seb, and he turned around to find his pillow bags of tricks.

He levered Samuelson's outstretched left arm and pressed below the elbow pit, searching for a vein. He pricked the skin with a needle, sending a sedative solution into Samuelson's bloodstream. He waited until he was certain Samuelson would not move. The liquor, the sleeping pills and the syringe of sedative were taking their proper toll.

The wait invited another series of flashbacks - first, to his medical school days . . to Hippocrates . . . to his professional oath . . to his *raison d'etre*. Then, far and a long way back to tying the fly by winding the leader around five times and then through the bottom loop and pulling tightly and double knotting and biting off the end with his teeth - just like Uncle Norm used to do . . when they went fishing together. Uncle Norm never had much to say, but when he did he always said the same: "Cast upstream and let the fly float downstream. The fish can tell the difference." And then in the evening, tired from a long day's fishing, Uncle Norm would sit at the kitchen table with an open can of beer, waiting for Aunt Bertha to fry the rainbow trout - along with some new potatoes - to a golden brown. He would give young Seb one-third of a glass of beer and, before long, he would say, "When you're not fishing, always go downstream . . whenever you can. Don't make life any harder than it is." And the boy would wonder and sip the bitter beer and watch his Uncle Norm.

Seb jarred forward to the present and, staring at the drugged Yahoo, he said aloud to himself, "Sorry Uncle Norm . . I'm going upstream . . . again."

He readied another syringe and pricked up and down - like a mosquito searching for supper - the little finger of Samuelson's left hand. He waited, only for a few minutes for the local anesthetic to have its full effect - freezing the entire finger. These minutes conjured up no memories, no flashbacks, as if Seb had numbed his mind to what he was about to do.

He held Samuelson's hand and tied a small rubber tourniquet around the base of his little finger. Then, in a swift, sudden motion he pressed the finger against the bedpost and, taking scalpel in hand, he cut deep - to the upper joint bone. Samuelson lifted his head and gave out a weak grunt. Seb immediately shot more anesthetic into the open cut. He waited . . . seconds only. Then, he gritted his teeth and, as the trickles of sweat turned into a stream down his forehead . . . into his eyes, he bore down on the scalpel and seesawed the blade through the tendons, severing the upper joint from the finger. Blood spurted up and out, staining the bedpost.

He moved quickly, applying an antiseptic compress to the exposed wound and wrapping it over with surgical tape. Then, he took several squares of gauze to blanket the severed joint. He examined Samuelson's hand, then stared coldly at his unconscious patient. He felt nothing. Spontaneously, he made his next move. He walked - without rushing - into the bathroom and opened the medicine cabinet above the sink. He returned carrying a small, squat bottle of Vaseline. Holding Samuelson's fourth finger - the one next to the amputation - he applied the Vaseline above and, as best he could, underneath the wedding ring.. It came off easily with one easy pull.

With the gauzed finger joint and the wedding ring - one in each hand - Seb moved - again without rushing, as if in a sleepwalk - out of the bedroom, down the first flight of stairs and into the study - opposite the sitting room. He sat down at his desk and took a piece from a ream of paper - common, nondescript writing paper sold in what he fondly called "typewriter alley" - a narrow, back-walled street where one could get anything typed - from a formal document to a love letter to a Viet Kieu boyfriend in Orange County, California - by male typists who two-fingered their war-era American typewriters.

He printed in large capital letters, careful to make the same letter the same way:

MR SAMUSAN IS HERE
WE CUT FINGER TODAY
ONE WEEK WE CUT HAND
TWO WEEK WE CUT HEAD
HE GIVE 1,000,000 US DOLLAR
TO CANTHO BABY HOSPITOL
HE NO GIVE MONEY WE KILL
YOU TALK POLISE WE KILL
HE GIVE MONEY
YOU NO TALK POLISE
WE NO KILL
GARANTE

Seb placed the wedding ring and the finger joint on the printed page. He folded it in half - bottom to top. Then, he printed on the front of a manila envelope:

MRS. SAMUSAN

He went - unrushed - upstairs. He shaved, took a slow, forgiving shower and dressed. Without looking in on Samuelson, he went downstairs to check on Hao.

Hao was sitting up, looking down. He raised his face when he heard Seb enter the sitting room.

"How are you feeling Hao?"

"I good now, Dr. Seb," Hao said without hope. The sorrow of life showed in his eyes as he reached out to touch Seb.

"Thank you Dr. Seb. You no let me die too much." Hao grasped Seb's right hand with both of his and shook it forcefully.

"No problem, partner," said Seb as his left hand joined the other three and held firmly. Then, he looked straight into Hao's eyes and spoke in a somber whisper, "Hao, I need your help . . now . . okay?"

14

The sun, through the lens of a humid early morning haze, was a deep tangerine disc vibrating above the tamarind trees. It promised that sort of day.

Gullens, having survived cultural dislocation, was just beginning to embrace the earthy physicalness of Vietnam. Seb had warned him that after the novelty of adventure wears thin, thick clouds of homesickness and culture shock storm the mind and emotions. Rungs on one's own cultural ladder don't hold - don't make sense in the new context, and the fall begins. For many, it's an early return to the comforts and conveniences of middle class life and a reunion with those who understand.. For some, it's a stoic determination not to quit, to see it through to the end, and a minor martyr complex takes hold. For the lucky few, it's an escape from self, leading to an epiphany of possibilities. Gullens was treading water somewhere between the some and the few. This morning he was captivated by the possibilities of intense physical beauty. He gave in to the sensual power of the sun's presence, and for the moment he felt at one with the few.

Marie called up to him, "Doctor Mark, you hurry. Dr. Seb call. He want you go to hospital now."

Gullens was out of his room and in the dining room within minutes - in perfect timing for Ba's greasy eggs and baguette. "*Merci,*" Gullens said, knowing that Ba - of the older generation - had been forced to learn French under their rule.

"*Bon appetit*, Monsieur Mark," replied Ba, knowing Gullens' command of French - even though he would argue otherwise in English - was limited to a few opening and closing gambits and the odd idiom.

Marie followed, carrying the common tin filter atop a thick glass. She backhanded him on the shoulder. "Where you last night Dr. Mark? Hung say you no come back until *trois heures du matin. Pourquoi?*" Marie's English spontaneously peppered with French made her all the more engaging.

"*Pourquoi? Vive la liberte*! I am a free man," Gullens countered. "Anyway, Hung was *tres* drunk last night. He didn't see anything or anyone."

"You *tres saoul aussi*," laughed Marie. "You no good for my Thao. No marriage - *jamais.*"

"O . . . Marie . . . so warm and tender . . .Marie . . ." Gullens sang badly in Seb's stead, and both of them clapped in mutual glee.

Following breakfast, Gullens walked out into the courtyard. Above, forty high-wire feet high in one of the old tamarind trees that fringed Thang Boulevard, he saw a wisp of a girl breaking dead twigs off thick branches with a stick. Below, her younger brother - about seven - collected the fallen twigs and laid them on two strands of string. Gullens had seen the two of them several times in the open market, hawking their bundles of twigs for a supper of rice and vegetables. He tried to imagine his nephew and niece, Tommy and Rebecca, doing the same in three years; he couldn't.

Seb was sitting at a desk in the staff lounge, which was sparingly furnished with three desks, three straight-back chairs - one leaning low to the floor, and eight metal folding chairs surrounding a metal folding table - forfeiture of the American withdrawal. One hanging bulb gave a dim light for Seb's work.

Gullens approached Seb from behind, unsure of himself and Seb's mood. "G'morning, Seb . . . How goes the battle?"

Seb did not look up from his paperwork. "Good morning Mark. Thanks for coming in on your day off."

"No problem . . What's happenin'?"

Seb placed the pen on the desk and arched the chair back on its hind legs. Still without looking directly at Gullens, he said, "A couple of things. Hao's been hurt . . . badly . . a gang attack."

"Why?"

"He tried to find Kim. The gang . . the guys who took her . . didn't want him sniffing around. They sliced up his face. Luckily, they didn't kill him."

"Oh hell, Seb . . ," Gullens paused. "What can I do . . to help?"

"Just cover for me today . . if you can."

"Sure Seb, no problem. Anything else?"

Seb set the chair down on all four legs and turned to face Gullens. His eyes were red and swollen and teary.

Gullens reacted immediately. "So sorry Seb . . about Hao. . "

"Thanks Mark. He'll be okay . . . It's just his luck . . his hard luck to be in the wrong place . . . And I asked him to find Kim."

"You couldn't have known what would . . ."

Seb interrupted. "One more favour . . . Could you take this letter . . uh . . envelope to Mrs. Samuelson. I found it here . . . at the hospital . . in my mail slot. I don't have the time or desire to see them right now." He handed the envelope to Gullens.

Looking at the envelope, Gullens read aloud, "Mrs. Samusan." He looked back at Seb. "Well, whoever it's from, they need a lesson in spelling."

"I know," agreed Seb. "Looks like a Vietnamese spelling of an English name. . . Happens all the time . . Me . . I'm Dr. Krastur . . .K.r.a.s.t.u.r."

"I wonder why it came to you, Seb."

"No idea." Seb paused, then added, "The locals assume all the foreign residents know each other . . . there's so few . . . Since I'm the old timer here, they must've figured I'd know the Samuelsons . . . And they were right."

Seb looked away, staring at the unpainted concrete wall of the lounge. "Anyway. . I'd appreciate your . ."

"Enough said . . . good as done."

Seb stood up and squeezed a grateful hand on Gullens' shoulder. He smiled without meaning to, and left the room. Gullens gazed at the envelope, pondering its origin and contents. "What would James Bond surmise?" he mused aloud to himself.

Hao opened the front door to an anxious Seb.

"Hao, is everything okay? Are you all right?"

101

Hao was standing upright. He leaned slightly on his left crutch and held the machete with his right hand, at the ready.

"Everything okay!" exclaimed a reborn Hao. "Mr. Sam . . . he wake up . . . he see me . . . he see face . . . he see big knife . . . he say no word . . . he sleep again."

"Thanks Hao," responded Seb, relieved. "Your workday is finished. See you tonight . . . about seven. Here's some money. Bring dinner from the Ninh Kieu - for three of us . . and some baguettes for tomorrow morning . . Tonight I'll look at your ugly face and clean it up a bit." Seb smiled slowly; yet again, the tears welled in his eyes.

"Okay Dr. Seb. You boss."

"Just remember Hao . . go home . . . go to sleep . . . no drinking . . . okay?"

"Okay Dr. Seb. I say before . . you boss." He smiled, self-satisfied with his new position, and handed over the heavy machete to a reluctant Seb.

The sharp sound of wood-on-wood alerted Seb to his guest. He climbed the stairs two-at-a-time, and entered the room to find Samuelson in a frenzied fit, twisting one way then the other - like a pig bound for slaughter. The sound that Seb had heard was the clap of two bed slats against the floor. The firm, thin mattress had sunk in the middle and, with it Samuelson - his back bent towards the floor. Upon seeing Seb, Samuelson sighed in relief.

"Thank God almighty!" He looked at Seb, trying not to show his panic. "Get me outta here, pronto . . . Some gooks kidnapped me . . tied me up . . . Jeezus Christ," gesturing to his bandaged finger with his chin, "the fuckers cut off my finger . . . Sonna-va-bitches . . . Hurry up . . . untie me before they come back! . . . Hurry up goddammit!"

Seb sat casually on the edge of the bed, looking down at his guest. "No rush Mr. Samuelson . . try to relax."

"Relax? Goddammit man, this is serious! We could both be killed! Untie me!" he bellowed as he sunk down again into the collapsed mattress.

"Serious for you, Samuelson . . not for me. Any more ruckus, and I will order Hao to cut off your hand . . your right

102

hand." Seb's words flowed steady and slow, like the mother river nearby.

Samuelson raised his head and opened his mouth to breathe in Seb's warning. His eyes glazed over with tears of fear and disbelief. He lay motionless, speechless and, after excruciating moments of waiting for Seb to do anything, he dropped his head and shut his eyes.

Seb waited patiently, wanting the reality of Samuelson's situation to take effect. Then, in a low and steady voice, he continued. "Listen carefully Samuelson . . . and say nothing." He watched and waited for Samuelson to react. Nothing.

"Gooks - as you call them - didn't kidnap you and bring you here . . I did. You were drunk last night . . . obnoxious and arrogant. I brought you here . . . this is my house," and with a bitter smirk, " you are my guest . . whether you like it or not." Samuelson lay frozen in silent fear.

"I cut off the tip of your finger . . Why? . . I also took your wedding ring . . . Why? . . . To prove to Mrs. Samuelson that you are a hostage and that your very life is at stake."

Seb's sarcasm and smirk were real . . . genuine . . . beyond his control, but his for certain - to his own astonishment.

"Why your life?" He paused. "Why not? To you money is life . . . so, I am demanding money . . . exactly one million dollars . . . for your life. Why? To pay . . . a pittance really . . . to pay for American atrocities against the people of Vietnam . . . . specifically, the innocent children of Vietnam. They are still suffering, even after all these years."

Seb stopped, thinking the patriot in Samuelson would emerge. Nothing. Only a quickened, heavy breathing and a slight quiver of the lips.

"The money is not for me . . . It's for Can Tho Children's Hospital. You see Samuelson . . . you are going to make a generous donation . . . to show your good faith as an investor in Vietnam's future."

He waited for his words to weigh in on Samuelson. "You rest now, and think about what I've told you . . . Then we will make plans . . . together."

103

Seb rose from the bed and went into the bathroom, leaving Samuelson to sag hammock-like in his mattress.

Seb lathered his face and slowly - absorbing the pleasant sting of foam and razor - shaved. He looked in on Samuelson, who lay more rigid than usual, frozen in his time of reckoning. Seb undressed and showered. He had no hot water . . . didn't feel the need. The cool, creamy brown river water washed away whatever troubled him. Today, it was Samuelson.

He went downstairs into the sitting room. He scanned his selection of tapes and, after choosing two, he took them - along with his portable tape deck - upstairs, into the bedroom. He set the tape deck down on the dresser top, plugged it in and pushed play: "The Three Tenors." He slouched down in the rattan chair in the far corner.

"Who is the greatest living tenor, Mr. Samuelson? Carreras? His voice has a romantic melancholy. Domingo? He is the most clear . . . crisp. Or Pavarotti? He has the greatest range and resonance."

Seb did not wait for Samuelson's appraisal. "Actually, like everything else, a combination of qualities equals greatness. Fortunately, no one has the perfect combination. Therefore, high praise goes to several, not just one."

Seb accepted Samuelson's silence. He was grateful for the interlude, and fell under the lyrical spell of the three tenors.

When the singing stopped, Seb started, again. "For example, Brahms could do a better lullaby than Mozart, but Mozart was the master of the requiem. Do you know Mozart's 'Requiem?' . . . Here, have a listen . . . it's possibly relevant to the moment."

He crossed the room, inserted the Mozart tape and turned up the volume to maximum. He returned to the corner chair, slumped halfway to the floor, his legs sprawled in a wide V. He rested his elbows on the round-wheel rattan arms and pressed his thumbs against his temples. The music took him away from Samuelson and himself.

At 7:30 Hao returned, carrying a large plastic bag with smaller bags inside containing the evening dinner. Tied to the hand-hold of his crutches was a bag of baguettes. Seb met Hao at the bottom of the stairway.

"Hao," exclaimed Seb in frustration, "this food's not from the Ninh Kieu; it's from your friends near the market."

"You right, Dr. Seb. Ninh Kieu too much money . . . I keep money for you . . then you happy!" Hao was pleased with himself.

"But Hao, this food will kill Mr. Samuelson. His belly is made in the U.S.A. He will get very sick."

"Okay, Dr. Seb. Mr. Sam sick. He die. No problem. You no like him too much. Okay?"

"No . . . it's not okay . . . Next time the *Ninh Kieu*."

Hao saw the concern in Seb's eyes. "Okay Dr. Seb. You boss. But you pay too much."

"*Ninh Kieu*, Hao . . *Ninh Kieu*," repeated Seb as he turned towards the kitchen. He took three bowls from the shelf, grabbed two pairs of chopsticks and a spoon and fork for Samuelson, and with the bag of dinner - along with the breakfast baguettes - returned to his bedroom and Samuelson.

"Here's the deal, Samuelson. Just listen . . . don't talk. You get one meal a day . . at dinner time. Eat as much as you want . . . cause you won't get another bite for twenty-four hours." Seb stared sternly at the supine figure, intent on maintaining the offensive.

"There's a method to my madness." He smiled ironically. "If you eat and drink at night, you'll shit and piss yourself empty in the morning . . . by the time I leave for the hospital. After I'm gone, you can't get up again until evening . . . when I get back. If you shit or piss while I'm gone, you lie in it . . . guaranteed." Even Seb himself seemed alarmed by his words and their tone. He paused to catch his breath and to reinforce his mood.

"Hao has the machete. He's ready to use it . . anytime."

Hao, in his own way, stood at attention, looking bravely at Seb, then fiercely at Samuelson. His stump-of-a-leg and carved-up face gave credibility to Seb's threat.

Samuelson swallowed fear as he spoke his first words in hours. "I need to go to the toilet . . . now."

105

"No problem." Seb undid both ropes from the bedposts and brought Samuelson's arms in front of his body and tied his hands together, the left cupped over the right - like those of an old man sitting on a park bench. Then, he stepped backwards to the foot of the bed. He unfastened the ropes and brought Samuelson's feet together and tied them, allowing only a fist's length between the ankles - just enough slack to shuffle from bed to toilet and back.

Samuelson raised himself, with Seb's help, from the sunken mattress. His entire body ached from inertia. He pivoted his legs in the direction of the bathroom, but the weight above his waist and gravity teetered him backwards onto the mattress. He struggled to raise himself again. This time Seb went around to the other side of the bed and, placing both hands against the top of Samuelson's shoulders, he pushed forward - lifting - while Samuelson grunted himself upwards. Once upright, the huge man waited to catch his breath. Then, in slow shuffles he worked his way into the bathroom and closed the door. The bathroom was empty of objects - especially objects of escape - except for toilet paper, soap and two towels.

"I can't wipe myself with my goddamn hands tied like this," Samuelson bleated through the closed door. Even his 'goddamn' had lost its bluster.

"Yes you can," retorted Seb. "You just change position and direction. Stand up . . . bend over and bring your hands under your ass. Wipe forwards, towards your balls."

Hao chuckled in understanding.

Seb continued, "I actually tried it myself . . . to make sure it was possible . . . It is. A simple matter of adaptation, Samuelson . . Who knows? Maybe in a millennium or two all of humanity will follow your lead . . . evolution of the species . . so-to-speak."

Seb and Hao heard moans - without words - from the bathroom. Eventually, the door opened and Samuelson stepped out - humiliated, full of hatred. He waited, unsure of what to do next.

"Before eating Samuelson, I think it would be a good idea to stretch your limbs and move about . . . to circulate the blood. I don't want you to clot . . . to end up in the hospital or the morgue . . " Seb studied the word he had just spoken and was momentarily stunned by the potential for real tragedy. He looked over at Hao, smiled weakly, and returned his eyes to Samuelson.

"I want you to live . . I really do . . . but not for your sake only . . . but for the hospital . . . for the kids."

Seb stood up and directed Samuelson in his forced exercise. Stepping-in-place, each foot raised the short length of the fist-wide slack. Knee-bends - back to the wall. Stepping sideways. Toe-touches - front to the wall. Waist twists. Stepping-in-place, again. Hand-over-head-holds. Neck-circles. Stepping sideways, again.

"Good enough. Now, let's chow down and enjoy." Seb motioned Samuelson back to the bed. "I'll be right back. Watch him Hao."

Seb seemed to leap down and back up the stairs, rejuvenated by the exercise he had shared with his guest. He brought back in a net bag four large bottles of BGI, several small packets of black-market processed cheese and a jar of jam. In his other hand he carried a pitcher of ice-water flavoured with the petals of jasmine flowers. For a brief moment Ky's image appeared to him, then vanished.

"Here's your choice. Vietnamese street food . . . Hao's special . . . goes in one foreigner's end and out the other in record time. Or baguettes with cheese or jam . . or both. The first will make you go, the second will plug you up. A mixture of both and you might be just right."

"Baguette with cheese," said Samuelson without emotion.

"Baguette with cheese coming up," chirped Seb as he set about opening the imported, triangular packets of cheese - a treasured find for foreigners looking homeward. "And what to drink?"

"Water," responded Samuelson.

"Water it is," and Seb poured out a glass, shards of ice inside.

They ate in silence - Samuelson the baguettes and cheese, Hao his own choice, and Seb a combination of the two.

Samuelson finished first. With his bound hands he took the bowl from between his legs, placed it to his side and lay back. Hao had replaced the fallen slats while Samuelson was in the bathroom. He felt the level firmness beneath him. He stared at the ceiling, moving his eyes in circles, in concert with the squeaky, tilted fan. A gecko, grounded upside down to the ceiling, watched Samuelson watching the swirling blades.

Seb broke the silence. "I've got to go . . to fax this letter. First, though, I need your cooperation. Read it.

All's going well with our venture here. Food's terrible though, and Sarah's got a bout of homesickness.
Business looks good. High unemployment means cheap labour. Hard workers for low wages. Big money! One snag. Temporary. Need $1,000,000 a.s.a.p. Government regulation - collateral - to prove long term commitment to the region. I know, we're doing them a favour coming here to do business. However, we have no choice. Money refundable upon opening of factory. Wire immediately to:

Samusan Shoes, Inc.
Account # 71169-44
Bank of Foreign Trade of Vietnam
(Ngan Hang Ngoai Thuong Viet Nam)
435 Hao Binh Blvd, Can Tho, Vietnam

Will be in touch.

Samuelson looked puzzled at first . . then defiant. "You can't make me cooperate. I won't sign this . . You can go to hell Doctor!"

Seb's response was well-planned. "Yes you will. Hao's friends - two of them - are with your wife . . right now. And they'll be there 'til the money comes. They both have machetes, just like Hao's. If you don't cooperate, they will kill her first . . then you . . . guaranteed."

Seb paused, watching Samuelson and trying to read his mind. Options? Strategy? He felt confident his threat had Samuelson cornered. "This is life or death, Samuelson . . If anything goes wrong - for whatever reason - both of you will die." He stopped, then added, "I took the privilege of rummaging through your wallet, which I now have along with your passport . . . You are nobody now, Mr. X . . get used to it."

Just as Samuelson let the letter fall from his hand, a waft of fan-cooled air caught it and blew it across the floor and under the corner chair in which Seb had lost himself to Mozart a few hours ago. Seb retrieved the letter.

"I want you to write in the name of the addressee - at the beginning - as you normally would . . . sign off and your signature . . . as usual."

Samuelson glared at him with loathing, and Seb reacted in kind. "Just remember . . one trick, even one mistake equals two deaths . . . guaranteed."

Seb handed the letter back to Samuelson, and then handed him a hard-bound book, one of his favourites - Dostoevski's 'Crime and Punishment' - to serve as the bound man's desk.

Samuelson's hand shook as he wrote in the proper places:

Jerry, ... Adios . . . . . . R.J.
"Who's Jerry?" asked Seb.
"Executive.V.P. My partner."

15

Gullens placed the envelope for "Mrs. Samusan" in his own mail slot in the staff lounge and began Seb's rounds. Surgery was less disturbing, less harrowing than walking the wards, especially intensive care. Surgery forced him to focus - to be in action, regardless of the outcome. At least he was doing what he did best. In the wards he became a mere spectator to the process of life and death - too often the latter. He adhered to the proper routine - a glance at the patient's chart, one hand to the forehead the other on the pulse, encouraging words for grief-stricken mothers - but he knew he was just marking time, waiting for the disease or injury to dictate the final terms. He found this ritual emotionally exhausting . . . defeating.

Just as he entered intensive care, Gullens heard Trang's voice . . . in Vietnamese. Still, he knew without doubt it was Trang speaking. He followed her voice to the last bed but one. Trang was sitting on a low stool, clutching with both her hands both hands of a young peasant mother. Their eyes met as Trang spoke the soft, slow words of regret, endurance and courage. Little Hanh had lived longer than any of the doctors had expected. Had she survived, she would have been bed-ridden for life - in constant pain. The little girl born without an anus. Dioxin . . . agent orange . . . dormant in the soil . . . more than two decades after the war's end.

Gullens left intensive care. He saw Vinh, a young intern, who was scheduled to assist him in his rounds, waiting in the corridor. "Dr. Vinh, I must go. Please do the wards without me today. I'm sure you'll do fine," he added as he back-stepped towards the lounge, "If you need help, ask Dr. Tri . . . Dr. Trang is too busy right now. Thanks."

He pivoted right and stepped into the lounge, grabbing the envelope and the palm-leaf fan he had hanging where others hung umbrellas. He walked out into the blinding, burning sun.

He returned to the guesthouse. Unable to eat or sleep, he lay on the bed, immobile. His eyes stared up - indifferently at first - at the whirling blades. Then, after a long spell of whirl, his eyes squinted narrow and seized upon the fan's swiftly spinning axis. Within minutes, he was swept into its vortex . . . into the void.

Hours later. A gecko chirruped in the darkness. Gullens washed away the day with a cold shower, then he dressed in the darkness, having picked out pants and a shirt without seeing them. He shuffled along the pitch-black hallway and down the stairway, tapping familiar walls and handrails to keep his balance.

When he opened the front door bats dove in, out and away, disturbed by his moving shadow. Then, the black blur of darting rats in the courtyard slowed his movement toward the road of belching sounds and blinding lights.

A cyclo driver took Gullens to the Quoc Te Hotel, where the Samuelsons had reserved the entire top floor for themselves and their American managers - John Murphy from Houston and Wayne Reynolds from Miami. Gone now - the managers back to the U.S. and Mr. and Mrs. Samuelson to a restored French villa in the city's northern outskirts, a suburb which housed high level government officials and foreign entrepreneurs - successors to the mandarins and military brass of French and American regimes. The hotel reception clerk wrote down their new address.

Gullens paid the cyclo driver and approached the front gate. The villa was bounded by high yellow-washed walls which were crowned with looping twists of barbed wire. A uniformed sentry confronted Gullens before he could use the intercom.

"I want to see Mrs. Samuelson. It's very important," Gullens enunciated carefully, certain he would not be understood.

"One moment . . . your name please?" the sentry asked politely.

Gullens was dumbfounded by the young man's command of English. "Gullens . . . Dr. Mark Gullens."

Within moments the gate opened automatically, and Gullens entered the front garden. A winding path bordered by terra-cotta pots of bougainvillea, mimosa and orchids led Gullens to the front door and Sarah. She was standing in the open doorway. Moths, seduced by the bright porch lights, winged about in a frenzy.

"Hi Sarah," Gullens stammered in a loud, awkward whisper. Her beauty weakened him. "Your guard speaks better English than I do. Where did you find him?" Gullens wanted, above all, to be casual.

Sarah responded in monotone, "Oh, him. He . . they . . there are three of them . . on shifts . . . can't remember their names. They were English teachers in Saigon. Richard offered them twice their salary. He hates using interpreters . . figures they could lie to him somehow." Her green eyes glowed as the porch lights haloed her face.

"Please come in. Richard's not here and the maid and cook have left." She closed the door gently behind them. "But, I can mix a mean margarita - my favourite."

"Sounds great," said Gullens. "But, how did you manage to find Tequila in Can Tho?"

"Not Vietnam . . . Texas. We came prepared. Richard doesn't like foreign food or foreign drinks . . . so he brought cases of this and that . . . almost like living at home. Anyway, you sit yourself down and get down-south comfortable." Sarah motioned towards the u-shaped sectional black leather sofa, situated centre-stage in the living room. "Two margaritas . . . maybe more . . ," she glanced back as she left the room.

Gullens could hear the crunching of ice in the blender. His mind's eye went back to the guesthouse, to Ny - cook Ba's unkempt apprentice - who would chisel away at a block of fast melting ice with a huge screwdriver. She would scoop up the pieces from the kitchen floor and put them in a bowl in the freezer - ready for lunch-time ice coffee for the foreign guests.

First, Gullens noticed Sarah's tipsy sway when she walked back into the living room; then, his eyes met hers - glassy.

"Four . . . just as you . .we . . . ordered," Sarah joked. "I wish this was Mexico. Richard has a grand hacienda on the Baja, and . . ."

"Speaking of your husband, where is he . . out with the boys?" teased Gullens, knowing Samuelson had no friends in Can Tho. He instantly regretted he had spoken of her husband, and tried to think of a diversion.

Sarah said, as if in court - under oath, "Richard is a drinker . . . not an alcoholic, really. He just goes on binges . . . about once a month. He calls it his time of the month . . . get it?" Silly, girlish titters followed.

"Yeh, I get it,"

Sarah continued, again in a tone of testimony regarding her husband's behaviour. "He's been gone since last night."

"You must be worried."

"No . . . not really . . . his benders are usually overnighters. Sometimes alone . . . sometimes not. Then he comes back home . . . no apologies . . . sleeps it off . . . and wakes up . . .that's it, end of story."

"I'm sorry, it must be hard for you," Gullens remarked in an attempt to console her.

Sarah leaned against the couch and threw her head back, looking complacent. "Not really. I like to be alone . . . sometimes . . . Don't you?"

Gullens was unsure of the conversation and of himself. He quickly gathered his thoughts and then blurted out, much too loudly, "Oh, . . . by the way . . . I have a letter for you. Seb found it in his mail slot . . . at the hospital."

"For me? I don't know anybody there." She placed the large manila envelope on her lap, and in an intentionally feminine way she opened the glued flap. Then, she pulled out the single page and held it under the lamp light. Gullens marvelled at the grace of her movements.

Sarah's face blanched and her slender hands began to shake violently. Her head, then her entire body shuddered in short, rapid convulsions. As she stood up, the envelope fell to the floor and a ring fell out. It spun once, twice, several times - like a top - then stopped. Sarah looked at the ring, gasped in one deep inhale and, putting both hands to her mouth, trembled uncontrollably.

Gullens rose, touched his hands to her shaking arms . . to steady her. She jolted towards him . . . then away, and rushed in jerky, tottering steps out of the room.

Gullens was paralyzed by Sarah's actions and the confusion of events. He heard retching followed by a run of heavy sobs. He bent to one knee and picked up the paper, reading the words . . . without recognition. His mind too was paralyzed. He gazed at the ring without recognition. Then, he picked up the envelope. He felt a bulge at the bottom. Inserting his hand, he touched the soft gauze, and he knew.

Shocked into action, Gullens methodically picked up the paper and the ring and returned them to the envelope, and then he folded the envelope over once, twice and once width-wise and put it into the right front pocket of his pants.

He walked, nearly tiptoeing, down the hall and stopped at the bathroom door, halfway ajar.

"Sarah . . . Sarah . . . " was all he could manage. He heard the aftermath of heavy weeping - long, dry, throaty sighs.

He opened the door and, standing behind her, he once again touched his hands to her arms . . . to steady her. She turned around limply and let her face fall against his chest, her sighs muffled in the folds of his shirt.

Minutes passed without movement. Gullens stared blankly into the bathroom mirror, puzzling over what to do next. The mirror reflected Sarah's sylphlike figure, and Gullens, his mind elsewhere, felt his body beginning to respond. It suddenly struck him that he had not held a woman, in any circumstances, for many months.

Hao - knowing Seb's habits - offered to stand sleepy guard, and Seb - knowing his own needs - gratefully accepted.

Before leaving, Seb spiked Samuelson's ice water with a heavy sedative. The sweet taste of jasmine hid any hint of medicine. Within an hour, Samuelson fell into a heavy night-long sleep. Seb tied his guest down again - to the bedposts.

Minutes past ten. Seb faxed Samuelson's letter from the international communications office, adjacent to the main post office. He was relieved. It was seven in the morning - on a Friday - in California. A business day.

In Can Tho - Friday night - at Venice. The music and lights of the first boat invited Seb to enter the floating lounge. Inside, laughing, drinking and dancing - only one couple cornered in slow step to a sultry jazz song. Seb guessed Billie Holiday. All but two of Ky's girls were paired. Business was weekend good. Ky sat alone, on a high stool at the bar. Seb saw her first and - nodding here, winking there - he wended his way past the lust-struck romeos and their charming coquettes to a welcoming Ky.

She spoke first. "A long night of poker and a long day of work. Welcome home."

"Thank you, Jasmine. I missed you."

Seb held out his left hand and Ky offered her right as she stepped down from the stool. They held each other close . . . gently . . . and then, in rhythm to the slow swing of jazz, they waltzed around and in between the other couples - towards, then out the door.

With arms around each other, they walked the length of the wide plank on to the canal road and down the short distance of seven bordello suites to number eight, Ky's boat of good fortune.

The bath water had been poured several hours before, in anticipation of Seb's coming.

"That's perfect, Jasmine, I need the coolness tonight." Seb undressed and pitched his bundle of clothes into the bamboo basket between the sink and the antique French tub. Jasmine smiled, seeing Seb under water. "Too cold for me, Chien Bot. You enjoy . . . Do you want a beer?"

"Not tonight. Too much booze in the last little while. How about a tonic with lime?"

"With gin?"

"No gin. Just tonic and lime . . . Thanks."

Ky prepared the drink, the same for herself, and proceeded to prepare his pipe. She kneaded the small, round pellet in the bowl of the pipe, then laid it on the bamboo bedstand.

"You are tired, Seb. I can see it in your eyes . . . what's wrong ?"

"I don't know." He struggled to find a quick answer, not wanting to revisit the past twenty-four hours. "Kim's gone." Suddenly, he remembered that Ky knew nothing about Hao. It struck him deeply strange that so much had happened in the short span of one day. It seemed more like a week - like a full month.

"Hao was badly beaten . . . I think by the gang that took Kim. He's at my place . . . resting. They totalled his cyclo."

"To-talled?" queried Ky.

"Destroyed. The bastards broke his cyclo into pieces. Gone."

"Poor Hao." Ky went quiet. She was aware of Hao's history. Words were unnecessary. She poured a teapot of boiling water into the tub, giving just enough warmth to encourage Seb to soak for a second twenty minutes.

Ky knelt beside the tub, and with light, massaging strokes she shampooed his hair. He leaned forward. With a scratchy sea sponge she scrubbed his back, then rinsed him with the softness of cool water cupped in her soft hand.

He soaked some more, consciously trying to drown Samuelson . . . to rid him from his mind. But the huge stiff body resurfaced and Seb, in silent resignation, stood up and pulled on the chain of the overhead urn. The cool water poured over him, like a baptism without faith.

He towelled off and sat on the bed next to Ky. Flame. Heat. Bubble. Smoke. First, second, third pipe. Ky encouraged the third and hinted at four, but Seb was already lying on his side in foetal repose, ready to return to time before thought.

Ky kissed his forehead, turned off the large light and nudged in next to him. Her breasts nestled softly against the middle of his back. One hand reached up to comb through his hair, the other rested on his heart. Their legs loosely entangled. The quarter moon was on its back, belly-up amongst the brilliant stars.

116

16

A series of rapid knocks, then smashing bangs against the door. Ky looked through the bamboo blinds at a still sleeping moon. It was some time beyond midnight, but long before dawn. A drunken Don Juan? A rejected Casanova?

She swiftly covered her nakedness in a silk sarong and, without words, she calmly opened the door.

"Ky . . . I'm Mark . . . Dr. Gullens . . . do you remember me?" In his agitation, Gullens momentarily stumbled on one of the several wooden slats which secured the two planks together and served as footholds during the rainy season. He recovered his balance, but not his composure.

"I must see Seb . . . now . . . It's very serious!" He shouted beyond Ky, wanting Seb to hear him directly. "I went to his place . . . Hao told me how to find you . . . I mean Seb . . . Is he here?"

Ky was neither alarmed nor amused. She had had many experiences with excitable, even combustible customers, especially foreign ones. Now, Gullens.

"Yes, Seb is here." She spoke simply, unhurried. "No, you cannot see him now. He is very tired and in a deep sleep."

To Gullens, her words came in slow motion. "Ky, this is very, very serious," he repeated, awkwardly stamping his foot for emphasis . . . and nearly falling off the plank again.

"Seb is very, very tired. He can't help you now . . ." Ky's firm words were mellowed by the softness of her eyes. She put one hand on Gullens' sticky-damp arm, patting it as she spoke. "In the morning . . . by eight o'clock . . . he will see you."

"Where . . . here?" Gullens was disoriented by harsh words in consort with kind eyes.

"Here, if you want," Ky offered.

"No . . . at Samuelson's . . . at eight. Here's the address." Gullens took out a crumbled piece of paper - the one he had been

117

given by the receptionist at the Quoc Te Hotel - and nervously handed it to Ky.

"I know the area." Ky flashed back to her teenage years - to nights spent at General D's villa in the absence of his wife. "Seb will be there at eight."

Seb stirred slowly to Ky's good morning touch. "Up, up and away," she teased. The smoke was still with Seb, and he resisted.

"Dr. Mark came last night, but I did not let him bother you. He was . . . how do you say . . . upsetting?"

"Upset." Ky's mention of Gullens spurred Seb to action. He reached for his clothes. "Sorry Ky, no time to lose . . . No breakfast . . . Got to go."

"Miss me?" asked Ky, knowing Seb's answer.

"Already do . . . already do."

"Wait Seb. Here . . . where Dr. Mark is . . . at the big American's house."

Seb grabbed the note and a fleeting kiss and ran out to find a cyclo-taxi. He returned home to a sleeping guest and his guard. Their snores seemed to be in dialogue, first one then the other in polite turns. Seb shook Hao forcefully and then released Samuelson for his toilet time. Within ten minutes he had Samuelson pinned down again to the bed and Hao drinking strong, black coffee.

"Hao, only half a glass of water for him. No coffee . . . no food . . . no toilet. I'll be back as soon as I can."

Other than Madame Guc's, Seb had never been - he had refused to go - to the villas of the elite. It was his feeble protest against the inequities in society - in this era, communist inequities. Now, made pliant by a pleading Gullens and by his own growing guilt as an extortionist, he found himself at the black iron gates of Samuelson's villa.

"Please enter, Dr. Seb," announced the sentry in anticipation of his arrival. Seb too noticed the sound of near perfect English, and wondered.

Before Seb was halfway up the walk the front door flew open and an agitated Gullens bounded out to face Seb.

"Thank God, Seb . . . you're here."

"Thank Ky. She . . . not God . . . got me here," Seb corrected. Then, seeing the panic in Gullens' eyes, he immediately softened, speaking kindly, "Sorry Mark . . . how can I help?"

Gullens and Seb entered the house together. They went directly into the living room and sat down on the sofa - in the exact positions occupied the night before by Sarah and Gullens. The young doctor confided in his senior colleague, his friend and - as Seb often teased - his reluctant father-figure. After Gullens' account of events, they both slumped against the sofa cushions, silent in thought. Seb had listened without showing emotion. Gullens put this down to Seb's Asian mannerisms. He knew he cared.

Carrying a pot of black coffee, a small pitcher of cream, a bowl of sugar, three cups with saucers and three spoons on a teak tray, which last night had held too many margaritas, Sarah entered the room. She was wearing a Japanese kimono - a honeymoon gift - pink with white cherry blossoms. The clinking of cups against saucers forewarned Seb of Sarah's condition. Her piercing eyes, reddened and swollen from a night's weeping, showed none of the sensuality that had so intrigued Seb upon their first meeting. And the TV smile - the girl-next-door look of seductive innocence - was lost in confusion and fear.

Sarah tried to sound strong. "I gave the maid and cook the next week off. Only the gate guards will be here until . . ." Her voice broke off.

While Gullens stood up to take the tray, Seb stepped forward to give Sarah a fatherly hug.

Then, all three sat down simultaneously, like marionettes in a puppet show. All three observed a telling moment of silence.

Seb broke the funereal spell. "There are no real options here. They . . whoever they are . . are in control. We must accept that. Life can be cheap here. But a foreigner's life is not so cheap - especially a rich foreigner . . . They know that, I'm sure."

Gullens, ever - especially now - the combatant, stiffened forward, ready to challenge Seb's compromising talk. Seb saw him coming and, without hesitation, pounced on Gullens before he could speak.

"No Mark . . no! Not this time. No heroics. No white knights. No goddamn Hollywood endings. This is Vietnam. It's different here . . . I know . . . I've been here a long time . . . maybe, too long."

Seb looked directly at Sarah. "Let it happen. Your husband will pay the money. With luck, he will be okay." He paused, long enough to give effect to his words of warning. "It would be foolhardy . . . extremely dangerous . . .to try to stop them." He paused again, then said, "First, we don't even know who they are . . . Secondly, they are demanding money for a hospital, not themselves. This, then, is a militant political act; they are totally committed to their cause . . . guaranteed . . . Finally, this is a life and death issue . . . maybe theirs . . . certainly your husband's . . . probably yours."

Sarah showed no responding emotion; she said nothing. She seemed empty of feelings, one way or another.

"What next then?" she asked.

Seb looked first at Sarah - gently - then firmly at Gullens. "Wait . . . we must just wait it out . . . and hope . . . hope for the best . . . ."

Long, lingering minutes of quiet. Even the chorus of birds in the garden outside ceased their chirping, stifled by the searing morning sun.

Seb rose from the sofa. "If I can help, please let me know. Afternoons and evenings I'm at the hospital. After eight, usually at Ky's. Any time is okay."

Sarah remained seated while Gullens accompanied Seb to the door. He had nothing to say.

Seb offered the closing gambit. "Thanks, Mark, for helping me out yesterday. And . . .thanks for just listening just now . . . I really do want to help . . . guaranteed."

"Guaranteed Seb," echoed Gullens without conviction as he closed the door between them.

When Gullens returned to the living room he found Sarah looking out the window, into the rear garden. She was crying quietly, subdued.

A storm, unusual in the dry season, was forming in the sky, high above. The sun still reigned, but dark, rain-laden clouds were closing in. The towering palms caught the gusty winds and the branches all bent in unison; the fronds scratched at one another - producing a clipping sound, like playing cards clothes - pinned to spinning bicycle spokes.

Gullens came up behind Sarah and gently gripped her arms with his hands. She gazed outward, transfixed by the storm's ominous movement. He spoke to her in a low, comforting tone, much slower and more careful than usual.

"Try not to worry too much. It will all work out in the end . . . Things usually do . . you know."

Sarah said nothing, but her body responded, leaning back against him.

"Seb understands how things work here. And . . . I'm sure he'll do whatever he can to help your husband."

Sarah stiffened instantly and her body straightened. She took a rigid step forward, breaking her body away from his. She didn't turn around to face him, but took a second step forward - up against the window glass. She seemed to be speaking to the storm itself.

"He's not my husband . . . We are not married."

Gullens froze, dazed in disbelief.

"I was his executive secretary. Now I'm his executive . . . He's been married twice. He wants me - third time's a charm you know. But doesn't want another messy divorce."

"And you Sarah . . what do you want?"

Sarah slowly swung around to face Gullens. And, again. as if in court under oath, she said, "I don't know what I want. I don't want a secretary's salary and the CEO's hands all over me. If he wants me he'll have to marry me. So we made a deal. One year as Richard's wife - a trial offer so-to-speak . . . fake an elopement to Mexico - wealthy executive and younger woman . . . fake marriage license . . fake honeymoon . . . fake love . . .fake life . . . fake-fake-fake . . ."

Sarah's eyes kept their focus on Gullens, watching for his reaction.

"But . . ." said Gullens.

"Richard's a pragmatist . . . and an opportunist . . . He's got what he wants . . .me . . . at least for one year."

"Then what?"

"I'm free to choose. Marriage . . . real and legal . . . and with it, fifty percent of the company . . . by inheritance . . . that's worth millions . . . or . . . nothing - no Richard . . . no company . . only me."

Gullens could no longer read Sarah's eyes. Her story had stunned him. He sank deep into the leather cushions of the couch. Sarah followed, sitting upright, at an angle to him. She continued - straight forward, like a witness at her own trial.

"It isn't working . . . never really did. We . . he tried . . . in Mexico . . . in Hawaii. It just didn't happen . . . never, for me . . . and now, not even for him. We haven't slept together since Japan . . . We're both just waiting . . till the year's over . . . in June . . . the month for weddings."

Sarah then slumped into a similar position to Gullens and closed her eyes. They both listened to the growing storm, the wind rattling the pane-glass window frames.

The light from the lamps - left on throughout the night - suddenly went out, and the slow, steady hum of the air-conditioner abruptly ceased.

Gullens recovered. "A blackout. Seb told me it happens often in the rainy season. Now too, I guess." He looked at Sarah - still, with her eyes closed.

"Perhaps Sarah, now's a good time to sleep . . . at least get some rest . . . What do you think?"

"Yes." She yawned in agreement. The winds picked up and a heavy rain began to fall, pelting the roof and windows. The rapid-fire drumming of the rain drowned out the whistle and swish of swaying palms.

"Please come with me . . ." Sarah said earnestly. "I don't want to be alone . . . Please."

They walked down the hallway. Before reaching the far end and the master bedroom, Sarah stopped and opened the door on the right. "This is my room . . . I'm . . We're both guests now."

Gullens followed her in, unsure of the moment. She grasped his hand and led him to the far twin bed. He bent over, slowly took off his shoes and stretched onto the bed.

Sarah carefully placed her sandals at the foot of her bed and slid softly onto the silk sheets and, within minutes, into a deep sleep.

Gullens gazed upon the sleeping silhouette, but saw nothing of her beauty. The morning storm had darkened the sky and the room. The damp air stood too still, too close. As he shut his eyes, he focussed on the beads of sweat cooling on his chest. He unbuttoned his shirt, inviting the wet, warm air to caress him. Once again, pure physicalness took over. Exhausted by a night without sleep and events beyond his control, he too fell deeply, soundly asleep.

The storm had won the day and moved on to the South China Sea, destined to gain in force and destruction before dying in the distant Pacific.

Sarah awakened to a subsiding storm and a slumbering Gullens, who - in seeming harmony with the waning winds - breathed in, then out in long whispering whistles.

She felt the heat in the room - wet heat from the warm rains. She stepped stealthily from her bed to his, trying not to break his sleep. Her whole being trembled as she touched his wet, naked chest lightly with the tips of her fingers. He half-opened his eyes in slow reverie.

"Trang." he whispered.

17

Following his encounter with Sarah and Gullens, Seb on an impulse to escape decided to purchase a bicycle, the famous Phoenix brand - imported illegally from Shanghai. The loss of Hao's cyclo meant inconvenient, often long waits in the overpowering heat for a passing cyclo-taxi. The bicycle meant immediate transportation and an opportunity to lose himself . . . at his own speed . . . in the dense traffic of humanity in the streets and alleyways of Can Tho.

Within the hour of his purchase, however, the cluster gear jammed time and again and the wheel spokes wobbled every which way. He realized a return to the Chinese store - specializing in the best of black market goods, along with the worst of service - would result in disagreement and disappointment. *Caveat emptor*, in hindsight. So, he pedalled with caution to the bike repair shop opposite the university guesthouse. A stagnant sewer pond linked to a dozen tin-roofed shacks separated the hovels in the rear from the street-front shops.

An old man was squatting low, his arms around his knees - one hand then the other swatting at the siege of circling flies. His wife was in the shade of the shop's interior. Dust-covered bottles - in a myriad of shapes and sizes - stood higgledy-piggledy on the dirty shelves. They contained liquor without labels: gut-rotting whiskey, flat beer and medicinal alcohol. Seb recalled years ago when he had paid pennies - in dong - for his first bottle of homemade brew from this very shop. It had stayed in him a matter of thirty minutes; then, stomach twists and turns and throw-up. 'Buyer beware' thought Seb as he greeted first the old repairman and then his wife, the liquor lady.

He left the bicycle for repair and crossed the noisy street to the relative quiet and comfort of the guesthouse. But, there was no peace to be had.

"Dr. Seb!" shouted Marie, as if lying in wait for him. "Dr. Mark no come back last night . . . I worry for him . . . too much bad man at night . . ."

"Bad women too, Marie," countered Seb. He could sense Marie's genuine concern. "I saw him this morning. He's fine . . . Just out too late with too many beautiful ladies."

Seb's banter relaxed Marie and, with renewed vigour, she turned her attack on him. "You tell me Dr. Mark is good man. You tell me he good for my Thao. He no good. He same like you, Dr. Seb. My Thao marry good man . . . no drink . . . no woman."

"No fun," Seb chimed in. He always knew, regardless of his own mood or circumstance, that Marie - with her mix of wit and wisdom - would lend proper perspective to the moment.

Sweet ice coffee followed - flavoured with Marie's guesthouse gossip. First them: This Professor . . . from Holland . . . that Doctor . . . from Sweden; then us: Mai . . . the Dean's wife . . . and Thuyen . . . the young official from Hanoi. Them . . . us. With Marie, Seb felt only us. He loved her - his big, little sister.

The repair bill (readjust clutch and cluster gear, replace rear brake pads and true spokes): parts - 8,000 dong; labour (2 hours) - 3,000 dong. Total: $1.10.

Seb cycled away on his now-new bike like an eight year old ready to race. He parked inside the hospital gate to the bewilderment of the parking lot attendant, who seemed to show disapproval of Seb's new mode of transportation as he chalked a permit number on the bike seat and handed him a torn paper receipt: #9.

Coffee with Marie and the bike ride - short as they were - had given Seb a fleeting reprieve from his responsibilities; yes, he would say to himself repeatedly over the following days - his responsibilities as a doctor and an extortionist. He would question in his wandering mind the pros and cons of his newly found role. Doctor Jekyll versus Mr. Hyde? Super-ego versus id? The end versus the means? And, to his benefit, he found solace in such internal discourse. Sophistry, perhaps, he would caution himself, but certainly, it served the purpose of keeping him on course. And, the very process of soul-searching purged him of absolute guilt. Absolutes - never, he would conclude.

Seb began his rounds - one full day plus four hours late - not complacent, simply composed. He checked charts, revised dosages and examined his patients more thoroughly than usual. His bedside manner improved. Rather than treating the disease, he took time to treat the person. "What's your favourite sport, Tin?" Then, "Anh, how about you and me sneaking out for an ice-cream? Our secret though . . . don't tell the nurses."

Trang had been watching Seb win timid smiles from one bed-ridden child, then another. She approached him from behind. "Good morning . . . excuse me . . . good afternoon, Doctor . . . Are you new on staff here? Your enthusiasm is contagious, and some of the old M.D.'s around here need an infection of energy and enthusiasm."

"Like me?" asked Seb rhetorically. "Rumour has it that I'm over-the-hill."

"Over-the-hill? What hill?" questioned Trang, puzzled.

"Old . . . past the peak, and going down . . . useless." Seb hunched over for full effect.

"You, Dr. Seb? Not you! I was watching you . . . you are full of vim, vigour and vitality!" Trang sang out in praise.

"Vim . . . vigour . . . where did you learn all that?"

"Dr. Mark taught me . . . he taught me many new words on our trip to Chau Doc."

"Well tell Dr. Mark to practice medicine, not English," Seb jested.

Here, within earshot of the sick children, Seb and Trang teased each other. And, although their words were not understood, their laughter was universal - enlivening the ward for nurses and children alike.

After completing their rounds, Trang and Seb walked in step to the staff lounge to discuss each child's condition and determine future treatment.

"We just received a letter from the Ministry," began Trang. "Two Canadian doctors are coming . . . They specialize in reconstructive surgery. They're with Doctors Without Borders."

Seb not only knew of the organization, he was once a member - during his first stint in Vietnam. 'Without borders' defined the organization's working philosophy: humanitarian medical work in third world countries - especially those ravaged by war and disease - without regard to political leanings. The volunteer doctors took time and money from their own practice to serve three week - three month - one year stints. Seb respected them and their work.

Birth deformities were all too common in Vietnam, especially in the south. Proof was not conclusive, but Seb and fellow doctors had collected sufficient evidence to support the strong suspicion that American herbicides - primarily agent orange - had poisoned pregnant women and punished their babies with a plague of deformities long after the end of the bloodshed.

"When will they arrive?"

"Tomorrow . . . or the next day," answered Trang.

"Great!" Seb blurted out, then added, "But we don't have enough anaesethetic . . . not for more than one day . . . two maximum."

"They're bringing their own," Trang reassured him. "Enough for one week. They'll each work in four hour shifts - three shifts a day . . . So, the operating room will be used all day and all night . . . for most of next week."

"No problem . . . unless there's a life or death emergency," Seb said, simultaneously thinking that so much about medicine in Vietnam is exactly that . . . life or death. "Just let me know if you need me . . . If not, I can catch up on my patients' records while they're here. . . You know Trang, in the U.S. I would not be allowed to operate until I had completed all the paperwork. . . . Paper matters . . . sometimes more than patients."

"I don't understand," Trang responded.

"Neither do I . . . By the way, how do you think my adopted son, Dr. Mark, is doing?"

Trang's body tensed, but her face showed no emotion. "I think he's doing very well. He's more realistic now."

"I understand. I had the same experience. Idealistic . . . then realistic . . . then skep . . ," Seb recounted without completion. "And, how was your trip upriver . . . to Long Xuyen and Chau Doc?"

"Well, Dr. Mark was disappointed . . . he thought they would . . . you know . . . just accept what he said . . . what . . ." Trang stopped in mid-sentence, remembering Gullens' disappointment in her - that last night on the boat.

"I know," Seb anticipated. "It's a simple matter of time and experience."

Seb grabbed a handful of files in preparation to leave. "Oh, Trang, it's Dr. Vuong's wedding tomorrow - right?"

"Yes."

"Would it be okay to bring Dr. Mark? It would be a good experience for him . . . different customs . . .traditions . . ."

Trang hesitated. "Dr. Mark? . . . of course . . . I'm sure Vuong's family would be honoured."

"Good . . . Tell Dr. Vuong I'll be waiting at the guesthouse . . . with Dr. Mark."

Seb walked towards the exit. "See you tomorrow, very early."

"Okay Dr. Seb . . . Don't be late . . . like today." Then she added," Better late than never!"

"Dr. Mark's words?"

"Yes, Dr. Mark."

18

Seb pedalled home, the new kid on the block - cocky on his new bike, faster than the others. He remembered back to his boyhood friend Earl, whose mother was divorced - almost unheard of then. Twelve years old; Earl six days older. They had spent that summer shooting baskets and riding bikes. Some mornings, when they felt brave, they would cycle to the train station, chain their bikes together with combination locks and - once out of sight of the yard crew - jump into an empty freight car for a free ride, sometimes with a hobo or two, to the next town, fifteen miles west. Then, they would jump off just as the steam engine entered the yard and the train shuddered to a screeching stop. Once Seb jumped too soon and his legs fell from under his body and he slid over the black cinders, blood streaming from both elbows. Told his mom he fell off his bike. Earl said so too.

Just as Seb braked his bike to turn left, he felt the weight of a small boy - no more than ten years old - on the flimsy rear carrier.

"Hello! . . . What your name? . . Where you from? . . . Are you marry? . . Do you like Vietnam?"

Within the length of one block and before Seb could even give answer, the boy swung effortlessly off the bicycle and landed with his barefeet firmly on the road. With a wave of the hand he wished Seb good luck, then turned the other way - into the absorbing crowd.

Seb turned right and, cycling more slowly now, maneuvered in and out and around peasant women - their backs bent forward under yolk baskets, young men - unemployed - in aimless stroll, graceful teachers in white *ao dais*, kids too young or too poor to be in school, and hawkers everywhere selling almost everything - food, drinks, birds - dead or alive, chewing gum, lottery tickets.

Seb touched earth when he saw Hao sitting in the shade on the front steps. Balanced on his stump leg was a flat, square object. His good leg stretched out, without purpose.

"For Christ's sake Hao, what're you doing?" challenged Seb in frustration. "Why aren't you upstairs with . . "

"Mr. Sam?" Hao answered elfishly. "You no worry. Mr. Sam . . . He good man now. He like me too much."

"Hao, what're you talking about? . . You must watch him . . all the time."

Hao just smiled back at Seb's crimson face. Then, he scowled in feigned defiance. "You no pay too much . . . I watch Mr. Sam . . For what? Rice dinner . . bad beer . . No money . . no work. Maybe, I work for Mr. Sam. He tell me he pay big money." Hao leaned back, braced on the steps by his elbows.

Seb stood above Hao, bewildered by his behaviour. Then he looked down to Hao's stump. Balanced on the stump was Seb's cutting board and on it, sliced into thick rounds, were the remains of a python. On the step, in a blue and white Chinese serving bowl, the snake's head floated in red water.

"Hao!" exclaimed Seb.

"Snake on bed . . Hao kill snake . . . Snake no kill Mr. Sam. Mr. Sam tell me he give me big money . . ."

Seb grabbed the machete out of Hao's hand and jumped up the front steps two at a time and up again to the bedroom upstairs.

Seb beheld an ashen Samuelson, sweat-wet and shaking. His eyelids were blinking rapidly - in rhythm to the whoosh, whoosh, whoosh of the overhead fan.

"Well," said Seb sarcastically, "Guess what's for dinner tonight? Skewered and grilled or in a stew? . . . Your choice." He seemed to delight in his guest's discomfort. "And for the record, don't try to bribe Hao. He would die before turning against me - no matter how much money you offered him."

Samuelson lay silent, still shaking slightly. Hao entered just as Seb finished, smiling confidently. He stood on his one leg, leaning forward on his crutch, as if ready for action.

Seb already regretted his anger towards Hao. "Here's the plan Hao. First, I'll take a look at your ugly face. Then, I'll check Mr. Sam's finger, and we'll take him to the toilet. After, you can go get some dinner for us - at the Ninh Kiew - for sure this time. Your friends can cook up the snake and you can have dinner with them. You have the night off . . . be back by five in the morning."

"Not good, Dr. Seb . . Mr. Sam pay big money . . you pay dinner - my snake . . I like work Mr. Sam," bellowed Hao, savouring his double victory, as he pirouetted on his one foot out of the bedroom and hopped down the stairs.

The afternoon moved slowly towards evening without one word from Samuelson, who had gorged and guzzled - beer this time - his way through a thoroughly Vietnamese dinner.

"How about some music Mr. Samuelson? Any requests?"

"That you come to your goddamn senses and let me go."

"Impossible . . too late . . . Sorry."

"But my wife . . ," pleaded Samuelson.

"Not to worry . . . As long as you pay the money and she doesn't talk, she - and you - will be fine . . free in five or six days." Seb surprised himself with his composure. He learned, perhaps for the first real time, that thinking is suffering; taking action is liberating. He felt a gradual loosening of his mind-forged shackles.

"One question," posed Samuelson, "Why me?"

"Why you? Well, Samuelson, there are several reasons. One, gut reaction. I detest powermongers of any kind . . you are a powermonger."

"What? I don't have the faintest idea what you're talking about," he responded, genuinely hurt by Seb's remark.

"You have an obsessive need to control people Samuelson . . your wife . . . even those you don't know. You forced two Vietnamese - at the Rainbow . . remember? You tried to force them to eat rare steak . . just because . ."

"It's the only way to cook a steak," interjected Samuelson.

"No, goddammit! That's not the point." Seb could taste the tension. "It's just that you think your way is the only way . . but it isn't."

131

Samuelson went on the defensive. "I didn't mean to . . "

"Insult them in public, bitch about foreign food . . Vietnamese food . . in Vietnam."

"But I don't have to like it," protested Samuelson.

"You don't have to be the ugly American either," argued Seb with rising anger.

"Hold on now Doctor. This ugly American is bringing big business to Vietnam . . jobs and money . . "

"Money?" broke in Seb. "Money? For whom? . . The workers? . . How much? . . Twenty-five dollars a month working twelve hour days. Twenty-five fucking dollars a month . . you bastard. You're making that much every five minutes."

"So? It's my investment . . my money . ."

"Shut up! Goddamn you. Shut up!" Seb felt the fury in his voice. "You'll make a killing on the backs of your workers. You'll make a huge American profit on Vietnamese backs. First, you tried to bomb them off the map and now you exploit them without conscience. You ugly, powermongering son-of-a-bitch!"

Seb tried to stand still, but his whole body vibrated in a violent catharsis. He turned away from Samuelson . . to the far corner of the room. He spit out the window to the street below, then stared out, without looking.

"Time for some soul music, Samuelson. How about Verdi's 'Nabucco?' Hebrew slaves then . . Vietnamese slaves now . . only difference - over two thousand years of fucking civilization."

Seb let the music take control. He sat down in the rattan chair, bending forward with his elbows on his knees and his hands holding his head, now dripping with beads of sweat. He pressed his thumbs to his temples to brake the pounding within.

The opera held Seb until - moved by the chorus, 'Va Pensiero' - he rose and, as if in a trance, walked over to the bed, carrying three pills and a glass of water in his left hand. In his right, he held the machete. He brought it within inches of Samuelson's left hand, bound tightly to the bedpost. "Take these pills or - guaranteed - I'll cut off another finger."

Samuelson lifted his head feebly and opened his mouth, like a dying Catholic taking communion. Seb placed the pills on

132

Samuelson's tongue and slowly tipped the glass, letting the water trickle into his mouth. Samuelson swallowed once . . twice. Drops of water leaked out between his lips, rolled down his chin, and mixed with the sweat on his chest.

Seb turned the tape over, turned up the volume and turned out the lights. He returned to his corner chair. A bright moon shone through the bamboo blinds, separating the two men with parallel planes of yolk-yellow light.

19

Startled, Seb jumped to his feet. He raised the blinds and opened the shutters to a steady banging below.

Hao looked up. "Dr. Seb! Four o'clock! I early . . . you can go now."

"Thanks Hao . . . I'll be right down." As he descended the stairs, he thought briefly of Hao's usual nightly binge and his chronic lateness. "Two wrongs must be right," he said aloud to himself.

When he opened the door, a new Hao saluted him. Clean clothes - ragged, but clean; a proper haircut, not the rough cut by his own hands with his cloned Swiss-army knife. Even his crutch showed signs of renewal - clean, white tape over the ever grimy grip. Sober and smiling. Only the hanging stump of a leg and the patchwork face of stitched wounds bridged the image of Hao - then and now.

"You hurry, Dr. Seb. Go wedding today."

"You're a good man Hao, and a good man is hard to find." And, on impulse Seb reached out and grasped Hao in a huge bear of a hug, and held him.

Seb returned upstairs to release Samuelson - still deeply drowsy - from the bedposts. He retied his guest's hands and feet in preparation for toilet and exercise time. Downstairs, Hao had dripped coffee and boiled water for *pho* - his everyday breakfast of meat bits in noodle soup.

Later, with Samuelson resettled in ropes and Hao in control, Seb jumped on his bicycle for a fast pedal to the university guesthouse.

"Go slow!" yelled Hao from the bedroom window, clapping his hands in praise of Seb's efforts. "You bad driver . . you die!"

Early, even before dawn, the city was in motion. Seb swerved to avoid colliding into two teenage boys - one pulling in front, the other pushing from the rear - a hand cart sardined with market-bound ducks. Seb thought once again about back-home days. Duck hunting in late Autumn . . . freezing, too-early mornings . . . trigger happy, restless waits - swift flutters of flight followed by booms of shotguns splitting the low sky . . arm wincing in black and blue pain . . . birds falling amongst bullrushes and cattails . . . gutting and cleaning . . . the too-long ride home . . . late supper . . . hot bath . . . sleep. Different ducks . . . different boys.

Marie had Gullens up, fed and waiting for Seb's arrival.

"Why so early?" objected Gullens. "How can you say 'I do' when it's too early to tell if you're dead or alive? Why not an afternoon affair? Much more civilized."

"Actually, it's an all day affair and often into the night, starting right now." He pointed to a bus edging off the road in front of the guesthouse gates. Seb and Gullens boarded the nearly empty, time-worn bus, chartered to pick up guests of both the bride and the groom. Seb did not recognize any of the passengers, all sitting in the first few seats.

"Vietnamese style," said Seb. "A special occasion . . . a matter of family status. No limos, but no bikes or cyclos either."

"Where to now? . . . The wedding?" asked Gullens.

"No . . . a scenic tour first - in and around Can Tho. Relax and enjoy."

Gullens noticed the pleasure in Seb's expression, but could not respond in kind. "Seb . . . maybe . . . what, with Sarah all alone . . . maybe I should . . ."

"Bring her along?" asked Seb caustically.

"Of course not."

"Then, what?"

The bus stopped. Three woman, elegant in formal *ao dais*, walked gracefully down the aisle. Seb and Gullens did not recognize the first two. The third was Trang.

"Good morning, Dr. Trang." Seb greeted her. "Perfect day for a wedding."

Trang smiled back. "Yesterday, today and tomorrow - in Vietnam every day is a perfect day for a wedding."

"Trang . . . uh . . . Dr. Trang . . . " interjected Gullens awkwardly

"Hello Mark . . . Dr. Mark," she teased, and then added, "just Trang . . . okay?"

Gullens ached with discomfort in the presence of Trang, and wondered if it showed. His mind ricocheted between Trang and Sarah - between the river ride with Trang and the night at Sarah's - between Trang's rabbit-in-the-moon and Sarah's storm - between what he felt he wanted and what he thought he shouldn't want . . . He found himself floundering, and, in self-conscious defense, he looked out the windows of the bus, hoping to become invisible.

Finally, the ancient bus, filled beyond capacity - three, even four, to a bench seat built for two - lurched noisily to a halt, blocking a narrow roadway. The driver opened the door and a nervous, handsome Vuong entered with his two older brothers. There was a spontaneous round of applause as the three men - in rented western tuxedos - greeted the wedding passengers. His parents and two sisters had left an hour before to welcome other guests who would be arriving at the Buddhist temple opposite the city park on busy Hoa Binh Boulevard.

After ten minutes of old women's chatter and young men's banter, the bus stopped in front of the Murirangsyaram Pagoda.

"No, no!" shouted an old peasant woman. Her farm-rough hands slapping at the driver's back. "Crazy . . . crazy," added her friends in chorus.

The hired driver had taken the groom and his guests to the Khmer Buddhist temple, three blocks away from the wedding venue.

Seb looked at Gullens, who sat silently, in obvious confusion. "Wrong church."

"I don't get it," said Gullens.

"Well, the driver - like most of the younger generation - has no religion. What with French and American Christianity, and now communist atheism - Buddhism, quite literally, has been forced to the back of the bus. Temples for most young folk are for weddings - not worship - so they might not

136

recognize the difference - at first glance - between a Khmer and a Vietnamese temple. Only the old folk - mostly women - have really kept the faith."

Laughter saved face. Even a nervous Vuong enjoyed the comic relief of the moment. The bus driver, aided by pointing fingers and shouting voices, found the destination, and the passengers - already in a ceremonial mood - began to exit.

"Stay seated," Seb advised Gullens. "Vuong has invited us to go with him to the bride's house."

"Why? Isn't she here . . . at the temple?"

"No. The groom must go to her home and formally ask her family's approval."

"But why are we going?"

"Well, because Vuong is a colleague . . . and one of my former students. Also, I would guess that - as foreigners - we bring a curious sense of good luck to the occasion. Auspicious guests . . . you and me."

Gullens, wrestling with his own sense of guilt in relation to both Sarah and Trang, was irritated by Seb's nonchalant behaviour in light of Samuelson's plight. "Shit, Seb . . . how can you play these games   good luck guests. . . when Samuelson's been kidnapped . . . Sarah's deeply distraught . . . and you . . . you just . . ."

"Act as if nothing has happened," Seb finished the sentence. "Well Mark, something is happening . . . right here, .right now. Two young lovers are getting married, and we have the privilege of participating in their happiness. Remember, when in Rome . . ."

"Rome . . . bullshit," countered Gullens. And - without another word to Seb, to Vuong, to anyone - Gullens leapt off the bus and ran towards the riverside market.

Seb remained seated, visibly unmoved. No one said anything - not even Vuong. The bus left, carrying Vuong, his two brothers and Seb.

Vuong carried a gift tray of flowers and fruit, and with a deep bow he presented himself to Viet Anh's parents. The bride was nowhere in sight. The father led Vuong and his two brothers up the outside stairs, gesturing for Seb to follow his lead. The ancestral altar loomed large in the small room. Several photographs of deceased loved ones held positions of honour on each side of the altar. Vuong entered the room and faced the altar, bowing low and lighting incense and bowing low again. The pungent smell permeated the room. Four men stood to the side. Vuong approached each of them - Viet Anh's uncles - and with his head half bowed he silently took in their words of wisdom.

Viet Anh, exotic in her rented western wedding gown, waited downstairs for Vuong. The modest bride and the nervous groom were ready, for the very first time, to show their love in public.

The wedding ceremony was a harmonious blend of religious solemnity and social activity: The bride and groom, kneeling and bowing before the gilded Buddha, guests watching and talking quietly - renewing friendships, the senior monk blessing Vuong and Viet Anh while eight others chanted the virtues of marriage, curious onlookers and temple devotees intermingling with invited guests - all bearing witness, and, the incessant cacophony of bus horns and street hawkers echoing through the open temple.

Following the formal ceremony, the bus made three trips from the temple to the pier near the bridge on Nguyen Troi Street. There, a fleet of long, narrow water taxis ferried the guests - along with the odd peasant seeking free passage - to a small island in the middle of the muddy Mekong.

Vuong's family farm was situated on the south bank of the teardrop island, less than half a mile from Can Tho City. Before the Americans came, his farm had been larger and more productive than now. U.S. army engineers needed sand to build the runways for the war planes. Vuong's farm - the entire island - was an enormous sand bar topped with fertile soil. Steel barges brought over machinery to claw away at the banks of sand. What land the Americans had left lay prey to the ebb and flow of the heavy, heaving river. The scarred banks buckled and tumbled into the water, and year after year - long after the Americans had left - Vuong's father and grandfather watched the monsoon rains swell the river and steal more of their land.

The wedding party formed a long procession up the short dirt path leading from the rickety dock to the farm. A red banner with gold lettering tied to an entry trellis of woven bamboo bade welcome to all.

Within the compound, under the shade of mango trees, young women knelt on a long makeshift platform of wood planks, cutting up fruit, vegetables, river fish, snake, chicken and pork in preparation for the afternoon feast.

The farm house was a weathered board building in the centre of the yard. Inside, the ancestral altar was decorated with garlands of flowers, bowls of fruit, small bottles of whiskey and pieces of candy. In front of the altar, at a long and heavy antique table extending to the open doors, sat the patriarchs of the island. They talked sporadically, between long drawn puffs on pipes and swallows of snake whiskey. Their skinny, sun-dried frames held up proud heads of white hair and weathered skin. Behind them, on wide bench-beds, sat their wives and a few widows - all old before their time, all chattering without the interruption of smoke or drink. Outside, in the adjacent orchard, tables had been set up in the shade for the guests.

Each cluster to his or her respective table: women here . . . Trang and friends, men there . . . Seb and fellow doctors - all male. A round table of middle-aged men - all heavy drinkers - toasted the bride and groom, toasted their proud families, toasted the future. Then, glass in hand, they wobbled and weaved from table to table in drunken twos or threes, toasting family and friendship, health and harvest.

The young women, in a rainbow of *ao dais*, sipped tea or soda or juice and talked freely but not loudly, their voices drowned out by the babel of drunken men.

After formal toasts, the feast began. From the north - from Viet Anh's family - spring rolls of pork and herbs, fish soup flavoured with fermented anchovies, skewered pork balls, duck curry and pickled vegetables. From the south - from Vuong's family - Mekong Delta specialties: shrimp salad rolls, turtle soup, ginger chicken, snake-in-rice hotpot and pickled vegetables. From both directions came a selection of sweet and spicy sauces.

Vuong's father, a short, rather stocky man in his fifties, had taken a liking to Seb. "You are Vuong's teacher. You are my friend," he announced in Vietnamese again and again to Seb and anyone else listening - louder and louder, drink after drink. Then, he grabbed Seb's wrist and led him away from the noisy orchard. He wanted to show Seb - the honoured guest - his farm, his family's land for generations beyond memory.

A massive big-hearted sow with her litter of eleven. "Three months, three weeks, three days for pigs," he advised the doctor. "More babies than women." A mosquito net hung above the pen, ready to protect the piglets from the nightly swarms.

Past the small irrigation pond with its toilet on stilts. Seb wondered if a tipsy reveller or two might not trip on - then - off the wobbly plank and into the stagnant water.

A long, low building with three rooms. In the first, a caged tangle of young pythons. In a bamboo cage of her own, the queen mother - curled in contentment. Outside the entrance, a caged duck awaited its end. In the middle room, rust-free tools of a farmer's trade: rice rakes, hoes, shovels, an adze and several axes, and knives, knives, knives - all hanging in their proper place. A flint-stone sharpening wheel attached to a wooden pedal, situated front and centre.

At the far end of the building, geese and ducks waddled to and from a second pond. Beaks into water, then a sky-high gurgle and down again to drink. They reminded Seb of the boozers in the orchard - first drinking, then toasting - heads held high.

A third pond, larger than the other two combined, held fish - a kind of carp - in the hundreds. At the far end, hanging between two trees, was a large rectangular three-man net. Fistful throws of dry feed towards the near end; then, from the other end, slow, steady steps with the net into the chest-high pond, cornering and capturing the gluttonous fish by the dozens.

They returned to the orchard from the other side. Behind the house, a mongrel dog on her side in the shade - five suckling pups , their eyes closed in daydream. Seb knew that, except for the bitch, they were market-bound along with the fish, ducks, geese, pigs, pythons and fruits of the season.

In a tiny, spindly bamboo cage were two quiet crickets, saving themselves for nightfall. Seb flashed back briefly to his boyhood days of grasshoppers in canning jars and horny toads in shoe-boxes.

Sure as Seb had thought, one of the drunk men had tripped his way to the toilet and into the pond. As Seb and Vuong's father finished their tour they saw four men at the river's edge, pushing and laughing and pulling and laughing their drenched, smelly friend in and out of the river water, then changing his clothes from shirt and tie to peasant pajamas.

As afternoon met evening, guests in their gender groups began to leave. The bride and groom stood on the makeshift pier, receiving final best wishes until the last of the guests departed. Then, they would leave, for a one-night honeymoon at the city's Quoc Te Hotel - the hotel for foreigners - for the price of a month's wage. Vuong had promised Viet Anh, "Perhaps next year . . . in the dry season . . . if father's harvest is good . . . we can go to Dalat. It's cool there at night."

The wedding guests were back on the bus with the driver, who had guzzled and slept through his long wait on the city side of the river. In a jerky, gear-grinding fashion, he found his way through the city, now loud with night-life.

Seb was sitting alone, across the aisle from Trang. "What a feast! We could learn a lot from you folks about wining and dining at weddings. Ours are too prim and proper." Seb could still feel the loosening effects of the liquor, and his words slurred their way out.

"Men drink too much here," Trang responded.

"And maybe the women don't drink enough," said Seb in repartee.

"I don't agree. I think we are changing . . . too fast. Many young people want to listen to western music and see western movies. They want to wear western clothes . . . jeans. Most young girls . . . teenagers . . . don't like *ao dais*. Even Viet Anh wore a western wedding dress . . . Her mother didn't . . for her own wedding . . . I'm sure."

141

Seb sympathized with Trang's concerns. "Yes, both Vuong's parents and Viet Anh's seem very traditional."

"Viet Anh's mother and father come from the north - the Red River Delta . . . Things haven't changed there much."

"And Vuong's parents?" asked Seb

"They're from the south, and the south is changing . . . But they're farmers . . . Farmers don't change . . . Sometimes their children do . . . if they move to the cities."

Seb took in Trang's view of the changing times, and looked back to the mid-fifties, when his mother had bought an automatic washing machine; her mother didn't trust it. Grandma preferred the wringer-washer. Clothes couldn't be wrung half-dry without a wringer. She didn't believe in spin cycles, and when Seb's mother's new machine switched automatically to spin, the old lady would check to see that it was done right. But the spin drum stopped every time she lifted the lid. It didn't work. So, she took the clothes out and put them through the wringer on the old standby washer and then hung them on the clothesline in the basement. Grandma, sometimes kind, sometimes cranky. "I mad on you," she would snap in broken English whenever Seb or his older brother provoked her. He remembered Grandma going to church to pray for the soul of a character who had died in one of the soap operas on TV. Then, when the actor appeared some time later in a TV commercial, she thought she saw a ghost. She prayed again.

Grandma didn't like change but things kept on changing: from Perry Como and Lawrence Welk to Elvis Presley and the Beatles, from butch cuts and levis to long hair and batik . . . and marijuana and protest marches and Kennedy's assassination. She had survived turn-of-the-century immigration, two world wars and the great depression, but she didn't survive the sixties. "She died just in time," Mom used to say.

The jerks and jolts and the bleating horns brought Seb back to Can Tho. Trang too had been thinking about the changes since her childhood days, a generation later than Seb's, in a land far removed from middle-class America. She was ready for Seb. "There have been good changes too . . . Vuong and I were able to go to university . . . to become doctors. Vuong's grandfather was a poor farmer when the French were here . . . and . . . his father was a poor farmer when the Americans came . . . Today, he's still a poor farmer, but his son is a doctor . . . Many of his friends can't read or write . . . but their children can . . . most of them. Good changes . . . don't you think Dr. Seb?"

"Good changes for sure," agreed Seb. He bounced back and forth on the bumpy ride - between Vuong's grandfather and his own grandmother, and then he sang in a voice so low only he could hear or understand, "And the times they are a-changin'."

20

Seb arrived home later than he had expected. When he entered all was quiet. He climbed the stairs, hoping not to disturb his guest or his guard.

As he approached the bedroom door, he heard a muffled snore. The lights were still on. In the corner, in the same chair Seb had used to escape his angst through opera, Hao slumped - asleep. His carved up face was tucked against his scrawny chest, and his sharp ribs were moving in then out in rhythm to his slow breathing.

On the bed sat Samuelson with outstretched legs tied to the bedpost. He seemed a Sunday morning American, reading a newspaper on the front lawn after a long, lazy breakfast. Seb recognized the paper, 'The International-Herald Tribune.' He stood in disbelief between his relaxed foe and sleeping friend.

"Haven't seen a paper for days," Samuelson said indifferently, without looking up. "How in the hell did you get hold of that paper?" Seb demanded, his voice strained by what he saw.

"Hao got it for me . . . told him I needed something to read . . . to pass the time."

Seb snatched the paper from Samuelson's hands. "You're not here to just pass the time . . . like a houseguest . . . you're my prisoner . . . goddammit!"

Hao awoke and wiped away the sweat that had glued his chin to his chest. "Hello Dr. Seb . . . you home now?"

Seb turned about -face and marched across the room, stopping directly in front of Hao. His tone was even, his words carefully considered. "Never do this again Hao . . . He must be tied down - both hands and feet - all the time."

"But . . . Dr. Seb . . ."

"Never again Hao . . . never!" Seb turned and marched back to the bed. He thrust his open hand against Samuelson's chest, knocking him backwards against the mattress. He took Samuelson's hands - first one, then the other - and bound them to the bedposts. Tight. Tighter than ever before. Samuelson winced as the ropes pinched his wrists, but he knew better than to voice his pain.

Seb then went to the bathroom and returned, carrying in his hands scissors, salve, gauze and tape. Without further word he went about his duty, tending Hao's facial wounds. "Hao, that's all for tonight. Go get some sleep. But first, go tell Ky I won't be going there. I'm staying here tonight . . . Come back tomorrow morning at seven."

Hao said nothing, realizing Seb's anger could not be broken by words, even teasing words of wit. But he couldn't fathom the depth of Seb's anger. It was just a newspaper, he thought.

Samuelson lay pinned to the bed like a victim on the torture rack, fearfully awaiting another turn of the wheel. His eyes stared upwards, following the circular whirl of the fan.

Seb settled down in his corner chair to read the paper - a Friday evening American checking the sports page for the weekend games on TV. His mien seemed to have shifted, from anger to indifference.

Minutes . . . an hour passed. Then, as abruptly as Seb had transformed from torturer to reader, he recast himself into a sinister synthesis of the two. He held the paper in his hands as the machete lay across his lap.

"So, Samuelson . . . you want to pass the time by reading the paper. Better yet, I'll read it to you . . . service of this establishment. This edition's a week late, but it will do under the circumstances." Seb's eyes squinted in anticipation. Samuelson closed his, not knowing what to expect.

"Front page news. Sex scandal in the White House. Rumours of impeachment . . . Impeachment, Samuelson . . . Can you believe that? Nixon lied to Americans about bombing Cambodia - thousands and thousands died. No problem - no impeachment. Reagan lied about the Contra Affair . . . thousands died - no problem - no impeachment. Then the president lies about a blowjob . . . now that's serious business . .

national security stuff . . . possible impeachment. God bless American values!"

He turned to the sports section. ".Bulls beat the Lakers 113-109 . . . You're a Laker fan, I presume."

"Yeh," responded Samuelson naively. "Got season tickets . . . for four . . . for clients . . friends."

Seb interrupted. "On to the entertainment page. Oscar nominations . . . Best picture .. . . best actor nominees . . . ah . . . who really gives a shit?"

Seb was building momentum. "Here we go . . . world news . . . Princess Diana's death . . . still making headlines years later . . . seems there might have been a conspiracy . . . looks like a good plot for another multi-million dollar Hollywood movie."

He looked over at Samuelson, gauging the effect of his performance. "Ah . . . here . . . the IMF . . . rules and regulations for poor countries that want to live the American dream . . . Nightmare for the poor folks . . . dreams for the rich only . . . No matter . . . stock market has been bullish this week . . . Into stocks, Mr. Samuelson?"

"Yes . . . I have stocks."

"What kind?" Seb asked sarcastically. "A.T. & T? Microsoft? How about Lockheed or General Dynamics?"

"Microsoft and G.D.," Samuelson admitted, as if under oath.

"Well, they'll save the world and make you money in the bargain." Seb's voice became dramatic. "A computer in every house by the year 2005 . . . Why not? . . . No electricity? . . . no problem. We have laptops now." Seb mimicked the door-to-door salespitch. "Imagine, my friends . . . right here in the Mekong . . . farm family of five . . . total income for the year . . . let's say $700 U.S. . . that's about two dollars a day . . . Farmer Ho Chi Brown . . . on his water buffalo . . . computer on his lap . . . no problem . . . lifetime payment plan . . . low interest . . ."

Seb stood up and saluted Samuelson. "And God bless America and General Dynamics . . . in the service of war . . . anywhere . . . for and against anyone . . . sell to the Arabs and sell to the Israelis . . . doesn't matter . . . a buck's a buck . . .

Hey, Samuelson . . . let's take a look at the Dow Jones . . . see how G.D.'s doing?" His eyes followed the index alphabetically. "Oh . . . here it is . . . up 1.5 . . know why? . . . I know why! Iraq! . . In God we trust? . . . Bullshit! . . . in Saddam we trust! . . . . Another war with Iraq will be good for business . . . especially good for the weapons industry . . and we all know . . .what's good for the stock market is good for America . . . and what's good for America is good for the rest of the world . . . isn't that right Samuelson . . .isn't it?"

Samuelson willed to react with the full force of his body, and he pulled at the ropes binding his hands to the bed. The bed swayed and the boards creaked, but the ropes held. Samuelson knew they would. He snarled as he returned the repulsion he had received from Seb.

"You're crazy!" yelled out Samuelson. "You're fucking mad! . . . I don't have to defend myself . . . what I do with my money . . . to you . . ."

"Your money?" asked Seb in a dramatic whisper.

"Yes . . . my money . . . and you're not getting a fucking cent of it, Doc . . . not one fucking cent."

"We'll see, Samuelson . . . we'll see . . . Want to bet double or nothing on the one million ransom?" Seb smirked as he stood up. He placed the machete on the chair, then calmly folded the newspaper lengthwise, exposing a narrow column titled 'World Notes'.

"To continue the reading service . . ." Seb heaved in and out a long breath before reading verbatim.

> **Wartime bomb kills six Vietnam youths (Hanoi).**
> Vietnam's deadly legacy of unexploded wartime ordnance exacted a new toll this week as a fragmentation bomb killed a group of six children in An Giang province.
> An official said yesterday the bomb - about the size of an orange - exploded as a group of ethnic Khmer children were playing with it. - Reuters

Samuelson listened, frozen in fear of Seb's bizarre behaviour. Seb was too intensely involved in the moment to notice any change in himself. He had always felt this way about the news . . . ugly reminders of the rich - the stock market . . . the mergers - and the poor - flooded farm fields . . . dormant bombs.

"Yes . . . you will pay the money . . . every fucking cent . . . or . . . we will kill you and your wife." Seb spoke in a remarkably matter-of-fact manner. "And now you will go to the toilet . . . then you will exercise . . . and then you will return to your bed - without eating . . . yes . . . you will go to sleep without dinner . . . Many Vietnamese, even children, go to bed hungry night after night . . . Now, it's your turn."

Seb took the few steps to the bed and leaned over Samuelson as if to untie the ropes. Instead, gripping the newspaper - now in a tight twist, he lifted his right hand high over his shoulder and swept it down sharply against Samuelson's face. The slap of paper against skin - like the pop from a boy's cap gun - stunned both men.

Ropes were untied. Toilet was taken. Exercises were performed, passively by Samuelson and not at all by Seb. Ropes were retied. The finger wound was cleansed and dressed. The pills and water were given and taken. Mozart's 'Requiem' - high bass, low volume.

Gullens had escaped from Seb, Trang and the wedding party only to find himself captured by Sarah. He found her sitting on the sectional sofa, paging through a fashion magazine. She looked stunning in her batik sarong - a honeymoon souvenir from Bali. She hadn't heard Gullens enter, and when she saw him she greeted him indifferently and her eyes returned to the magazine.

Gullens tried to read her mood, but lost his way watching her vacant look and passive posture.

"How . . . are you . . . feeling, Sarah?" Gullens stammered.

"Okay."

Gullens heard a tautness in her tone. She was not okay. "Have you eaten today?"

"No. I'm not hungry," she replied.

"But . . . you've got to keep your strength up, you know."

"No, I don't." Sarah's eyes met his. "I can't . . . and I can't just sit here either . . . doing nothing."

"What would you . . ."

"Find out where Richard is . . . try to do something . . . anything," insisted Sarah.

"There's nothing we can do . . . nothing."

Sarah threw the magazine at his feet. "Nothing . . . You can do nothing . . . is that it?" Her eyes had found their focus. They revealed a stormy sensuality, and as they searched Gullens, he faltered.

She stood up. Her hands seemed to caress first her waist and then her hips as she smoothed down her sarong. Gullens' eyes fell helplessly on her, and she knew she was in complete control.

She spoke softly now. "We can try Mark . . . without going to the police. Seb has contacts . . . connections . . . and . . he's supposed to be your friend. He should help you . . . help us." She targeted his eyes with hers as she waited for his answer.

"Okay Sarah . . . I will talk to Seb again. He's gone to a wedding . . . but should be back sometime tonight . . . I'll see what I can do . . . I really will." He could think of nothing else to say, and he sensed there would be nothing else they could do.

"Would you like a drink now?" Sarah asked suddenly, engaged in casual conversation. "Scotch? Gin? Beer?"

Gullens followed her mood swing. "Gin and tonic, please. It's a tropical thirst quencher . . . This heat can sure sap the energy."

"G & T - just what the doctor ordered. This should recharge your energy. Yes?"

21

Hao arrived early, before seven. He found Samuelson awake in bed, his pupils revolving with the fan. He saw Seb in his corner chair - asleep, the machete hidden behind his back. Seb had not taken advantage of the bed Hao had made for him on the floor, below the shuttered front window.

Hao brought with him breakfast for three. The *pho* was swimming about in plastic bags collared at their tops with rubber bands. They were swinging precariously from the handle of Hao's crutch.

After toilet and mandatory exercise, Samuelson's legs were rebound to the bed and he was served a bowl of *pho*, which, after an entire day without food, tasted almost Texas-good. Seb noticed Samuelson's awkward effort to eat with chopsticks, and he could not conceal his glee. "Well now Samuelson, last week you refused to go anywhere near what you called 'foreign food'. And now, you are sucking down Vietnamese breakfast like it was the finest of cuisines. Seems you're beginning to bridge the cultural gap . . . or . . . are you just downright hungry?"

Seb did not expect an answer. After breakfast Samuelson was fully bound, leaving Seb free to make his hospital rounds and check on the progress of the Canadian surgeons.

The two doctors, full of enthusiasm and energy Seb could only vaguely recall, were feeling the intoxication of their work - purposeful goals, children in real need, appreciative parents - to a degree they had never before experienced.

Seb felt genuine happiness in their happiness, and, for a brief interval as he walked his rounds, he relived the rewards of his past twenty years of work. He was, nostalgically at least, at momentary peace with himself.

150

He dropped into the staff lounge to complete the required reports - bureaucracy which he felt took time and energy from hands-on work. He scribbled indecipherable notes, his lone act of professional rebellion. He knew that the reports would be rubber-stamped by some weary official waiting for his meagre pension. Work rituals, he thought, kills real work.

Just as he was finishing the final form, he heard light footsteps approaching from behind. He smiled without turning around. "How goes the battle, Dr. Trang?"

"Victory, victory, victory!" exclaimed Trang in controlled excitement. "There will be many new and beautiful smiles on many children very soon. The Canadian doctors are doing wonderful work."

Seb recalled his training of Trang as she spoke, and felt a swell of pride within. "You always make my glass full, even when I think it's empty."

"Are you thirsty? . . . One moment Dr. Seb." Trang knew what he meant, but a mixture of modesty and playfullness propelled her out of the hospital and on to the street.

She returned carrying three coconuts. "Two for you and one for me . . . To each according to their needs . . ."

Seb smiled warmly. For years Seb had been entranced without end by the Vietnamese: resilient, resourceful and generous beyond their means. And, by way of contrast, he had been outraged time and again by the trait of many garden-variety tourists and ex-pats: haughty, loud, suspicious and cheap beyond belief - cultural bargain hunters.

"Why?" He had asked himself many times. The poor seem generous; X is generous; therefore, X must be poor. A valid syllogism? Then, by way of deduction: the rich are miserly. Therefore, a false syllogism? Yes . . . but what about Dickens' Scrooge . . . or . . . Shakespeare's' Shylock? Literature; not reality . . . Whose reality? Harvard University receives donation of $23,000,000 reads the front page. Two homeless men - both Vietnam war veterans - die in sub-zero Chicago reads the last column on the last page, just preceding the social obituary of John P. Smith III (April 1, 1908 - March 15, 1998), founder and CEO of XYZ, Inc. Will be sadly missed

by loving wife A and daughters B and C. Interment will be held
. . .In lieu of flowers . . .

Only Ky and opium could provide Seb an escape from
the guilt of his culture; he found release in the pleasure of love
and the peace of smoke.

And Trang, more than anyone else, rekindled his
embers of energy for his work, his raison d'être. Today, she did
the same.

"Well, Dr. Trang, cheers!" he toasted as he banged his
coconut against hers.

Their chat was broken by the sound of loud, speedy
steps in the corridor. "Hark ye, gentle Trang! I hear mischief
afoot . . . know ye that heavy pounding on the floor? Why . . .
none other than the gallant Gullens . . . Lo and Behold! It shall
follow . . . as the night the day . . . that Dr. Mark shall follow
me . . . wherever I may go . . . mark my words." Seb let out a
staged belly-laugh in character with and in obvious self-
appreciation of his dramatic wit.

Gullens barred the doorway with his frame and glared
past Trang to Seb. "We've got to talk . . now . . . right now," he
demanded.

Seb saw the angry squint and the combative stance. He
hoped to save the moment, especially for Trang. "Dr. Mark, it
is my pleasure to introduce you to Dr. Trang . . . pediatrician
without peer . . . Dr. Trang, this is Dr. Mark . . . potential
unlimited . "

"Enough Seb. This is serious." Gullens looked over at
Trang. "Sorry Dr. Trang, I won't be in today . . . or tomorrow . .
. or the day after."

Trang responded immediately. "Okay Dr. Mark. I will
take care of everything . . . please don't worry." Then, she said
so very gently, "Can I help you Dr. Mark? . . . I want to help if I
can."

"No, it's not your problem," Gullens replied abruptly.
"It's his," and he turned back to glare at Seb.

"Okay, Mark, okay." Seb looked kindly towards Trang.
"Dr. Trang, will you please excuse us? I'll be in tomorrow, as
usual."

Trang smiled weakly, first at Seb and then at Gullens. With a graceful retreat she left the two men to themselves.

"Not here Mark. They - the doctors, nurses, kids - shouldn't have to listen to our troubles . . . they have plenty of their own."

Seb led Gullens out of the hospital and across the street to the coffee house, the same one where they had had a give and take about the risks of romance in Vietnam.

Seb ordered two *cafe-sua* - coffee with sweet, condensed milk - and they sat down inside, beneath the cooling blades of a squeaky fan. They faced each other in a long silence, both aware of the perils of words going wrong.

"Well Mark, remember my rambling discourse on the pitfalls of cross-cultural love . . . right here, not so long ago?"

"Sure . . . I remember. And, as usual, you were right . . . That doesn't make it any easier though. Theory versus practice . . . you know what I mean?"

"Yeh, I know . . . only too well."

"Well Seb, " Gullens said, sensing an opening, "theory versus practice about . . . this Samuelson situation . . . you know what I mean . . . Well, your theory won't work in practice . . . in reality."

"No, I don't know what you mean," responded Seb, even though he could guess the gist of Gullens' point.

Gullens' small eyes narrowed, squinting at Seb as he spoke. His words shot out like gunfire. "Samuelson's been kidnapped - held hostage. Sarah's over the edge. Their lives - both of them - are in danger. You - we - do nothing. Just wait. It's impossible . . . crazy."

"Okay Mark," Seb questioned in a slow, steady voice. "What should we do?" Go to the police?"

"No, not that . . . I know that could backfire . . . But, Jesus, Seb . . . can't you do something? . . . I'm really worried about Sarah." Gullens was visibly agitated. A rush of blood had reached his neck and face.

"And what do you think I should . . .can do?"

"Seb, you know the city, the people . . . so does Hao . . . and Ky . . . You could ask some questions . . .carefully . . . to get some leads."

Seb was dumbfounded by Gullens' naiveté. "And if . . . if we can get some leads . . as you say . . . then what do we do?"

Gullens began tapping his right foot rapidly, in rhythm with his voice. "Then, with some info we can . . . well . . . we will have some leverage to negotiate . . . to make our own demands. They . . . whoever they are . . . don't want to get caught . . . right?"

"Right," agreed Seb. "But wrong . . . dead wrong, if you think you'll be able to save Samuelson . . . He'll be dead before you find him . . . Sarah too most likely."

"Why?"

"Because, Mark, these guys mean business - guaranteed. To them, it's a simple matter of life or death . . . theirs or yours . . . theirs or Samuelson's . . . Sarah's . . ."

"But we can't just sit around and do nothing. We've become cowards," argued Gullens.

"No, not cowards Mark . . . Just two doctors in over our heads. Please . . . really think this through carefully . . . logically . . . They have the only real leverage - Samuelson; we don't. They have the plan . . . the weapons . . . we don't. They have everything . . . we have nothing. We have no choice but to wait it out . . . It will be all over in a few days . . .if the money comes. . . and . . if they keep their promise - I'm counting on it - Samuelson and Sarah will both be alive . . . let's just wait it out."

"Like cowards," snapped Mark.

"Like cowards? Your words Mark . . . This isn't Hollywood . . . this is Vietnam. No heroes here."

The waiter had just brought the coffee to the table when Seb rose from his chair. "I'm not in the mood for coffee or for any more chit-chat . . . I'm tired Mark . . . I'm going now." Seb turned to leave, then stopped. "Another thing Mark. What you did in the hospital . . . in front of Trang . . . was unacceptable. She'll worry now - about you . . . she shouldn't have to. She has

154

enough on her plate without us weighing her down. You owe her an apology."

Gullens watched the slow but steady drip of water draining through the coffee filter. Then he looked outside to lose himself in the slow, steady parade of people zig-zagging their way across the sun-baked street.

22

Seb crossed the street cautiously, dodging buses, trucks, cyclos and bicycles, and entered the hospital. Trang was sitting in the staff lounge, pen in hand.

"Dr. Trang . . . may I treat you to lunch today, down by the river?" Seb spoke softly, sensing that the earlier incident with Gullens would be with her still.

"Thank you, Dr. Seb, but, I'm very busy now." She was quietly unconvincing.

"Too busy to have lunch with your teacher?" Seb knew he would win with these words. From Confucian ideals promoted during China's one thousand year rule over Vietnam came the time-honoured concept of teacher as moral guide. Twentieth Century western values - via the French and the Americans - had invaded Vietnam, but had not been able to dislodge the most deeply rooted beliefs - from ancestor worship to a deep respect and loyalty to family and community.

"Oh, Dr. Seb . . . I am very sorry. I was thinking too much. Of course I would like to have lunch with you."

"Good. Let's go then, before you start thinking again. Here's the plan. Let's walk - doctors say it's good for one's health - to the temple and eat a bite here and there along the way."

"Of course! You are my teacher . . . I will follow you."

"Anywhere?" teased Seb.

"Anywhere? . . . Well . . . at least to the temple," parried Trang with a hesitant giggle.

They left the hospital grounds by way of a side entrance which opened onto a small market, protected from the sun by dozens of tattered cloth umbrellas - one scratching the next in sequence. Sleepy food vendors were squatting on their haunches in the hot shade, fanning away the heat and the flies. This was fast food at its best: rice and noodle dishes with meat, fish or vegetables, bottled water, beer, weak sodas and strong whiskey.

Seb and Trang chose from the variety of dishes, sharing a smorgasbord of sweet and spicy tastes. Much more satisfying - Seb thought as he devoured a spring roll - than the hamburgers and hot-dogs of his small town days.

He was too immersed in the feast to notice that Trang was just nibbling her way through lunch, showing less than her usual enthusiasm for the joy of the moment. Only when he went to drink down his food, did he look up to see the worry Trang was trying to hide. "What is it Trang?" he asked with concern.

Trang didn't respond.

"Is it Mark?"

"I'm worried about Dr. Mark . . . He's not happy now."

"Mark is going through a bad spell right now,"

"What do you mean . . . spell?" asked Trang.

"Sorry . . . bad spell . . . a bad time. It's hard to explain Trang . . . because you have never lived away from Vietnam . . away from your culture. Mark's suffering a bit of culture shock." Seb knew it was more, but his concern for Trang outweighed the details.

"Culture shock? I don't understand Dr. Seb"

"It happens all the time. It hit me a few months after my arrival. Too many differences between our own culture and another . . . different customs . . . different ways of doing things . . . sort of like looking at the same tree with different eyes. Confusion . . too many questions and not enough answers. So the negatives - for me it was the heat and the noise - began to take control . . . and the positives - the goodness of the people and the importance of my work – didn't seem as positive as they first were . . . when I was fresh and everything was new and exciting."

"I think I understand," Trang said between tiny bites, "but today . . . at the hospital . . . Dr. Mark was really angry about something . . I know that."

"Yes . . . you're right Trang. But, for sure it had nothing to do with you. In fact, it's to do with me . . . I haven't had much time to . . ."

"I don't think only you, Dr. Seb."

"Why not?"

Trang placed her bowl of noodles on the table and laid the chopsticks across the rim of the bowl. "I think I made him sad . . . even angry . . . last week on our trip to Chau Doc."

Seb anticipated what was coming, and he realized it was their teacher-student relationship, rather than their professional association, that gave voice to Trang's concern. He began walking slowly, feeling that movement would ease her telling. "Why? What happened in Chau Doc?"

"Not Chau Doc, really," replied Trang. "On the way back . . . near Can Tho." She paused, then continued nervously. "I like Dr. Mark . . . maybe he likes me too . . . because . . ." Trang's voice broke as she tried to hold back her tears.

"Did he touch you Trang?" Seb asked protectively. "He shouldn't have . . ."

"No Dr. Seb . . . not really . . . I wanted to tell him . . ." she turned her face away as a slow trickle of tears streaked her cheeks.

"I understand . . . I understand Trang." Seb visualized the scene: the river, the moonlight, the motion of wood on water, Gullens' impulsive urgency, Trang's appropriate reticence, the awkward silence, the misinterpretations, the farewell, and the painful loneliness of doubt and guilt about right gone wrong.

"Trang . . . listen to me . . . very carefully." He waited for her to acknowledge him, and she did so with a slight swerve and bow without losing a step. Several blocks away the gilded roof of the temple sparkled too brightly in the soft blue sky.

"Whatever Mark did, it was a mistake . . . an innocent mistake . . . a cultural mistake. You've seen some movies - Hollywood movies . . . and I know your customs - Vietnamese customs. Mark was in the movies - made in the U.S.A., but you were in reality - in Vietnam. You were right . . . this is Vietnam. He was wrong . . . I know that, and I'm sure he knows that too . . . now. But he doesn't know what to do . . .and maybe . . . maybe you don't know what to do either."

"What do you mean . . . what can I do?"

"Nothing . . . I know. But, if Mark tries again . . . to see you . . ."

"I don't know. Perhaps Mark won't want to . . ."

"Wrong, Trang. I'm sure he will . . . He likes you very much . . . He wants to see you . . . he enjoys your company. He just must learn . . . the Vietnamese way."

"Too late now," Trang said with finality. "He is angry . . . You saw him today."

"Trang, it's never too late . . .and Mark's angry with me, not you . . . Listen . . . please listen to me."

They passed by a row of houses between the market and the temple. Cyclos and bicycles were blocking the narrow street, and a crowd was milling about the entrance to a small yard. Seb's words were suddenly lost in a din of band music. As they approached the entrance, murmurs moved through the crowd, and it parted - as if in invitation. Seb looked into the yard and beyond, to the open front doors of the house. There, in the middle of the main room, was the corpse of a man in an open coffin and, on both sides, a small cluster of mourners. Immediately in front of the coffin was a woman of about sixty years, dressed in a loose garment of white linen. She was lying prostrate on the floor, and, in unearthly moans followed by ghostly wails, she mourned beyond relief the death of this man.

Seb reeled, stung by the loudness of the brass band and the eerie mourning of the woman. He turned towards Trang, who touched his arm gently. She led him slowly away from the gathering crowd and the shrill sounds of grief.

"Trang, what's happening there? I've been to many funerals here . . . I've seen folks mourn and I've heard the band music . . But, this woman wailing . . I've never . . "

"The woman is mourning for the family, not for the dead man,"

"But she is so terribly sad . . . Was it her husband?"

"No, she's a stranger."

"A stranger?" Seb was incredulous. "A stranger?"

"Yes. She's hired to weep. She gets paid to cry over the death of someone she doesn't even know."

"No," countered Seb. "I've never heard of . . ."

"A long time ago some rich families paid older women to mourn the death of someone they love. It was a public show of affection . . . of respect . . . Then the government stopped it because it was showing off wealth - money . . . not really showing sorrow . . . real sorrow."

"And now . . . why are they doing it now?"

"Well," Trang said disapprovingly, "today things are changing . . . Families are changing . . . married children don't want to live with their parents, like before . . . and they want only one . . . or two children. They are too busy trying to make money in the new Vietnam . . . so a family isn't so important."

"But, why a paid mourner? I still don't understand."

"Because . . . now . . .when someone dies, the family with money can rent a mourner - for one or two or three days - to show their friends and neighbours that they really love the one who died . . . and to also show that they have money."

"But, what about the government . . . the law?"

"The government is changing too . . . Money is the new king." Trang paused, then added, "Not all changes are good, Dr. Seb."

They walked together in silence the short distance to the temple, giving them both time for reflection.

Before they entered the temple gates, Seb slowed Trang to a brief stop with a gesture of his hand. "Listen Trang . . . please listen to me."

"Yes?" she waited for his words.

"Mark made a mistake . . . two mistakes. Last week on the river and today, at the hospital. All I ask . . . if you really do like him . . . still . . . is to let him see you. Okay? . . . But, only if you want to." Seb muddled through his suggestion, at a loss for the words to right an innocent wrong.

Trang's face broke into a gracious smile. "I am listening to you Dr. Seb, and I will see Dr. Mark if he wants to see me."

"Only if you really want to," Seb repeated, almost in caution.

"I think I really want to."

As they passed through the wide, open gates of the temple a throng of beggars - old, wrinkled women, young mothers with babies, street urchins and war-mangled men - surrounded Seb, pulling at his arms and legs in pursuit of small change.

Trang stood alone, watching.

23

Following the temple visit - for Trang making merit by lighting incense and for Seb by passing out money - they returned to the hospital. En route they skirted round the funeral scene - much louder than before and with a growing crowd of the sad and the curious.

Seb waved a thumbs up goodbye to Trang as he pedalled away from the hospital. It was mid-afternoon and the relentless sun was getting the better of him. Even the cooling cruise of cycling could not check the pinch of prickly heat as his shirt pressed wet against the heat rash riding his collar bone. He sweated less than most westerners in this delta sauna, but much more than the locals. "Their blood's thinner," an alcoholic old Asia hand had once told him. "That's why I drink the hard stuff; it thins the blood so I'll sweat less." When he had started his first stint in Vietnam, he would bring a change of shirt to work as one might bring a bag lunch. Usually too hot to eat, he would sponge wash his upper body and put on a clean shirt which would soak through within an hour. Back then, he had been self-conscious about his perspiration problem, aggravated all the more by the curious concern of his Vietnamese colleagues who diagnosed every possible cause for his 'sweat-fever' as they called it. Now, he just poured - much like a dog pants - oblivious to the reaction of others.

This time all was in order. Samuelson was in his proper place, pinned to the bedposts. Hao was suitably stationed in the corner chair. Although illiterate, Hao knew his numbers and he was checking to see if he had won the lottery.

"I no lucky," Hao greeted Seb. "I buy ticket too much! I no get money. I no lucky man."

"What's the prize Hao?" asked Seb. "How much money can you win?"

"*Dong* too much . . . 1-0-0-0-0-0-0," answered Hao.

One million *dong*, thought Seb. That's one hundred bucks - at a dollar a day, that's four months' wages here; in the U.S. that would be a day's pay - minimum. Interesting ratio: 100 to 1 . . . really?

He turned to gaze on Samuelson. The numbers which had just bounced about in his head came tumbling out of his mouth like numbered balls in a bingo cage.

"Think about this Samuelson. An American - even a lowly paid labourer - makes about one hundred times the money of a Vietnamese worker. Middle-class equals two hundred times more. A doctor four hundred times . . .even more . . . imagine that!"

Samuelson was vigilant, not wanting to stoke the anger burning within Seb. He pretended he didn't hear the words, the numbers.

Seb began to bait him. "Just a bit off-balance, a bit out of whack . . . moral whack . . . don't you think? Twice as much, four times, ten times . . . these multiples we can live with. But two hundred, four hundred times . . . can we live with that Samuelson . . . can we sleep at night? Say something Samuelson, goddammit, or I'll cut off all your fucking fingers so you can't count all your fucking money!"

"I don't know . . . that's quite a difference . . . I guess," stammered Samuelson nervously.

"Yeh Samuelson . . . a dollar a day compared to four hundred is . . . how did you describe it - 'quite a difference'."

Seb had already been agitated. Gullens, the sun and prickly heat, and now Samuelson - and what his very presence conjured up - rekindled in Seb a long smouldering disgust for the mathematics of life. He was good at math - too good for his own good - because all too often the numbers made him think and thinking made him suffer. He regularly played with numbers and, regardless of the method - ratios, percentages, flat figures - this obsessive quirk stole from him what little peace of mind he might have had before the counting began. Now, he began counting again.

He retreated to the bathroom and after a shave in silence he emerged, having purged the venom from his mind. He had stopped counting.

"Hao, let's get Mr. Sam going . . . toilet and exercise. Then, you take the evening off . . . I'll be fine until about eleven or twelve . . . When you get back I'd like to go to Ky's . . . okay?"

Hao's quiet concern about Seb's angry numbers vanished and his old self surfaced in his spontaneous reply. "You lucky man Dr. Seb. You go Ky. You sleep Ky. She beautiful! I sleep Mr. Sam. He not beautiful too much."

Seb could not contain himself. "You are beautiful Hao . . . you are one beautiful guy!" And without holding back, Seb hugged Hao, almost crushing his scraggy frame.

After the routine rituals, now firmly established by Seb and adhered to without protest by Samuelson, Hao left the two foreigners to their mutual enmity.

Although Seb was in control, the pressure of Samuelson's confinement and their confrontation was wearing. He wanted out of this web of hostility he had spun. Such hate gave rise to self-loathing, and he feared its self-destructive persuasion. He chose life in his music that evening, the vibrant voice of Andrea Bocelli's 'Romanza'. He turned the volume high and then proceeded to prepare for his evening watch. He grabbed a bottle of gin from his seldom-used liquor cabinet and tonic and ice from the fridge in the kitchen. He returned to the bedroom and to his reserved seat, the corner chair. The song, 'Caruso', began just as Seb took the first swallow of forgetfulness.

Samuelson lay passively on the bed, but his eyes, looking from one ceiling corner to another - from spider web to spider web, indicated an active mind. From time to time, he glanced furtively at Seb, who, with each drink, slipped more deeply into the sea without memory.

When Hao returned shortly before midnight he found Samuelson wide awake but Seb slouched into an intoxicating slumber.

"Why you no sleep?" Hao challenged Samuelson. You no take Dr. Seb pill?"

Samuelson smiled sociably. "No I didn't. The good doctor fell asleep before treating his patient."

Hao couldn't understand Samuelson's gist, but he could hear the change in his tone. The arrogance was gone and a strange friendliness showed. Hao braced himself, remembering Seb's anger from the day before. He didn't trust Samuelson or himself.

"Why you nice now? . . . Dr. Seb tell me you no nice . . . Dr. Seb tell me you trick me too much."

"No tricks Hao." Samuelson's voice held its friendly tone. "Just want someone to talk to."

"No talk . . . You sleep."

"I'm not sleepy . . . Hao . . . Why do you work for Dr. Seb . . . Why do you help him?"

"Dr. Seb good to me. He save me."

"How did he save you?"

"Long time . . . I boy. U.S. bomb try kill me . . . kill leg . . . very bad. Dr. Seb no fix leg . . . but fix me . . . I lucky boy."

He looked over to Seb in a spontaneous gesture of gratitude. "I love Dr. Seb too much."

Then he turned his attention back to Samuelson. "Dr. Seb tell me you bad man . . . you kill Vietnam people."

Samuelson gaped at Hao, open-mouthed. Hao in turn riveted his eyes on the bound man. "Dr. Seb tell me you rich man. He tell me rich man buy bomb. Rich man make poor man go Vietnam. Bomb Vietnam. Kill people too much."

"That's a lie Hao. I haven't killed anyone . . . Dr. Seb lied to you."

"Dr. Seb no lie me!"

Hao jumped one-legged from his standing position and, before he could stop himself, he was leaning on his good leg against the bed and hammering blows at Samuelson's chest with his fists. Hao's angry howls and the howls of pain from Samuelson stirred Seb from his slumber, and in a sleep-like trance he shuffled to the bed to try to restrain Hao from behind. They both collapsed on top of Samuelson, crunching his chest

165

with their weight.. Heavy breathing from Seb and Hao and short, raspy breaths from Samuelson filled the room.

Seb, in short, jerky motions, raised himself from the bed and pulled Hao off a terrified Samuelson. Then, he removed his shirt, went to the bathroom, and put his head under the cool water to wash away the gin in his head.

Samuelson's bound body was still shaking when Seb returned to check on his prisoner's injuries. He gently touched his hands to Samuelson's chest and ribs. "You'll be a bit black and blue by morning, but there's no broken bones. I'll make an ice-pack to keep the swelling down." Seb loosened the ropes which bound Samuelson's hands to the bedposts, easing the pain of his breathing.

Hao stood crazed, leaning against the wall, soaked in the sweat of violence. Seb picked up the crutch and handed it to Hao, and with a pat on the shoulder he said, "Hao, I think it's better for you to go home . . . get some sleep - I can watch him."

"I sorry Dr. Seb . . . I . . ."

"No need to be sorry Hao. Everything's okay . . . Don't worry . . Go and get some sleep . . . See you tomorrow - at seven . . . okay?"

"But Ky . . ." stammered Hao.

"Ky will understand," Seb said with kind finality.

24

Ky had waited up for Seb until the need for sleep conquered her desire for his company. When daylight came without him, she began her morning routine without whys and wherefores. She took a slow soak in her antique tub, dressed and went out, walking down the canal road to Bia's tiny *pho* stand on the corner.

There, where she had her breakfast whenever Seb was not around waiting for his traditional breakfast of bacon and eggs, Ky was always welcome. Twelve years earlier Ky had befriended Sau, Bia's teenage Amerasian daughter. Sau had been sentenced to a life of serving *pho* to those who refused to accept her. A living reminder of America's war, she was one of thousands born out of unwed love, prostitution or rape. Some found reluctant acceptance in the United States. Most, like Sau, were ridiculed as 'children of dust' and as adults ostracized in Vietnam. Social outcasts.

At Venice, social taboos were taboo, and Sau, at Ky's invitation, apprenticed not in the arts of love but in the art of business. Now, Ky could leave Venice to Sau's management.

After a bowl of *pho* and the young day's new gossip, Ky walked down a narrow alley - fringed with birds in bamboo cages - to an *ao dai* seamstress shop. She had her fourth and final fitting. Her pink *ao dai* with white jasmine blossoms falling from shoulder to heart would be ready by evening.

Ky exited the alley and casually crossed the main street, seemingly oblivious to the oncoming traffic. On the other side she entered another alley - this one a sequence of small beauty salons. Here, two middle aged women took charge - one, of her fingers; the other, of her toes. After a trim and a polish, Ky slid back as they levered the chair to a reclining position. A five stage shampoo followed by a facial.

Seb found her there. "I guessed you'd be here. How's my Jasmine?"

Ky's head was angled back, her hair awash with shampoo and her eyes closed to the world. "I'm fine Chien Bot." She smiled easily. "And how are you?"

Speaking in English allowed them some intimacy, even in public. "Okay," said Seb, "except that I couldn't see you last night and . . ."

Ky's smile grew wide as she finished his oft-repeated line, "and I really, really missed you."

"Well, I really, really did . . ."

"Miss you," teased Ky, then added, "Me too, me too."

Seb blushed with embarrassment, giving invitation to the salon ladies to laugh in chorus, in conspiracy with their gender.

"Anyway," said Seb feigning shyness, "I'm free for a few hours . . . how about a date?"

"And darling, where will we go?" The women caught hold of the 'darling' and spontaneously repeated it between easy giggles.

Seb mused for a moment on the universality of romance and the engaging world-wide words of love. "Well darling, this is your town . . . you be my guide."

Again a chorus of giggles as the women pretended to work, their ears tuned in to the odd word they might recognize and react to.

And again Seb mused briefly, this time puzzling over the supreme modesty of the traditional Vietnamese woman, the sweet coquetry of the salon staff and the erotic magnetism of the ladies of Venice. The Asian woman seems more simply herself, in contrast to her complex counterpart a sea and an ocean away in North America.

Seb and Ky left the salon to mirthful applause and flagged down a cyclo to take them to the market pier. After a lunch of papaya, mango, banana and yogurt - another French leftover - they hired a boat to take them downriver to what once was a bird sanctuary. They sat near the boat's bow, silently absorbing the bustle along the riverbank: Children swimming in the slow eddies; a man sinking below the surface in search of river stones to sell - his wife waiting in their rock-laden dinghy; old men fishing without poles - the lines wrapped around wooden spools - letting the current control the hooks' drift, weather-beaten women in peasant pajamas and conical hats pushing then pulling the oars - taxiing sellers and buyers to and from the city market; police patrolling the river in motorboats - in pursuit of contraband goods; dozens of houseboats - grandmothers safeguarding grandchildren for their fisher sons and vendor daughters-in-law. As the oarswoman rowed the boat away from the city, the rural reaches offered new sights: farmland and rice-paddies, the odd exotic bird and nesting turtle, and small gangs of monkeys.

Ky had come to know the bird sanctuary well when she belonged to General D. He had taken her there many times - to a bird viewing tower on high stilts - out of sight of his jealous wife. There, watching in yearning the free flight of wild wings, Ky had found brief release from her life's bondage. That had been so many years ago, long before Seb's coming to Vietnam.

Now Ky led Seb along the same pathways General D. had shown her. But the sanctuary's past beauty had withered with the scars - not of years - but of the war's Agent Orange. Dioxin had dealt death to the flora and fauna of this tropical refuge on the banks of the Mekong. Trees grew stunted and scraggy, and the mangrove swamps swelled with the litter of tortured tree trunks and rotten roots. There were birds, but only a few, and their half-hearted shrieks seemed to decry their poisoned lot in life. An eerie silence punctuated by distant squawks told of past wounds and future doom.

Ky ached in empathy with the birds' plight, even as she felt the pain of her distant past. She wanted out. Without telling Seb why, she took the left fork in the trail, away from the bird tower and back towards the sandbar pier. The oarswoman was waiting in hiding from the sun under the canvas canopy on the boat. The return upriver took more than twice the time of the easy downriver row. The slight woman strained at the oars as they cut smoothly into and out of the heavy current. She searched for the odd eddy along the long bends in the river, brief spells of rest from the relentless waves of work ahead.

The boat docked just as the early evening sky turned a pale rouge, softened by the haze of heat above the water.

Seb and Ky, in a rare show of open intimacy, walked arm-in-arm along the river's edge to the canal road and home, to Venice #8.

They bathed together, washing, touching and towelling one another in gentle ways. In bed, Seb lay on his side, his arms propping up his head as he watched Ky prepare his pipe. Even at this moment his boyhood came to mind as Ky's quiet, orderly movements brought Uncle Norm into focus. The way - without words - he had taught Seb how to fish well: to rub the base of each rod segment behind the ear to give just enough skin oil for an easy slide out at take-down time, to tie fly to leader without leaving a bubble loop, to whip the rod back to ten o'clock and release at two, to jerk hard - but not too hard - to set the hook, and to let the little ones go till another day.

And then Seb returned to Ky, who - without words - taught him once again how to love well within the pain of life.

25

Gullens stood at the crossroads: to the left was the hospital, the sick children, Seb and Trang; to the right, Sarah. With Seb, there was both duty and friendship; with Trang, duty and the whisper of a romance lost; with Sarah, duty to Samuelson and the siren song of desire. His mind tried to dodge the pricks of duty as he scurried diagonally across the intersection. He was racked by conscience, self-doubt and lust, and he could feel the pull, piece by piece, of each tortured thought. He wanted wholeness again.

Time took priority. Sarah was alone, desperate one minute, defiant the next. He had to be with her regardless of her moods; in fact, because of her moods he reasoned with his heart.

Sarah was reclining on the sofa, her head resting high on an overstuffed pillow showing a Picasso print of eyes staring every which way. She held a gin and tonic in one hand, a cigarette in the other.

Gullens immediately saw the glaze of her green eyes and knew she was well on her way. "I didn't know you smoked," remarked Gullens, hoping to engage her in light conversation.

She looked up at Gullens. Her green eyes tried to dance, but the wobble of her head broke any rhythm of seduction. "I do and I don't," she slurred, louder than she realized. "I don't when Richard's around . . . He says it's not lady-like . But, I do when he's not around and . . ." Sarah sat half-up and moved her arm in a royal sweep of the room. "As you can plainly see, he's nowhere to be found. Isn't that grand . . . just grand."

"Sarah," Gullens spoke cautiously, "you've been drinking."

"Of course I've been drinking . . . You're quite the private eye . . . can tell when a girl is soused!" She tried to sit upright, but swayed against the sofa arm for support. "And, if I may ask . . . what have you been doing, Inspector Gullens?"

"What do you mean, what've I been doing? . . . I've been at the hospital this morning."

"You know what I mean, Mark. I'm not talking about playing doctor . . . What did Inspector Gullens find out about my husband . . . my loving husband Richard?"

Gullens searched for words - any words that would quiet her, comfort her. Truth, he thought, seemed irrelevant now, even destructive. "I saw Seb. He's making contact with friends . . . but he said we must be patient . . . and he told me to tell you that it's better to just wait it out."

"Wait for my loving husband?" Sarah rose to her feet and approached Gullens, each step meant to be one step closer to seduction. But, just as she spread her arms to welcome him, she tripped and fell against him, like a lost child stumbling into her father's arms.

Gullens guided Sarah gently back to the sofa. She turned her head into the pillow to muffle her sobs in the folds of Picasso's surrealistic eyes, He butted her cigarette and took the ashtray, drinking glass and bottle of gin to the kitchen. He returned with a dishcloth and towel to wash and wipe clean the end table, dirty from the glass circle stains and dusty from the cigarette ashes of Sarah's day alone. He wished they could both start over again.

Sarah's drunken sobs slowly ceased as she entered an inner limbo between the hell of what is and the heaven of what might have been.

Gullens sat on the side section of the U-shaped sofa, watching Sarah's heavy breathing and listening to her sporadic sighs. When the sighs stopped and the breathing eased, he knew she was asleep. He also knew what he had to do as a doctor; he must sedate her through this traumatic time.

He waited, awake through the night, until morning. After serving a light breakfast of baguettes and coffee, he offered her a sedative - only one. Sarah, the alluring enchantress became the compliant patient and the dutiful wife awaiting her husband's return. Gullens imagined that the real Sarah was an intriguing composite of the wholesome girl next door and the amorous woman upstairs

By the time he returned to the guesthouse all was quiet. Only Hung, already several swigs into his night watch, was there to greet him. Gullens slipped quietly up to his room, turned on the fan to slice up the hot, thick air into thin wafts of breeze, and collapsed on the bed. Within minutes he was in a deep, dreamless sleep, the purely physical sleep of exhaustion.

He was abruptly awakened by the hoarse crowing of Judas, the resident cock. Several years ago, John, an American missionary in the guise of an English teacher, had given this innocent fowl the name of Judas. In a failed attempt to convert the guesthouse staff, he even gave them Christian names. John himself was a convert and, as most who cross over to another side - religious or political, he became rabid in his beliefs and unrelenting in his preaching. In the end he departed, embittered by the kind disinterest of the locals in his heavenly ways. Life at the guesthouse continued in a familiar flow of give and take, - as it had long before Judas got his name.

After a breakfast of baguettes and eggs - peppered with teasing reprimands from Marie, a flirtatious punch from Ny and a French tête-à-tête with Ba - Gullens caught a cyclo to the hospital. On the way, he flashed back to his first few weeks in Can Tho: the oppressive heat, the strange food and stranger customs, the losing battles of his child-patients, the sense of being beyond the buffers of comfort and confidence.   He flashed on Trang: their first meeting at the hospital, the joy of travelling with her and Seb to the bat temple, the temptation of moonlight and river and her graceful beauty on the boat from Chau Doc, the awkward silence and lonely sorrow.

The cyclo coasted to a slow stop in front of the hospital gates, bringing Gullens back to the present, to his work and to Trang.

He found her in the intensive care ward, sitting on the edge of a bed. She was taking the pulse and temperature of a ten year old boy who just that morning had been admitted to the hospital suffering from dysentery, acute dehydration and brain-burning fever.

"How's the little fellow doing?" Gullens asked, already knowing the answer.

Trang turned her head towards Gullens and her moist eyes met his. "It's not good . . . He's burning up."

"Can I help?" offered Gullens, again knowing the answer.

"There's nothing we can do; only wait. He can't hold anything down. . . it goes right through him. Maybe . . . with the i.v. . . . maybe he'll be okay . . . But, he's had a very high fever for too long, I think." Trang put her hand to her lips and then to the boy's hot cheek, tapping it lightly with encouragement.. He lay motionless, his eyes vacant - without recognition or response. Trang then looked at the silent mother and smiled sadly; the mother, clutching her son's hand, returned only sorrow.

Trang and Gullens walked out of the hot, hushed room of children and their mothers. This time Trang needed to let it out. "It's only water . . . clean drinking water, and he would be in school today . . . instead of . . ."

"I know, Trang."

"Well, why won't they listen? It's just . . ."

"It takes time," Gullens reminded her gently. "Remember, you told me it takes time for them to accept . . ."

Trang's voice broke sharply. "Too much time for this boy . . . for so many others . . . it's taking too much time."

Gullens said nothing more. He could only stand by, waiting for Trang to recover herself.

"I've got to do my rounds now," she said, her voice still quavering.

"Me too. See you in the lounge . . . later . . . maybe," Gullens said, almost as a question.

"Maybe," replied Trang as she walked away, down the stark, humid corridor.

Gullens finished his rounds first and found himself alone in the lounge. A pile of forms to be filled in and filed were stacked in waiting. He could not put pen to paper. His mind would not move, still stationed as it was, with Trang.

Half an hour later Trang entered. Her slow, unsure movements cautioned Gullens to say nothing. He stared blankly at the forms. It's all so irrelevant, he thought. Paperwork, meetings . . . all irrelevant.

Trang sat down at the other table, underneath a large portrait of Ho Chi Minh. She looked up at the picture, then down at her papers.

The silence seemed to disable both of them from further dialogue. Gullens tried, without interest, to scratch out words on paper. Trang was numb; she stared at the wall, her mind elsewhere.

Finally, Gullens interrupted the long silence. He spoke louder than necessary. "Trang, I want to apologize for the other day."

"The other day?" asked Trang, still numb to the moment.

"Yes . . . I was angry . . . confused. Dr. Seb was the innocent victim . . . and you were the innocent witness. I'm sorry if I caused you any trouble."

Trang felt her feelings return. Butterflies within when she spoke. "No trouble for me Dr. Mark . . uh . . . Mark. But, I was worried about you . . you seemed so sad." She wanted to say more, but the words weren't there.

"Trang, it's been a difficult time for me . . . I'm only just beginning to learn about Vietnam... I know I've made some mistakes, but I don't know what to do about them." Gullens voice slowed noticeably, fearful of another fault

"Please don't worry Mark. Yesterday is gone and tomorrow never comes." Trang was regaining her self-confidence with each exchange.

"What a beautiful proverb. Vietnamese?" asked Gullens.

"No... just my mother's way of seeing life. Maybe, because she saw so much . . . the war . . ." Trang stopped short, regretting her final words.

175

"Well . . remember . . you were going to teach me Vietnamese and I was going to give you some American slang. Is it still a deal?"

"Of course Mark . . ."

"Well, how about Sunday then . . . Bring some friends and we can go to Sandy Beach . . . by the stadium. We'll trade language lessons over lunch."

Trang's eyes brightened, sensing the opportunity of renewal. "You've got a date Dr. Mark . . . Mark."

Gullens laughed, realizing the irony. "Well, not really a date . . . just a Sunday picnic with friends."

"Okay . . . a Sunday picnic. I will meet you at the guesthouse at eight, before it's too hot."

"Eight it is," confirmed Gullens with bridled excitement.

They parted, . . . both thankful that there would be another time, soon.

26

It was late night - after midnight - when Seb shook off
the sleep of smoke and love. He could hear the courtly
croaking in the paddies on the country side of the canal.
Usually, this signalled sleep, but this evening's tryst reversed
their choral effect; they awakened him to the reality of his
responsibility to Hao and, reluctantly, even to Samuelson.
Seb covered Ky with gentle kisses, from her silken
tresses down to the two dimples below the small of her slender
back. He had to pull himself away from her, pushing back the
urgency of desire.
Plastic bags of fast-food rice and noodles hung from the
handlebars as he bicycled his way back home following his
afternoon rounds at the hospital.
Samuelson and Hao - bound guest and crippled guard -
were positioned as usual. A wary distance - an ocean larger
than the stuffy room - separated the two men.
Seb went about his responsibilities methodically,
sensitive to the sullen stand-off between guest and guard. He
treated their wounds - Samuelson's finger and Hao's face - and
served them dinner in the good company of Chopin.
For a fleeting moment, which he intuitively
acknowledged would not last, he relished his position - that of
objective observer, a scientist amongst the lab rats. It had
evolved into a controlled experiment in human behaviour: the
corporate executive in chains versus the cripple in charge. The
rules had changed and the playing field had a different tilt.
What would the meek do if they were to inherit the earth? Be
the revolutionary and dispossess the wealthy? Establish a
hierarchy of reverse oppression? Or rather, become the rebel -
the slave who denounces the master, yet denies himself
privilege and power? The man who simply wants to be equal

amongst all? Schmaltzy idealism? Social realism? A bit of both? Possible? Probable? Significant?

Seb looked again at his two subjects under study - microscopic grains in the sands of humanity. Of no cosmic value. And what of the scientist himself, the one who observes and records and researches ad infinitum . . . ad nauseam. Of cosmic value? If anything, a pimple rather than a grain - pus full of knowledge without wisdom, function without feeling . . . circa 2000 a.d.

For several hours - with Chopin and Mozart - he meandered through the mazes of his mind - paths of what was, what is and what ought to be. He had done the same for years, and at the end of his wanderings he had found - if not clear direction - at least the energy to meander more. As years passed and experience muddied his innocent outlook and exhausted his idealistic energy, a curious cynicism grew - curious in that it caused him to think in near-spiritual terms yet to act in more physical, more primal ways than he had ever before imagined. Ky was his muse, inspiring him to live rather than think life. And, in his deepest moments of doubt, she became his anchor, shielding him from his inner storms of anger and angst.

Samuelson, as if a predestined part of Seb's fate, took centre stage now - the *el Nino* of Seb's storms. His very presence battered at the refuge given by Ky, and Seb found his primal self becoming more disposed towards death than life. He could never have held anyone hostage in his twenties, thirties or forties. He wondered why in his fifties - when memories were just beginning to mean more than the moment at hand - he would take a course of action so desperate and destructive. The primal pull was downward - he could feel its strength - and Ky and Hao, Trang and Marie, Mozart and Verdi were losing their life force over him. When he reached out for them they were always there for him, but lately he wasn't there himself.

Morning came - as it always does in the Mekong - in a slow, sweltering gesture towards life. The high whines of the cicadas and the kissing chirps of geckoes gave way to the crowing of cocks and the warbling of birds. And they in turn gave way - without wanting to - to the jungle of voices and the thunder of machines - humanity in motion under the silent, scorching sun of day.

Samuelson was the first to stir. Hao was asleep on the floor, barring the door with his body. Samuelson looked over at Hao. "I've got to piss. Wake up and get me to the toilet - fast."

Hao stirred, but did not respond. Seb noticed that Samuelson had not seen him sitting in his corner chair, and he decided to keep silent. He wanted to observe his subject under study.

"Goddamn bastards!" yelled Samuelson, loud enough to alert Hao. "When this is all over, I'll get my due . . That quack won't see the light of day for the rest of his life . . . I'll have him pushing rocks in prison. Goddammit! Wake up you fuckin' gook!"

Seb had simply wanted to observe, but Samuelson's outburst was too much. He had to respond.

"First of all, Hao is not a fucking gook. He's Vietnamese. You use words loosely Samuelson . . . much too loosely . . . just like millions of your redneck friends - gook, nigger, spic. The day will come when white skins will pay a heavy price for their racist ways. As for you - here and now - I should get Hao to cut off your penis - that way you'll never need to piss again."

Samuelson lay stunned - both by Seb's presence and his shocking statement. It took him some time before he could say, "I didn't know you were here."

"Doesn't really matter, does it? If anything, it speaks to the truth of your nature - who you really are. A man talking aloud to himself is his true self, isn't he?" There was a rhetorical rhythm to Seb's words, the rhythm of interrogation. "And tell me truthfully Samuelson, how did you plan to punish the quack . . . as you called him . .uh . . me, I presume? No light of day? Pushing rocks? Prison?" Seb sounded out every word of each short sentence as if he were speaking to a very young child. He had come to enjoy his absolute power over his prisoner. It was only in the abstract that he continued to

179

question the probity of his actions. Once in motion, his primal momentum carried the conversation.

Samuelson blanched. He knew he had no power, no options under the circumstances. He also sensed in Seb a growing hatred towards him, and he could not hide the complexion of fear on his face. Even his bound hands began to tremble against the bedposts.

Seb sat down on the bed and began untying the ropes. "Looks like you have a case of the shakes . . . What's the quack's diagnosis? A - withdrawal symptoms due to alcohol? B - the loss of power and control? Both of the above? None of the above? . . Come on Samuelson, tell the quack what ails you."

Samuelson remained silent, barely able to breathe.

"Must the quack give the diagnosis?" Seb asked, inviting an answer from Samuelson. "Okay then . . . here goes . . . It's terminal I'm afraid . . . malignant cancer of the whole being. It's the cancer of power - B above . . . It feeds not only on the ego, but on the heart - the desire for power - and on the brain - the manipulation of power . . . Money and prestige, beautiful women - these are the rewards of power, but it is the obsession with and the pursuit of power that are the sources of your disease."

Seb helped Samuelson, who had stiffened from long hours of lying on his back, to stand up. While Samuelson shuffled weakly to the bathroom, Seb continued his discourse.

"Well, that's the diagnosis . . . Now for the treatment options: A - the prognosis is not good. We could save time by just putting the patient out of his misery . . . mercy killing . . .uh . . . murder, I suppose, since the patient has not agreed to his own demise. B - cut out the heart and brain, thereby eliminating the desire for and manipulation of power. Problem is, the patient would be of benefit to no one, including himself."

Samuelson sat on the toilet, trying to block out Seb's harangue. His hands were bound together, but he managed to press his middle fingers to his ears to muffle Seb's loudness to a murmur. Yet, he could not help but hear the words.

"C - ego therapy . . . balance the ego. That's the ticket to good health. With all of our scientific advances and with our state of the art medical technology, we can transplant hearts and clone sheep. Surely, we should be able to balance the ego, don't you think?"

Seb waited, though not expecting a response. He wanted the heavy seconds of silence to serve as an answer. "Well, regardless of outcome - acknowledging options A and B are unacceptable . . . from a pragmatic point of view - we will meet the challenge and attempt an innovative, experimental treatment in a Herculean effort to balance an ego gone terribly out of kilter . . . Samuelson, can you hear me? . . . Do you know what we're going to do to cure you of your disease - a disease considered malignant and terminal? Do you know Samuelson? Do you? . . . Well, here it is: We will attempt to save you - to balance your ego by a surgically social procedure called sharing. Sharing, Samuelson, will not only save your life; it will save your soul . . . what's left of it."

Again, long seconds of silence. Seb noticed that Samuelson was still in the bathroom. "Mr. Samuelson, please come in here so I can announce to you directly that you will be the beneficiary of this miraculous treatment - Option C."

Samuelson shuffled back into the bedroom and stopped in front of Seb, who was now standing between the doorway and the bed. Samuelson's face had regained a tinge of colour, but his hands still trembled slightly. The two men faced each other.

Seb resumed the monologue, his eyes flashing and his hands gesturing in rhythm with his words. "Share what, one might ask? Well, Shakespeare and Mozart shared their creative genius . . . Socrates and Confucius, their philosophical insights . . . Gandhi, his instinct for social justice . . . everyone has something to share . . ."

"Sharing?" Samuelson whispered in reflex.

"Don't interrupt me, please! Doctor . . .uh . . .quack knows best." Seb's eyes glowered. "Now listen. Obviously you're no Mozart or Socrates or Gandhi. But, in a big frog in a small pond sort-of-way, you are a petty John D. Rockefeller or

J. Paul Getty, with a genius for power through money. Well, Mozart shared with us his music and Socrates shared his wisdom and Gandhi, his justice. You, therefore, will share your money. And, in sharing your money you will begin to balance your ego, and in balancing your ego you will purge yourself of your cancer - the pursuit of power. In consequence, you will be healthy - alive I should say, as I will have no reason to kill you."

Seb hesitated just long enough to look over at Hao who was listening, without understanding, to Seb's every word. He sat spellbound still.

"Hao, would you please get us some *pho* for breakfast . . . Looks like a full day ahead of us . . . Thanks."

Hao hobbled down the stairs and out of the house. The nearest *pho* cafe was on the corner, only forty metres away. It would not take long.

"To continue," Seb said after Hao departed. "The treatment itself. First, we visit the hospital. This will be shock therapy, hard on your present condition but a necessary procedure if your ego is to be cured of its cancer. Immediately after the hospital visit, we will go to the bank - so different from the hospital on first impression, but in one way quite similar: They are all suffering disease. - the children at the hospital are physically bankrupt, and the big business types - like you - are morally bankrupt."

Samuelson, although fearful of Seb's strange, menacing behaviour, protested. "You can't say that . . . paint everyone with the same brush. It's not fair."

Seb snapped back. "One, I'm not a painter . . I'm a doctor dealing with an epidemic - the greedy ego. Two, you have no right to judge what's fair and what's not. Remember, you are in the top one percent - financially speaking - in the world. Children starve while you eat steak . . . So, so much for fairness . . . " Seb's voice weighed heavy with anger. "So, shut the hell up or I will cut out your tongue!"

Samuelson recoiled, then shuffled in a wide circle around Seb and sat down on the bed, passively waiting for Seb's next volley of words.

"Good. Now to continue again . . . Just as one gives blood to help others survive - I'm sure you've donated blood Samuelson . . . you will give money - one million dollars - to help save the children at the hospital. And, in the process of sharing your wealth and your power, you will balance your ego. . . . You will be cured Samuelson . . . at least for the short term. However, you could suffer a relapse if you don't follow the long term treatment: making money to help others . . . I call it the altruistic ego effect. It's only in the experimental stage now; in fact, you're the first guinea pig. But, I'm confident that with further research and application it has the potential to cure the cancers of power and money. Only time will tell, but you may be part of medical history in the making."

Seb finished and bowed slightly, as if he had given a lecture at a doctors' convention and was awaiting polite applause. None came - only Hao, hopping one-footed up the flight of stairs, the bags of *pho* swinging from the handle of his crutches.

After a quick breakfast, Seb released Samuelson from the ropes which had choked his wrists and ankles for almost a week. Samuelson instinctively rubbed his wrists and raised his eyes, like a slave given freedom.

Seb's look had not lost its loathing. "You can dress yourself. Your clothes have been washed . . . you know, the ones you puked on last week when you came here drunk. Then we'll go, first to the hospital and then to the bank. One very important point Samuelson . . . a matter of life or death - yours and your wife's. If Hao's friends don't hear from us by dark, your wife is dead . . . by machete . . . guaranteed. So no Hollywood escape . . . not if you ever want to see your wife again."

Seb's face contorted into a Faustian smirk, self-satisfied in his capacity to deceive, to control.

"Yeh, I know. Your wife . . . she's somewhat the innocent bystander . .so what? . So was the Vietnamese mother shrieking in agony while helplessly watching her child die from the burns and blisters of napalm . . . Thousands of mothers and thousands of children . . ."

Seb felt his whole being shake, his anger on the edge of full explosion. "Let's go Hao. Find a cyclo . . .now . . . right now." Seb could sense Hao's hesitation and could only hope that Samuelson would not play the hero.

Seb and Samuelson sat in the seat of the cyclo and Hao, also a passenger, leaned against the front frame, facing them. Seb spoke the only words en route to the hospital. "Remember Sarah . . . dead or alive, and the same goes for you."

Samuelson stared straight ahead, silent. Trang saw them as the cyclo skidded to a stop in front of the double doors. "Hao, how nice to see you! It's been such a long time," said Trang in Vietnamese.

Hao's eyes brightened and a broad smile swept across his face.

Seb seized the moment. "Dr. Trang, I would like you to meet Mr. Richard Samuelson . . . from the United States."

Trang, having been schooled by Seb in the ways of modern western women, offered her hand first. "It's nice to meet you Mr. Samuelson. Welcome to our hospital."

Samuelson stiffly held Trang's hand as he stuttered. "Dr. Tra - Trang . . .uh . . . thu - thank you . . ."

Seb interjected. "Mr. Samuelson wants to help. He's here in Can Tho on business . . . you know, that new shoe factory being built near the stadium. But, he would like to do more . . . to donate some money to the hospital."

"That's very kind, Mr. Samuelson," said Trang. "We need so much . . . to treat the children . . . medicine, equipment, surgical supplies. Thank you for your kindness."

Samuelson's body seemed to contort as he made an awkward attempt to smile. He didn't even try to respond this time.

Seb smiled, sensing victory. "I thought it would be a good idea for Mr. Samuelson to see for himself . . . the hospital . . . the children . . . then, he can decide how much he can help us."

"Of course, you are very welcome. Dr. Seb can be your guide."

Again Seb spoke up, before Samuelson could respond. "Thank you Dr. Trang." Then he looked directly at Samuelson. "I am your tour guide . . . at your service."

The two Americans entered the hospital, while Trang and Hao remained outside, catching up on city gossip.

Samuelson saw a desperate hope in most mothers' eyes, but only a dull resignation in the vacant stares of the children. He saw the ravages of disease and the ugly work of deformities. He could not avoid their eyes - pools of pain looking towards the unlucky likelihood of death.

Seb watched Samuelson as they moved through the wards. All these years had not steeled Seb to the agony of knowing the children's fate. He had become a part of their lives and their deaths. He had saved some, lost many more. Too many eyes closed, and there were always more eyes waiting for him . . . endless eyes of suffering . . . excruciating . . . unnecessary.

As the tour proceeded from intensive care to the burn unit and, finally, to a twelve-bed dormitory - a home to children bearing deformities of a long ago war - Samuelson's eyes changed. At first, they had shown a studied indifference - the prisoner's protest against his punishment. Then, his eyes had narrowed in an attempt to squint beyond the children's stares. Slowly, the row upon row of suffering eyes shattered his nerves, and his eyes finally met theirs in a well of acknowledgement.

His large, stiff body slouched passively forward, without a will of its own. Only when he saw Trang, waiting to bid them goodbye, did he find his voice. "Dr. Trang, I will do what I can," he stammered tensely.

"Thank you Mr. Samuelson. And thank you for visiting the children. It is not often that we have a foreign guest."

Throughout the tour, Seb spoke matter-of-factly about this disease and that deformity. He appeared to be programmed, like so many tour guides numbed by the very routine of their work. He had not expected Samuelson to respond visibly to what he witnessed. Seb was caught off-guard, unprepared for Samuelson's slightest change of heart.

He suddenly wished he could start over or change course in midstream.

As they left the hospital, Seb looked to Hao for resolve - the blast of a landmine, the missing leg, the long recovery. And he flashed back beyond Hao to the hundreds of helpless children waiting to die, and then he returned, renewed for the moment, to Samuelson.

"Okay . . . time to do some banking."

Seb realized that a money transfer of this amount would have to be done by Samuelson in person and in the presence of the bank's director. Seb had known Huynh Bao Tri for years, ever since he had arranged a biannual currency exchange and deposit of his inheritance from Uncle Norm and Aunt Bertha, who had had no children of their own. There were eight nieces and nephews and Norm and Bertha had bequeathed an equal amount to each, but they also had established a trust fund for Seb for - as the will literally read, ' services rendered: baling hay, docking sheep, shovelling manure and fly fishing for ten consecutive summers.'

Seb had advised Director Huynh of Samuelson's intended donation and had requested a pre-approval for a post-dated transfer of one million dollars from Samusan, Inc. to Can Tho Children's Hospital. The stage had been set.

"Welcome Mr. Samuelson," greeted Ms. Huynh, a short, stocky masculine woman of forty-five. She had closely cropped hair and wore a grey pin-striped pant suit - unusual, even in postwar Vietnam. She led the two men into her office on the second floor. There, the customary tea was ready and the obligatory enquiries regarding family and mutual friends were observed before Ms. Huynh broached the subject. "It is my honour to meet you, Mr. Samuelson. Dr. Seb told me of your generous intention to donate money to the Children's Hospital. You are a true friend to the people of Vietnam."

Samuelson nodded his head in awkward appreciation of the director's words, but Seb spoke for him. "Mr. Samuelson has just visited the hospital. He understands the serious situation there and wants to help."

Ms. Huynh reached for an envelope lying on the round table behind her ersatz colonial chair. "Yesterday I received a fax from the Bank of America in New York. The money has cleared and it is only a matter of hours before we can officially transfer the funds."

Both Ms. Huynh and Seb waited for some response from Samuelson. None came, and Seb found himself struggling through the tense void by breathing in and out a mantra he had learned during his meditation days while at university. Once situated in Vietnam, he had further developed this practice to see him through the emotional stress of watching his patients die so young. He had never before imagined that he would take refuge in his mantra in a bank.

Ms. Huynh, after waiting for a response from either man, took the lead again. "Here are the forms, in triplicate." She pressed her finger to three different lines on the page. "Mr. Samuelson, initial here and here, and your full signature at the bottom, with today's date . . . Dr. Seb, please sign as a witness, on the left side . . .Thank you."

The entire process took several minutes as Ms. Huynh insisted on translating the Vietnamese on the forms. Only after Samuelson gave his signature and Seb bore witness did she present Samuelson with three copies written in English. "These are not official because they are only translations. But I thought you might want them for your records."

Seb caught the pride in her voice when she emphasized the word 'translations.' She knew her English language skills were high. Her father had been one of North Vietnam's interpreters at the Paris peace negotiations with the Americans in the early seventies, before the fall of Saigon.

Samuelson was elsewhere. He stood up abruptly and without shaking hands or looking at Ms. Huynh, he walked towards the door.

Seb wasn't sure what he should do next. In an attempt to smooth the exit, he bowed slightly towards Ms. Huynh who, anticipating a western handshake, had held out her hand. Seb's ancient bow nearly grazed her hand and, as he straightened up, he reddened with embarrassment. "Sorry . . . and thank you . . . I'd better be going as well . . . Thank you again."

Seb rushed out in search of Samuelson. He saw him already seated in a cyclo taxi and yelling at Hao, who was entertaining the driver with an emotional re-enactment of the destruction of his own cyclo and the injury to his face.

Seeing Hao centred Seb, and, interrupting Hao's performance, he called out, . "Let's go home now and wait . . ."

Samuelson spewed out angry words. "You sonna-va-bitch! You made a deal . . Once I signed over the money I could go free. Don't you dare . . ."

"Sorry Samuelson . . . I'll keep my promise . . . once the money's actually transferred to the hospital's account. Until then, it's not a done deal. So settle down . . don't blow it now . . . for your wife's sake . . . Understand?"

Seb turned to Hao, and in a voice growing progressively more weary, he said, "Hao, as soon as we return Mr. Sam safely home . . . to my place . . . we can tell your friends to return Mrs. Sam to her house. Then, we'll just sit and wait till the money comes."

Hao looked at Seb, questioning, "Friends?....Mrs. Sam?"

Seb shot back anxiously, "Yeah, that's right. Good."

Then, he looked directly, almost sympathetically at Samuelson. "That's the best I can do."

And the two Americans threw their heads back against the cyclo seat, too tired to test one another one more time.

27

By mid-afternoon Seb began to feel the coming relief as he envisaged life without Samuelson. The money for the hospital - for medicine and equipment - would revitalize a work-weary staff. He would have more time with and for Ky. He would buy Hao a new cyclo, restoring their partnership and renewing Hao's sense of purpose. He looked over at Hao, curled up on the floor by the bedroom door like an old dog in its favourite sleeping spot. Seb sighed out loud in one long, lingering breath, "If only I could get him to quit smoking."

Seb walked over and gave Hao a shake. "Hao, I'll make you a deal . . . one that's good for both of us."

And, just like an old dog, Hao opened his eyes without lifting his face from the floor. "What deal, Dr. Seb . . . I no trust you too much. You trick me too much time."

Seb had always found an invigorating joy in their repartee. Often, the subject was secondary to the process. "Here's the deal Hao. You quit smoking and I'll stop eating eggs for breakfast. This way you'll save your lungs and I'll help my heart."

Hao didn't move a facial muscle. His retort was instant. "You no fair, Dr. Seb. You no eat egg; I no smoke. You sad in morning. I sad day and night. I sad too much more to you. You trick me again."

Seb yielded to Hao's logic; he knew he could not win. He turned his attention to Samuelson. After their visits to the hospital and the bank, Seb came to realize that his guest was near the breaking point, and he didn't want him to unravel, not now - not in the final lap. He had given him a double dose of sleeping pills, sufficient to secure him in sleep long past midnight.

"Hao, Mr. Sam is dead to the world . . ."

189

"Dead!" exclaimed Hao, jumping up on his good leg and peering at Samuelson stretched out on the bed. "I no kill him! I no kill him!"

"Easy Hao . . . easy. I meant he's asleep . . . sound asleep . . . not really dead . . . okay?"

Hao twisted his face in bewilderment, and he could only show a frightened, hesitant smile.

Seb saw the puzzled look in Hao's eyes. "Sorry Hao . . . sorry." He bent down to pick up Hao's crutch and the machete. "I have to go to the bank about the money, and I want to visit Ky . . . I'll be back tonight."

"Okay, Dr. Seb. I happy money come and Mr. Sam go. I no like kill . . ."

"I know Hao . . . Don't worry, there'll be no killing . . . I promise."

Seb jumped on his bicycle and began the sweaty zigzag through the noisy streets teeming with walking feet and rolling wheels. The burning sun bent his neck down towards the ground. He did not see their faces.

The money draft had arrived, had been exchanged into Vietnamese dong and transferred to the hospital's account. The deal was done.

A different Seb cycled from the bank towards Ky's. The sun seemed not so unbearably hot now, and the streets of feet and wheels became streets of hopeful faces - resilient and resourceful.

A slight detour took Seb to the city's only newspaper office. There, he left an envelope for the managing editor - an old friend for whom he had often helped translate articles from Vietnamese to English. The articles were published in the monthly newsletter, 'Vietnam Today' - a government propaganda sheet for spreading the gospel to foreign residents of the country's commitment to perestroika Hanoi-style.

Seb found Ky in her floating home, sitting in front of the mirror and looking down at the fold of her hands in the fold of her lap.

"Jasmine, Jasmine, Jasmine," echoed Seb as he moved towards her, excited in anticipation of her smell, her touch, her love. Then, he stopped. Even his breath ceased. In the mirror's image he saw tears streaking her cheeks - slow, separate, silent tears. Ky never wept; at least, he had rarely seen her weep. He couldn't remember when he last saw her face show such sorrow. He stood still, unsure of himself.

Ky whispered her words. "Kim's gone . . . from Vietnam."

"What?"

"Kim's gone . . I don't know where."

"Where? What do you mean?"

"She's young . . . beautiful . . . a virgin."

"A virgin?"

"Yes. For many men for a few more years."

"Ky, I don't understand."

"She was sold in Saigon . . . Sent somewhere . . Germany . . America . .Canada."

"How do you know?"

"I know!"

"How? How Ky?"

"Friends in Saigon . .. friends from Venice . .police . ."

"They did it?"

"No. They only found out about it . . . too late."

"Who then?"

Ky pivoted on her stool, turning towards Seb. "I don't know. Does it matter?"

"Who Ky . . who? Tell me who?"

Ky could not understand his need to know. "Gangs, Seb . . .brothers . . .cousins. During the war, they made good money in Vietnam - drugs, gambling, prostitution. Then, when Saigon surrendered, they had nothing . . . their American customers went back home and their Vietnamese customers lost power and money. So they left too . . . and . . . now, they have everything again in Los Angeles, Toronto, Hamburg . . . many places. Their brothers and cousins in Saigon send them girls . . too young to understand and too poor to care. Big money for the gangs."

Seb was stunned. "But Kim . . . How do you know that she . . ."

191

"I know Seb . . . I'm sure. They call her Sweet Coconut." And the slow, separate tears began to flow in a stream of sorrow only Ky could understand.

Seb stood still for Ky for a long time. The only movement was of his own tears, slow and separate as Ky's had been.

Without words he stepped forward and knelt before Ky, opening his arms to her. She closed in, trying to hide against his chest.

Seb knelt there for her for a long time. And, when her stream of tears went dry, he gently lifted her by the waist and turned her towards the bed.

She slipped over to the far side and curled sideways and bent her knees up to touch her elbows. She wrapped her arms around her belly to hold her pain in - out of Seb's reach.

Seb slipped beside her. He watched over her for a long time. Then, he circled one arm to cradle her head and the other to hold her arms tightly to her body - for a long, long time.

Ky sighed for sleep and then slept, and Seb slipped quietly away.

28

Both Samuelson and Hao were lying on their backs, snoring. Samuelson's heavy, heaving snores harmonized in a weird, rhythmic way with Hao's pursed whistles.

Seb shook Hao out of his dreams. "Hao, my son, wake up! It's finished. Mission accomplished."

Hao, naturally slow to awake to reality, groaned out incoherently, "What you mean 'me-son?' I no understand. You no have son."

Seb ignored Hao's interpretation. "The money's here. Mr. Sam can go home . . . You can go home. It's over. It's all over."

Samuelson's eyes opened, staring out in every direction to find his bearings.. He was still feeling the effects of the double dose of sedative administered by Seb. He raised his head drowsily, but said nothing.

Seb saw Samuelson's slow movement and reacted in kind. He assumed the role of ponderous judge, and his words resonated with the weight of power. "You are free to go Mr. Samuelson. You have served your sentence and paid your debt to society." Samuelson simply gaped at Seb, baffled by his erratic behaviour and afraid to say anything that might rouse his anger.

Seb continued in judicial solemnity. "In lieu of a formal declaration of release, I have prepared the following article for publication in Vietnamese and English."

American Gives Gift of Reconciliation

Richard J. Samuelson III, President and CEO of Samusan Shoes of Liberty, California, has

donated US$1,000,000 to Can Tho Children's Hospital. In offering the money - to be used to purchase essential medicines, update diagnostic and surgical equipment and provide specialized training for hospital staff - Mr. Samuelson released this statement. "When I came to Vietnam just a short time ago, I planned to open a shoe manufacturing plant in Can Tho. This plan is on track and we expect to begin production in three months. The result will be 300 new jobs, a definite boon to the local economy. However, we want to do more. My time here has opened my eyes to the tragedy of war and its aftermath. Therefore, I also want to give to Vietnam a significant donation to show first, American goodwill and, secondly, our acknowledgement of and apology for the loss of nearly three million Vietnamese lives during the war. It seems appropriate that this gift is given on March 16, in commemoration of those who were massacred in the village of Mai Lai in 1968. I hope that in the future the American and Vietnamese people can establish positive relations based on mutual respect and understanding.

Samuelson bristled in disbelief. "You can't print this! It's a goddamn lie! This was extortion . . . not a donation . . .and I am not going to - in any way - criticize my country. Don't you dare print that!" As he roared, he pulled violently at the ropes binding him to the bed.

"Sorry . . . too late. It's already gone to press . . . and will be in tomorrow's papers. Not only that, . . . the article has been wired via Reuters for syndicated circulation throughout the U.S."

Samuelson stammered, "You can't just . . ."

"Already done. They'll probably contact you for verification. Of course, you can deny the whole story . . . but, you'll have to explain everything - to set the record straight. . . . It will take time and - guaranteed - you'll lose your investment in your factory here. More importantly, your life and your wife's will be worthless . . . Tomorrow, next month, next year - here or in the U.S. - you will both die if you blow the whistle - guaranteed."

Seb walked over to the small table beside his corner chair. He poured himself a glass of cool water from the red thermos. Then, he took a second glass, filled it and offered it to his guest.

Samuelson, his mouth parched from the effects of the sedative, too long a sleep and the tension of the moment, nodded a sullen yes. Seb untied his right hand and gave him the glass of water. He then cleaned and bandaged Samuelson's finger for the last time.

Hao watched the two men, now in passive confrontation, and he mixed his love for and loyalty to Seb with a distant compassion for Samuelson. He wanted everything over.

Seb released Samuelson's other hand and then his bound feet. "Hao, take Mr. Sam out and get him a cyclo . . . to take him home."

Hao hobbled down the stairs and out of the door ahead of an unsteady Samuelson. He went to the corner and whistled awake a dozy cyclo-driver and gave him money and directions to Samuelson's house. "Goodbye Mr. Sam. Next time we friends. . . .Okay?"

Samuelson, his stiff body seized up from disuse, stepped feebly up to the rear seat. He looked straight ahead and said nothing to Hao. The cyclo slowly turned the corner, out of Hao's sight.

Seb was leaning against the front door when Hao returned. Both men looked wearily at each other, searching each other's eyes for the possibility of the way things used to be.

Seb spoke first. "Hao, thank you for all your help. I know it wasn't easy, and I'm really sorry if I made you do . . ."

Hao cut in. "No sorry, Dr. Seb. I okay . . . but I worry you okay. You no same like before."

"I'll be okay Hao. We both need a holiday - a few days of rest. We could go to Dalat - cool this time of year . . . What do you think? . . . Then, we'll get into a new business together. Okay?"

"Dalat okay. New business no okay. I cyclo man. I no want new business."

"Right Hao. Cyclo it is. We'll get into the cyclo business again . . . partners, okay?"

"Okay Dr. Seb. I like you my partner."

Seb stepped down the front steps, level with Hao. He clasped him with both his arms and pulled him tightly against his chest. The top of Hao's head barely grazed Seb's chin. Slow, separate tears wet Hao's dry, dishevelled hair. Seb held him for a long, lasting moment. Then, he released Hao and, without looking at him, turned around and entered the house, closing the door behind him.

29

Mid-point in his extended stay in the tropics, Seb had been seduced by the addictive effects of gin and tonic. The results for him and his work and his relationship with Ky had been damaging - almost ruinous. Too much liquor had brought to surface the dregs in Seb's soul, and angst had turned to anger, and anger to aggression. Only Ky's steadfast love and comforting counsel had saved Seb, his work and their bond. Under Ky's guidance he had traded alcohol for opium in an effort to defeat his demons, and its amnesiac effect had come to promise him a more mellow, more compassionate tomorrow.

Tonight, however, Seb took to the gin and tonic. Then, he sat down at his desk in the study and began to write, one long letter followed by a short one. The gin actually sharpened his mind as he chiselled out his points on paper. But it betrayed his body, and the more he drank, the more his hand shook for more. The monkey of his past was back and bent on climbing him again. He could see that the words he had written were impossible to read, and in desperation he resorted to his trusty typewriter, yet another momento of the American war and withdrawal. During his former bout with booze, he had two-fingered his way through several short stories in the heat of countless sleepless nights. He had sent them to the U.S. for publication, but had never had a reply - not even a letter of polite rejection. He always detested any state of suspended limbo, so with impulsive finality he had shelved his typewriter- along with his hit-and-miss muse- in the closet, above his single rack of clothes.

Tonight he felt forced to return to his two-finger typing, tap-tap-tapping out the written drafts with only the odd error. Like riding a bicycle after years without one, he thought, as his mind wandered far away to the tune of the tapping keys. Biking with the southside gang, howling out the coyote call to regroup after summertime suppers, kicking the can, hiding and seeking, telling terrifying tales of One-Eyed Gimpy in the cozy comfort of sleeping bags under a prairie sky and within safe earshot of his or another boy's sleeping mom and dad.   Seb's mind wandered from the twisted present to a good-time past long after his two fingers stopped their waltz of words.

He had typed - into the night - three letters and addressed three envelopes and slipped them into one large manila envelope marked 'Gullens'.   Then, he marched upstairs in slow motion, as if under orders.   He entered the bathroom and opened the medicine cabinet and took out a small bottle of pills and placed them in his briefcase along with the large envelope.

He turned off the lights, even the bedroom light he usually left on when away, and closed the front door.   He balanced the briefcase on top of the old typewriter, which he held with both hands in a heavy lean against his chest.

"Should I catch a cyclo or ride my bike?"   Seb asked himself aloud.   "Of course, the bike,"   remembering the gang of eight-year-olds too young to worry about the dangers of real life or accidental death.   He manoeuvred the small briefcase diagonally into the handlebar basket and secured the typewriter onto the rear carrier with two bungy cords.   Leaning towards drunkenness, he balanced himself on the seat and pedalled with a calm detachment towards Ky's.

The streets were eleventh hour eerie: The cyclo drivers, dozing or half-drunk, waiting for their final trick - men, young and old, too besotted by rice whiskey and the cunning charm of short-time lovers to question the double fare; the lonely women - no longer a charming catch - bending swayback against lampposts, willing to reduce their rate rather than risk a night empty of food and sleep. The working women, bending double under the shoulder yolks of baskets filled with pineapples, mangoes and papayas; the sweaty sinews of stevedores, working overtime for pieces of chicken on their children's rice; the cluster of homeless children circling the statue of Bac Ho, waiting for another lost tomorrow; the old man sitting on a low wooden stool, his crooked hands cupped over his bamboo cane, waiting out another sleepless night watching , and wondering what might have been if only . . ..

Seb stopped where the canal flowed under the bridge. He lifted the typewriter off the bicycle and, kneeling down, he lowered it gently into the murky water.

Ky was awake, waiting for him. She heard his footsteps on the plank and when he opened the door - bending down to clear his head - she kissed the v hollow below his throat, tasting the salt of his evening's travel.

The bath had already been poured, the water welcome-cool to draw out the heat from his weary body.

She intuitively read Seb's posture and movement, and she knew what salve would soothe the wounds within him. Tonight she knew, by the way he stepped into and out of the water, that smoke only was more than enough.

Seb towelled himself lethargically, watching Ky remake the bed and prepare his pipe. He poured a glass of water from the blue and white porcelain pitcher - Guilin style, from Ky's mother's dowry. He studied the images of mountains and mist, and pondered the possibilities of having been born in another era, another culture. And then he moved on to the coincidences of life - the meeting of a prairie boy and a brothel girl in a delta city in Southeast Asia. Beginnings. In betweens. Endings. He sipped in the velvet-soft jasmine blossoms which floated in the water.

"Jasmine, I love you . . . I really, really love you," whispered Seb across the quiet room.

"Me too, Chien Bot," Ky whispered back, raising her head to meet his look.

With a large towel wrapped securely around his waist, Seb crossed the room. The slow sway of the boat gave a waltzing rhythm to his walk. He opened his briefcase and took out the large manila envelope marked 'Gullens' and placed it neatly on Ky's dressing table, careful not to knock over the chaos of cosmetics strewn about. Again, he turned towards Ky.

"Really, really love you," he said.

"Me too."

He took the small bottle from his briefcase and picked up the glass of jasmine water and entered the bathroom and closed the door. When he came out, Ky was waiting on the edge of the bed, ready to light his pipe. Seb slipped around Ky onto the smooth silk sheets. He lay sideways, facing Ky, and held up his head with one hand; the other held Ky's thigh under her kimono.

"I have something for you. But first you must close your eyes."

"Oh Seb! A mystery gift!"

"Yes . . . a mystery, for sure." He pressed his lips to Ky's forehead as his hands moved to encircle her neck. "Okay . . . you can open your eyes, my Jasmine."

Ky blinked tears. Slowly, she moved her hands to hold the pendant. "Oh my Chien Bot . . . it's so beautiful . . .*cam ong* . . . thank you."

The gold chain held high a single angelwing jasmine flower - its eight gold pinwheel petals spreading delicately over the creamy bronze skin just below her throat.

"Seb . . . why this? Why now?"

"Because Ky . . . just because I'll love you forever."

Seb smoked once, twice and a final third time. Ky too, this time, shared his third pipe. He rolled over onto his other side to the far side of the bed - his knees bent towards sleep, and Ky snuggled against him - the curve of her belly caressing the curve of his back. She circled her right arm around his waist and pressed her palm to his chest. They closed their eyes and fell silently asleep, together.

The only sound, the croaking of the bull frogs in the paddies on the country side of the canal.

30

Gullens was late for his rounds at the hospital. He managed to manoeuvre his way past several other doctors and seek refuge in the wards, amongst the innocent, ailing children. Their dull eyes tried to shine in recognition, as shy smiles slowly worked their way to greet him.

Gullens completed his rounds, punctuating his genuine concern and professional attention with self-conscious smiles and awkward attempts at conversation in a language the children would never come to know.

Trang was in the staff lounge, waiting for an update from Gullens on the condition of his patients. He entered, knowing that Trang knew that he was both late and deeply embarrassed.

Trang, as always, also knew how to make the difficult easy. "Any changes Dr. Mark?"

"Only two - No food for Tho for twenty-four hours - surgery tomorrow, and for Hue - I've doubled her glucose intake . . . she's very, very weak."

Trang's eyes met Gullens'. "Will she be okay?"

"I don't know . . . I really don't. They brought her here so late . . . maybe too late."

They both lowered their eyes and sat in silence to write the brief reports required of them every day.

An hour passed before Trang spoke. "Dr. Mark, Dr. Seb didn't come in today. In fact, he's missed his rounds three times in the past week. He never used to miss work . . . I'm worried about him."

Gullens studied her face, then considered his words carefully. "He's been unusually tired lately . . . seriously so. And, I think quite depressed."

Trang spontaneously voiced concern. "Why? Can I help?"

"I'm not sure why . . . exactly . . . so, I don't know what we can do. However, I feel that a holiday . . . maybe a leave of absence for a few months . . . would do him a world of good."

"He can go anytime," Trang said, and then added emphatically, "He knows that."

"Of course," agreed Gullens. "But it's not easy for him to take a leave, and I doubt we can convince him."

"What about America?" suggested Trang. "He hasn't been home for a long time."

"Over twenty years," Gullens said. "Home for Seb is here, Trang. You know that better than I do. After nearly half his life in Vietnam, he doesn't think of the U.S. as his home."

"It must be hard for him . . . not going home."

Gullens could sense Trang's deep affection for Seb, and he wished he could ease her concern. " 'Home is where the heart is' . . . a famous saying. Have you heard it before?"

"No." responded Trang, and she took time to ponder the proverb's meaning. Then she looked directly at Gullens and spoke so gently. "In Vietnam we say ' The heart never leaves home.' "

Gullens absorbed the words in his mind, trying to understand. Then his voice whispered back, "I'll go now . . . to check on Seb. Please don't worry Trang. . . . He'll be all right."

"Thank you Mark." As he was leaving the lounge she spoke up loudly, wanting him to hear her every word. "Sunday picnic. Meet you at the guesthouse . . . Eight in the morning, Mark . . . not at night . . .okay?"

Mark stopped at the door and his eyes travelled the length of the room.

"Okay. It's a date - eight on Sunday morning."

Finally, he felt he understood.

31

Gullens took a taxi cyclo to Seb's, thinking on the way that Seb simply was stressed out over the emotional intensity of recent events: Kim's disappearance, the assault on Hao and the kidnapping of Samuelson. Gullens also realized that Seb was the pivotal player - the one the others relied on - and the raging torrent of one event after the other was pulling him under, into a whirlpool of defeat and depression. In less than three months they had become lifetime close, and Gullens valued their friendship: their father-son link of then and now, experience and naiveté, realism and idealism. Now, Gullens felt instinctively that it was his turn. He wanted to help Seb in any way he could. He would adjust his own schedule so Seb could have time - at least three months - and space - freedom from the encumbrances of others - to rekindle his spirit, his impulse to live each day as if there were no tomorrow.

Gullens found the front door closed, but unlocked. He entered, calling out Seb's name from first floor room to room. Nothing. He climbed the stairs, pounding down loudly with each foot; he did not want to alarm Seb - awake or asleep. He reached the closed door of what he guessed was Seb's bedroom; he had never before been upstairs. He knocked first - loudly - and again called out Seb's name. Nothing. He thought of an amusing entrance - a la the British butler - but the very silence of the house muted him as well. Then, with trepidation, he pushed open the door to see a room in disorder. This, Gullens thought, was not the methodical, meticulous Seb. Clothes were strewn over the floor and several days of dishes were stacked high on the dresser top. The small waste basket was stuffed with empty plastic food bags. In the tropics, yesterday's smell equalled today's stench.

Gullens scanned the room for signs of Seb - even of his absence. His eyes fell upon the bed, glimpsed, gazed, then squinted and shut. He tried to visualize what he thought he had seen: strands of rope hanging from each bedpost and the mattress - like a sliced loaf of unleavened bread - with round wads of raw cotton coming out of each long gash, and a machete sliced into the centre of the headboard. He opened his eyes to the same, and he felt his belly bottom out and his bowels begin to run.

In the bathroom he found Seb's leather medical bag chock-full of the basics - not for house calls but for mobile surgery: anaesthetics, syringes, scalpels and sutures. Gullens' mind ping-ponged between Seb's bedroom and the hospital, and images of Seb, Hao and Samuelson surfaced - floating, frightening images of torture and death. Who? By whom? Why?

And, where was Ky? He lunged down - two steps at a time - the flight of stairs, and age-old dust flew out of the floorboards when he landed. He raced through each first floor room to see for himself, again, that nothing had been disturbed and no one was there. Nothing, no one. He threw open the front door and ran into the street, shouting for a cyclo as only a foreigner in a frenzy would do. Passers-by turned their heads in his direction, then moved on indifferently.

Sweat seeped from every pore, his hair was shower-soaked and his wet clothes a darker tinge. The blazing midday sun shone high in the azure sky, oblivious to life below. Even the cyclo driver - in seeming collusion with the universe - showed a lethargic apathy towards Gullens as he taxied him - for double the fare - to Venice.

Gullens, his mind still reeling from what his eyes had seen at Seb's, could not remember Ky's boat. First, he crossed the wooden plank to the front boat - the lounge, but it was daytime dark. He tried the second - no answer. He crossed the plank to the third boat. He could hear the drone of two voices, low and lazy after a spell of love. He whispered Ky's name through the green shutters, but no answer followed. He tried again - this time in a whispered shout - and waited impatiently. "*Tam*," a woman's voice called back. "*Tam*," she repeated with impatience. Gullens had learned his numbers from Marie, who knew he would be bilked time and again until he could bargain with the street vendors and cyclo drivers.

He scurried back up one plank, past four more boudoir boats and down another plank to number eight. He rapped repeatedly with his knuckles, shouting for Ky - unconscious of the racket he was making.

Ky opened the door. She looked directly into Gullens' eyes for a brief moment, then moved to the side to let him enter.

The bed appeared awkwardly large for such a small room, and, on the bed Seb's body seemed smaller than life. Even at a room's distance, Gullens immediately recognized death: the pallid face, the position of the arms to the side, the absolute absence of any movement - the flicker of eyelids, the purse of lips, the slightest rise and fall of the chest.

Gullens sat down lightly on the edge of the bed, as if not wanting to wake him. He picked up Seb's heavy hand and pressed the limp wrist with his two fingers in an effort to find what he knew wasn't there. He bent his ear to Seb's heart, hoping in vain he was wrong.

Ky had arranged the room for another day; nothing, other than the briefcase by the side of the bed, indicated change. Seb had always made a point of not bringing his work, personal or professional, to Ky's. Theirs was an affair beyond the reality of the other world.

Gullens looked towards Ky. She had rearranged a garland of jasmine on the small ancestral altar stationed high against the bow-wall of the room, and was lighting three sticks of incense to place in the tiny vase at the base of the altar.

He waited for her to finish. Then, he rose from the bed and walked, almost tiptoeing, over to the altar. Ky turned to Gullens and her eyes showed her silent anguish. He brought her against him, holding her kindly close. She stood motionless, her head pillowed against his chest, her arms at her side. They heard only each other's deep, mournful breaths of loss.

Slowly, Ky stepped backwards, away from Gullens, and walked around him over to the bed. She bent low to pick up the briefcase and then pivoted her body gracefully towards Gullens, holding out the briefcase with both hands. After he took it, she gestured for him to sit down on one of the two low stools in front of the altar.

He opened the briefcase. On one side, in a small pocket usually reserved for business cards, he found an empty bottle of sleeping pills. On the other side, in a file pouch, he saw a large manila envelope marked 'Gullens' in black ink. Each letter, much larger than necessary, had been traced twice over with a shaky hand - like that of a child practising his capital A, B, C's. He briefly held the empty bottle, rolling it with his fingers, then returned it to its pocket. He placed the briefcase on the floor and lifted the envelope to reading level. He felt a knot, already tight, strangling his insides. His hands began to tremble as he opened the envelope and removed its contents. Everything, save the signature, had been neatly typed.

The letter was for Gullens.

Dear Mark:

As you can see, I took the pills. Violence was never my forte, so guns, razors and ropes were out.

I addressed this envelope to you for two reasons. I trust you, and I am confident that whatever you choose to do, you will do it well.

Enclosed is a copy of three letters bound for America - a dead man's bluff. If you decide to send them, please do so from within the U.S. - a matter of keeping a clean trail. If you decide not to send them, burn them. I understand.

The last envelope is for Ky, the executor of my will. Please help her in any way you can.

I'm content, knowing you are here - at the hospital. It needs new blood. I regret I was not a better mentor. I failed in giving you that 'basket full of wisdom'. Nonetheless, I'm sure you'll fill it yourself, in time.

Take good care 'my son' and go downstream whenever you can.

Love,
Seb
p.s. Trang would love to have coffee with you

Gullens wept openly as he read the letter several times, wondering why . . .why . . why.

Ky was watching him, but said nothing. She was sitting on the bed, holding Seb's right hand in her lap - one hand under, the other over his.

Gullens then read the master copy of the three letters bound for the U.S.

Mr. President and C.E.O:

In Vietnam today, millions of people, too many of them children, are suffering disease and death due to the lack of basic medical supplies.

American babies are born healthy. Too many Vietnamese babies are born with severe deformities - even to this day, a legacy of your involvement in and profit from the U.S. invasion of Vietnam.

Before making demands of you, it is important that you are made aware of the damage you have done in the false claim of patriotism and democracy.

You sprayed over 40 million litres of Agent Orange on villages, farms and forests. This Agent Orange contained dioxin, the most toxic chemical ever developed. Remember 'Operation Ranch Hand?' Remember the motto 'Only we can prevent forests?'

You dropped many thousands of bombs on millions of innocent civilians. More bombs than in World War II - 500 pounds for every man, woman and child in Vietnam.

You killed 3 million and injured millions more. Imagine the bombing of the San Francisco Bay area - with no survivors.

Why are we accusing you? You weren't piloting the planes or pillaging the villages. Why should you be held accountable?

Because you were in your corporate boardrooms counting your profits from the war. Your children were going to private schools while Vietnamese children were dying from the bombs and bullets. Your wives were playing bridge at the country club while Vietnamese mothers were mourning the destruction of their homes and the deaths of their loved ones. You made billions of dollars killing millions of innocent people by manufacturing bombs, landmines and toxic chemicals.

And, why now, over a quarter century later, do we find you guilty?

First, because what you did was a heinous crime against humanity. You should have been forced to stand trial before an international wartime tribunal - along with American political and military leaders. You should have been found guilty of mass murder bordering on genocide and sentenced to life imprisonment.

Secondly, not only have you not been punished, you have continued to profit from the cruelty of war elsewhere. Today, the United States has the world's largest arms industry - responsible for 70% of the weapons of war sold to third world countries. Your greedy boardroom decisions have caused death and destruction for innocent families throughout the world - Bosnia, Mozambique, Guatemala, Cambodia, the Middle East.

Consequently, you must pay. By the deadline of July 4th - U.S.A.'s Independence Day - $10,000,000 must be sent to <u>*Victory*</u> *for* <u>*Victims*</u> *- a non-profit organization committed by conscience to right the wrongs of the American war in Vietnam by offering assistance to innocent victims and their families. Notice must be given in the* <u>*New*</u> <u>*York*</u> <u>*Times*</u>*, publicly announcing this gift of life.*

If you comply, you will live and no further demands will be made of you or your company.

If you refuse our demands, you will die. If you go to the police, you will die. After your death, other executive officers and company board members will die.

It is your decision.

    GUARANTEED!

"Guaranteed," uttered Gullens. "Guaranteed," he repeated, and he seized the word and ran back with it through his many conversations with Seb and took it all the way back to the words in the ransom note regarding Samuelson. "Guaranteed." He sat stone still, frozen in the shock of knowledge, without understanding why. Why Seb?

Ky waited on the bed, still clutching Seb's hand, often smoothing down the hair on his arm, just above his wrist. She stared out the tiny window above the bed, at the indifferent sky.

Stung by what he had read and come to realize, Gullens looked mechanically at the three envelopes destined for the U.S.: General Technologies - United Electronics - Jonnix Industries. He put them back in the large manila envelope.

Then, he picked up the last envelope, addressed to Ky. "It's for you . . . from Seb . . . his will."

"Will?" asked Ky, her thoughts elsewhere.

"A letter about what should be done with his possessions . . . his money."

"I don't care . . . You read it."

"I understand Ky . . . but . . ."

"I don't care. Leave us alone now . . .please."

Gullens returned to the guesthouse and, alone in his room, he wept through the words of Seb's will.

To Whom It May Concern:

This is my first, last and only will and testament.

The money (approximately $50,000) held in my trust account (# 542-2210, West Coast Credit Union, 1975 Van Ness Blvd., San Francisco, California) shall be dispersed as follows:

1.   *A case of the best scotch to Hank at Rainbow Cafe. I'm sorry I missed our poker game this past Thursday. My forfeit.*
2.   *A new cyclo for Hao from your silent partner. Drive carefully, and don't smoke too much.*
3.   *$10,000 in trust - to be administered by Ky - to Tin and Sau, Kim's brother and sister. Address: Bac Ho statue on Hai Ba Trung Street, Can Tho.*

4.   *All my professional effects and $10,000 to Can Tho Children's Hospital - to be administered by Dr. Trang, my dear friend and colleague. My sincere gratitude for your kindness and patience. You are a doctor's doctor.*

5.   *All my personal effects and the remainder of my trust fund following the above disbursements to Ky.*

"I really, really love you, my Jasmine."

Seb Kloster

32

Trang had arranged for a car and driver to take Gullens to Saigon. It was too early for Gullens - a six a.m. breakfast at the guesthouse. He nibbled at a baguette but couldn't eat the eggs, and only sipped his coffee until it cooled. Even Marie was quiet, pretending to be busy in the kitchen with Ba.

Gullens reluctantly pushed his chair backwards from the table and picked up his backpack. "Marie, I've left two suitcases in my room - okay?"

"Your room, Dr. Mark?" Marie shouted from the kitchen. "You go away . . . no more your room . . . room for rent."

"But Marie . . . I'm just going home to visit family and get my work visa . . . one month . . .max."

Marie refused to leave the kitchen. "You no come back. Too many foreigners come once . . . say they come again . . . then never come again." she shouted with finality.

"I'll come back Marie. . . I promise ," insisted Gullens. He felt their meal time teasing uncomfortable this morning.

"I think he'll come back Marie. I hope so," interjected Trang, having just entered the dining room through the wide open double front doors.

"Trang, why are you here?" asked Gullens in surprise. "Shouldn't you be at the . ."

"Hospital?" Trang completed his thought. "Well . . . yes I should. But, today we brought the hospital here." She gestured with open arms towards the courtyard.

Gullens was bewildered. Weighed down by his backpack, he walked out of the guesthouse and into a small crowd of doctors, nurses, support staff and seven children, whose elfin grins and shining eyes expressed what words could not.

"Just a few of your success stories, Dr. Mark. There's many more to come . . ." Trang's voice cracked as she spoke.

Gullens tried to say yes, but said nothing. His mouth went desert dry and his throat swelled closed. He tried to manage a smile, but could only nod tight-lipped as he shook each extended hand with both of his and half-hugged each shy child in turn.

Marie was waiting behind the well wishers. When Gullens saw her, he tried to wink, hoping to lighten the moment. As he shook Marie's right hand, she slapped him squarely on the chest with her left and then gave him a quick, rough hug. "Okay. One month I keep your room."

Words would not come. Gullens could only squeeze her wide, round waist. He turned to face the waiting car and Trang, who was standing near the open back door. Their eyes met, but only for a moment. They both looked down as their hands touched. Finally, Gullens found his voice. "We still have a picnic date . . .don't we?" His eyes stayed down, focusing on her hands.

"The first Sunday after you return . . . . I'll meet you at the guesthouse . . . . . eight o' clock."

"In the morning." he added, and their eyes lifted in unison and locked.

"In the morning, Mark."

The car, a 1968 four-door Ford Galaxie - the very vehicle used by the United States Information Service in Can Tho during those eternal years of war and ruin - belched out black smoke as it backed out of the guesthouse gates and into the disorderly flow of traffic.

As Gullens glanced back at his circle of friends, his eyes found Hao, standing alone in the shade of a towering tamarind. With his back solid against the trunk and his good leg rooted to the ground, Hao held his crutch high in a slow wave of farewell.

The shocks showed no signs of life as the car bumped metal to metal down the road to Saigon - Ho Chi Minh City.

"What is a rebel? A man who says no."

Albert Camus (1951)

ABOUT THE AUTHOR

David Kos was born in the United States, but has called Canada home for the past thirty-three years. He has taught English Literature and English as a Second Language in Canada, the United States, Nigeria, China, Japan, Thailand and Vietnam. He also has worked in First Nations education as a teacher, counsellor and administrator. He and his wife, Kay, live on Salt Spring Island, British Columbia, Canada.

ISBN 141200573-6